STONEBRIDGE MANOR

BY

PETER C. BRADBURY

To Danielle

Many thanks

Peter B

This book is dedicated to all the people who have shared or influenced my life, including, but not

limited to, my wife Debbie, my family in England

and the U.S., my mentor Leslie, and all the people I

have worked for and worked with as a Butler. I

would also like to thank Jason Davis for his cover

drawing, Samantha Davis Darrin, and Rebecca Poma.

CHAPTER ONE

Lady Baldwin was lying face down on the bed, a white sheet barely

concealing her modesty but not her figure. Despite being in her

middle forties, she was still sought after by enough men to keep her

happy. She still had her looks, her small waist, her large breasts

helped by some minor operations and her long slim legs. Although

her shoulder length blonde hair was extremely disheveled and her

lipstick smudged, she didn't particularly care at this moment. She'd

just had sex and wanted some more. She raised herself up onto her

right elbow and rearranged the sheet around her to the best effect,

highlighting the length of her legs and the roundness of her bottom.

Today, she knew she was irresistible..

Her blue eyes quickly took in the surroundings; a tiny bedroom with

limited furniture, the biggest of which was this queen size bed which

she herself had bought, just a couple of nightstands on either side in

natural pine, a dressing table and chair in the same pine, and a small

wardrobe. The walls were plain white and curtains stood out in a

dreadful chocolate. They were closed at present, thankfully keeping much of the daylight out. After all, it was still only 3pm. Her clothes were scattered all about the beige fitted carpet and she smiled as she recalled how hurriedly they'd been discarded.

Lady Baldwin heard him flush the toilet and turn the faucet on to wash his hands from the bathroom next door; then the faint sound of his bare feet padding away toward the kitchen. She knew he loved her, worshipped her really, but she didn't love him back. He was just a lover.

In the tiny kitchen he busied himself getting a couple of glasses and a bottle of champagne out of the fridge. Champagne was her usual beverage, she'd even sent a crate to this apartment purely for her frequent visits, along with other personal supplies. She'd probably have the whole place redecorated and refurnished soon but he didn't mind, just as long as she visited.

Simon had worked for her once as her butler. He wasn't very good as a butler though so her husband, Lord Baldwin, had let him go. Little did he know that it was her decision. She liked him working for her but felt claustrophobic with him around all the time and was certain her husband was suspicious. Besides, Simon wasn't her only lover.

Simon had returned back here to London. He resumed his old job of looking after a single American man who was very rarely in Britain and therefore needed very little in the way of service. Simon was very good at paperwork and organizing but was poor with valeting and serving meals so working full time for Lord Baldwin, who expected his suits pressed and shoes shined on a daily basis, was a disaster. Thankfully, he'd managed to get his old job back. As Lady Baldwin didn't like to visit him at his new residence, she'd found this tiny apartment for them and whenever she was in town she'd call and they'd meet . It wasn't the most perfect arrangement for him. He'd prefer a more permanent situation but he understood it was better than nothing and she was very generous. If only he could get her husband out of the picture..

Simon was almost twenty years younger than Her Ladyship, nearly six foot tall, handsome with short black curly hair, and blue eyes, slim and muscular, very well spoken, good mannered, and always well groomed. He was an ideal young gentleman with an eye for the older ladies. Scatter- brained young women were not for him. His ideal was Lady Baldwin or C as he called her now, a scheming devious woman who knew exactly what she wanted which at the

moment was he..

"Simon, where are you with the champagne?" She called from the

bedroom. At times like this her voice was very soft and sexy

without accent, a classic English lady. Yet at other times she was

able to cut people to the bone with it, a completely different person.

"Be right there, C," he replied as he popped the cork, holding the

bottle in one hand and the two glasses by the stems in his other. He

made his way back naked, apart from the striped boxers he'd slipped

on when using the bathroom. It was going to be a long afternoon.

CHAPTER TWO

Approximately one hundred and sixty miles away in a small terraced one-bedroom house, a telephone conversation was just starting.

"Good afternoon," said the deep baritone voice on the other end of the line from another suburb of London.

"Hello Ken. What's all the racket in the background?" replied Phillip in his amused northern accent.

"Hang on a minute, you moron. I'll just turn it down."

There followed the sound of the receiver being put down and shortly after the volume of Beethoven's Fifth Symphony being drastically reduced. Ken loved Beethoven. Before the phone rang he was probably sitting in his armchair conducting the orchestra with his baton. He had actually conducted an orchestra once, only a rehearsal, but he'd done it and was pretty good at it. Of course, Phillip would never tell him that. They were too good friends to start complimenting each other; instead they traded insults and jokes which made them both laugh.

Ken was much older than Phillip, 81 years to Phillip's 37. Ken was a retired butler, had taught Phillip several years before. They'd immediately hit it off despite being total opposites. Ken was outgoing, rotund, enjoyed the arts and cooking, loathed sports. He was also a real ladies man. They did however share the same sense of humor, honesty and belief in staying true.

"You know," said Ken as he picked the receiver up again, "I'll never understand why a person of your intellect can listen to that brain numbing noise that you call music rather than Beethoven, who was the greatest musician ever to live."

Phillip laughed. They argued about music all the time and whenever they visited each other they played their own sounds just to bait each other. He generally subjected Ken to some Rolling Stones.

"So how are you doing, buddy Is the wicked witch of the north still driving you crazy?" continued Ken, referring to one of Phillip's employers, Lady Baldwin.

"No more than usual. But then I've been here before. I must be a glutton for punishment."

"Well, I keep telling you what her problem is. You should introduce me to her and I'll charm her into bed, give her what she needs."

"Get out of here, Ken. You're 80 years old. If you got her into bed, she'd be waiting a month for the erection.." Phillip's sarcasm dripped from his words.

"Well I think you should introduce me or else do the dastardly deed yourself. She's not unattractive, is she?"

"No, but no thanks. She needs someone old, decrepit, and without morals." Phillip pauses and teasingly adds, "Perhaps I should introduce you?"

"Okay, insult taken; but I'll be glad to service her."

"Sure, Ken. I'll keep you in mind for when she gets really bad.."

"So you old bean, is this just a social call or do you require my expensive professional expertise?"

"Actually, I was wondering if you fancied coming to the World Cup this year."

"The World Cup?"

"I know you're ignorant of all things sport but surely you've heard of the world cup?"

"Nope."

"It's a football competition, or soccer as the Americans like to call it, between all the countries of the world"

"You mean that silly game where grown men chase a little white ball around a field?"

"Yes, but it's not silly."

"It is to me. Why on earth would I want to go?"

"Because it's being played in the USA."

Ken just loved the USA. He and Phillip had previously been on vacation there together.

"Now why didn't you say that to begin with rather than all that World Cup stuff?"

"You want to go?"

"Of course I do. Just tell me when and how much. I'll leave the details to you. I didn't think you'd be going back there after buying that stupid car."

Phillip had recently purchased a Toyota MR2 in a color he liked to describe as 'the color of the sky on a cloudless day'.

The car was brand new, his first ever sports car, and he loved opening his garage door to take it out, even if it was just to go to the local store. Mind you, the payments were exorbitant, but as he was single and earning good money, 'then what the hell.'

"My car isn't stupid."

"It's only got two seats."

"I only need one."

"That's selfish. What if you go on a date?"

"Then there's a seat for both of us."

"Where would I sit?"

"If I was on a date you'd be sitting at home."

"That's selfish."

This was a normal chat between Phillip and Ken, nothing was ever intended or taken as an insult.

"Whatever. So will you want to see any of the games in America?"

"I don't know. If it's going to be expensive, I won't."

"I'll find that out. I want to go for a month. Is that okay with you?"

"Sure, but how on earth did you get a month off? The wicked witch doesn't like you taking holidays."

"When I came back here, I told them that if I didn't get decent holiday time I'd leave again. His Lordship keeps asking me when I'm going on 'walkabout' as he puts it so I told him July, all of July. She'll have a fit about it but she can lump it."

"Do you think he's told her yet?"

"Not a chance. I'd have heard about it if he had."

"Has he any balls?"

"She had them cut off a few months ago. He came home one day walking like a cowboy who'd spent a month in the saddle so I asked him what was wrong. He'd just had a vasectomy."

"God almighty. I thought they were too old to have more children."

"I think she just wants to prevent him from meeting someone else and having kids. That's how she snared him in the first place. It's not like she's stopped taking the pill."

"How do you know that?"

"Ken, we're butlers. Remember, we know everything.."

"Forgive me, Phillip. Retirement dulls the senses."

"I'll remember you said that, Ken. I thought you were getting Senile.."

"You'll pay for that one." Turning serious again, Ken asks, "So you think the wicked witch is

playing around?"

"Of course she is. She doesn't bring them here but I hear her on the phone sometimes talking to a couple of them. I think His Lordship suspects. He doesn't seem to like it when they call and she leaves the room to talk to them but he never says anything."

"Amazing. I can't believe he never says anything."

"Beats me why he doesn't. With his money, he could easily find someone else."

"Right, it's not like he's as ugly or as poor as you."

"Very true. Anyway, enough of that. So you're coming to America?"

"Try keeping me away. Fran will be thrilled when I tell her tonight."

Fran was Ken's closest friend, as she had been to his deceased wife who'd died after a long illness. Were it not for Fran, Ken would have taken his own life as he was lost after her death , Fran had gotten him back on track and enjoying life again. She also had the ability to see people for what they were whereas Ken trusted everyone and could be easily conned. Phillip liked Fran. She always spoke her mind no matter what.

"She'll be thrilled to get rid of you for a while."

"I don't know why she likes you so much. All you ever do is insult me.."

"That's why she likes me."

"She's coming over tonight so I'll tell her then. Are you working tonight?"

"Not tonight, he's going down to the Cotswold's, to their other house so I've got the night off. Although it means I have to spend it with the dogs."

"You still have to spend the night in their house when no one is home?"

"Yes, it's a real pain and pointless but that's what they want so I have to do it."

"You do what you have to. I won't waste anymore of your time then, Phillip. I'm so happy we're going to America again. Tell me when you need some money for my fare and keep me up to date with your plans. I can hardly wait to go."

"We'll have a ball, Ken. Give my love to Fran and I'll call you soon."

"Have a good night, Phillip, and thank you."

"You too, Ken. Speak to you soon. Bye."

"That's that then," thought Phillip as he hung up the phone wondering now how he was going to raise the money and find the tickets for the soccer games he wanted to see.

He knew he probably wouldn't be able to see as many as he'd like but he was single, he didn't have a mortgage or utility bills so he could always use credit.

Despite thinking of himself as ugly, Phillip wasn't that bad looking and many folk thought he was quite handsome He was slim, 5' 10", wore a warm smile with mischievous hazel / green eyes, a roman nose, and a moustache. At twenty, his hair had grayed and he'd lost most of it apart from a little on top and around the sides. He'd recently stopped worrying about his hair so he was more relaxed these days which probably explained why he came back to work here.

This was his second stint here. He still wondered why he'd come back, especially as it was only a few months ago that he'd gotten away. When he left, he made it clear that it was because of Lady Baldwin's behavior toward him. Her mood swings, anger, and the constant switching from the routine that she said she wanted was unbearable. He told them both why he was leaving, knowing His Lordship would be furious with her. Phillip had been the only person they'd found who could not only do his job, but everyone else's as well. He was well-liked by everyone and could press suits and polish shoes promptly just as Lord Baldwin liked. If Her Ladyship had actually asked him personally to stay, rather than give him a message through the nanny, then he may actually have stayed. But he was quite miffed with her attitude so he had left.

When Phillip returned to his mother's apartment, they'd already been calling her asking for him to reply but he ignored the messages. He went back to his previous job of working for the High Court and its judges. It was only itinerant work but despite its low wage, it paid the few bills he had and was fairly easy. He didn't spend much of this period actually at his mother's home but she continued getting calls so he caved in and spoke to them before going down to see them. By this time, Lady Baldwin had more or less moved to their new house in the Cotswolds in Gloucestershire, and his Lordship went there for some weekends . They'd found a butler for that house but still wanted someone for Crompton Hall in Derbyshire. As Lord Baldwin would still spend time there and the shooting parties would continue as before, a butler was needed. Given the new scenario, he agreed to see them down at their new house.

The new house, Stonebridge Manor, was at least twice the size of Crompton . Unlike Crompton, it sat right in the middle of its own property so it wasn't easy to find. He eventually found and drove through the tiny village that no doubt belonged to the estate. It's one road brought him directly to the open gated entrance to the main house itself. They were obviously expecting him or perhaps just left the gate open during the day, . The gravel driveway crunched under his tires as he wound his way toward the house, a drive of about half a mile. He passed three other houses which belonged to the estate and no doubt were occupied by various staff. He knew a few of the staff here, had worked with them at Crompton, but there were still a few he wouldn't know and he wondered how long they'd last.

He caught a few glimpses of the house as he made his way. A big three storey Georgian stone manor with the full basement making the rear of the house four storey tall. This was much bigger than Crompton. As was customary for a servant, he figured out which was the 'service' entrance, parked, and stepped out of his car. He wasn't in uniform, which for him was a traditional morning suit; but he did wear a dark gray lounge suit, white shirt and conservative striped tie. Though he wasn't here to impress anyone. He didn't care if they offered him his old job back; he was more interested in what Lady Baldwin was going to say.

"Hey Phil, I thought you'd escaped us all.."

Phillip turned around, putting one arm into his jacket. He knew who the friendly greeting was coming from, it was Cathy the maid but made sure before making a smart and sarcastic reply.

"I did, but I keep getting calls saying my freedom was actually only parole and that I needed to finish my sentence." They both laughed and gave each other a hug.

"Good to see you again, Phil. We've missed you."

"Thanks, Cathy; but I do wonder why I'm actually here. Good to see you as well."

"Kay will be here in a second. She's missed you as well."

"There's no one to make fun of you both anymore; that's why you miss me."

"Even Lady B has missed you." Cathy commented, quite seriously.

"Now I know you're joking" he laughed.

"Phillip!"

"Kay, how are you?"

"Give me a hug. Welcome home."

Cathy and Kay were the two closest servants to Lady Baldwin, who was always referred to as Lady B when she was out of earshot. Cathy worked as her maid and Kay was her children's nanny and general confidant and organizer. These two were the go betweens for everyone; they'd tell Lady B stuff that she had no right knowing, but could also tell you things about Lady B if they so wished. It was a game really, but a game that Phillip could play.

Both women were of the same height, 5'4", both blonde, but that's where the similarity ended. Cathy was very slim, her hair longer, brown eyed, a mother and wife, very emotional. She wasn't unattractive, but apart from fixing the curls on her hair she didn't do much with her face or perhaps she'd been told not to by her ladyship.

Kay's hair was short and straight, struggled with her size and figure, single, better educated, frightened most people with her manner, and not prone to being tearful. Like Cathy, she wasn't at all ugly and she made better use of her make up. Her skin was good and despite how she liked to come across, she was prone to blushing.

Both of them should have left years ago, in Phillip's

opinion, but they were very well rewarded and didn't have

many other options.

Phillip had arrived early so they gave him a quick tour of the

place before finishing up in the kitchen where his old pal Rene,

the chef, was busily preparing lunch.

"Rene, it's bad enough I am here but I thought you'd opened a

restaurant in Paris." said Phillip smilingly and offering his

outstretched hand to be shook.

Rene was tall, over six feet, very slim, a mop of black hair

but no facial hair. He had the uncanny ability to always

appear unkempt, no matter what the situation, yet his wife,

also French, was the epitome of elegance.

Rene took his hand and smiled back. "Someone fuckin

gazzumped me at the last minute," he replied in his strong

French accent, "I swear I'll kill them if I ever find out who

did it. But no matter, here I am again." He paused, "and of

course it's nice to see you ."

(Gazzumped is a British term for settling on a price for something and then at the very last moment, another bidder comes in and offers more.)

"Your family is well?"

"Yes, very well. Maybe you'll have chance to go see them before you go home, eh?"

"I hope so, but what exactly happened to the restaurant?"

"Oh, we went back to Paris thinking all the contracts had been settled. I was buying equipment for it and we'd actually moved in. Then the agent told us we had to leave as someone had paid more money at the last moment. I don't know who but it's since been resold, I believe," Rene shook his head, "so here I am again."

"I'm sorry, Rene. I know how much you were looking forward to having your own place, but it's very nice to see you again."

They'd worked together previously at Crompton and Rene had often spoken of his desire to open his own restaurant. He had found one just outside Paris and when Phillip had left he was working out his notice, full of excitement about returning home.

Rene was a great chef. He was the best Phillip had ever worked with and he'd worked with quite a few. He often wondered how Rene put up with Lady B's penchant for being late for meals, as he very often had to re-cook. Behind her back he would cuss and complain about his food being ruined by her lateness, 'fookin beech' he would grumble in his French accent. But when she put her head into the kitchen to say she was sorry for being late, he would always turn around and say "that's okay milady; it's no problem." Phillip always chided him for this, jokingly, as Phillip, when he had to cook would not re-cook if she was late. He'd just keep it warm and if she didn't like it, then tough. He would always ask her when she wanted dinner and would have it ready by then. If she then decided to wait another hour and not inform him, then so be it, she could have it burnt.

Normally in private homes there are set times for meals and if they're missed, a good excuse is needed. Even then a snack is all that is offered. In this house, that was not the case.

Very often, breakfast would still be required at lunchtime and dinner could be anytime from 6 to 9pm. Dinner parties could be even later which caused much consternation amongst the staff, especially the chef.

"So Phillip, are you coming to work here with Tom?" Phillip had heard of the household's butler Tom, by all accounts a very good one. His wife worked here as well doing maid duties but Tom had picked up the pieces here after the first two men had walked out. He had gotten the place back in order.

"Not that I've heard of. They just want me back at Crompton looking after his Lordship and doing the shoots. Have you any idea who'll be doing the cooking?"

"I think you will. The only time I'll be going back there is when they have parties."

"I see. I can cope with him. If she comes up, I'll do what I usually do when she's late. I'll cremate it."

Cathy, who'd remained in the kitchen standing with her back against the aga cooking range listening to these two , spotted Tom as he passed by the kitchen and called him over.

"Tom, come and meet Phillip."

"Hello Phillip. Very nice to meet you. Your reputation precedes you."

"Hello Tom. Nice to meet you, but don't believe what you hear unless you're being told just how bad I am."

Tom was a little younger than Phillip. A little larger, neat short black hair with a parting down the left side. No facial hair, but probably had to shave twice a day as he already had a shadow around his chin. A nondescpript but pleasant man, he very much preferred to stay in the background. He was wearing an apron over his jacketless uniform and looked like he was busy.

"I don't mean to be rude, Phillip, but I just need to go and make a call. We'll chat after your meeting if that's okay?"

"That's okay, Tom, I understand. I'll see you later."

With that, Tom hurried away, passing by Kay as she entered the kitchen.

"They're ready for you, Phil. Shall I show you the way?"

"You'd better. I'd get lost in this place."

Although he'd had a quick tour, this was a big house. It was a mansion really, approximately 40,000 sq. ft. and quite daunting. He'd actually seen the house just after they purchased it but it was a lot different then. It had since been remodeled, redecorated, refurnished. It had been very unique, a mixture of modern décor with old fashioned furniture. Now it was like a classic design magazine, open any page and you'd find some part of this house in it. They came to the library. Mahogany floor, large stone fireplace, frilly plain curtains, sash windows looking out over the lake and its stone bridge, books from floor to ceiling and mainly unread, a big desk, lamps and occasional tables, a huge Persian rug, and in two of the overstuffed armchairs sat Lord and Lady Baldwin. They rose in unison as Kay showed Phillip into the room.

"Good morning Milord, Milady."

"Good morning to you too, Phillip. Nice to see you and thank you for coming down," responded Lord Baldwin, smiling and shaking his hand. His Lordship was dressed as he usually was when he was at home, corduroy pants, check shirt unbuttoned at the neck, slippers. Slightly overweight at about 5'10", his ruddy cheeks clean shaven and his mousy hair short and parted down his left side.

"Good Morning, Phillip," said the not as happy Lady Baldwin, although she did offer a smile of sorts.

Her ladyship wore a white blouse, the obligatory white pearls around her still elegant neck, a flowery skirt, stockings and high heels. She looked like she was ready to go out for lunch somewhere. Phillip guessed she was, but first she had to do this 'interview'.

"Come and sit down, Phillip," beamed Lord B motioning him to the couch alongside the two armchairs they were occupying, "Would you like a coffee or anything?"

"No, I'm fine thank you." Phillip took his seat after they did, with Lady B in the middle. Kay left the room with a little wave.

"So Phillip, now that you've had a break, you're here to ask for your old job back?" continued Lord B, conveniently forgetting that Phillip's presence was requested.

"No milord, I came here because I was asked to. I was told you wanted me back at Crompton and that the situation had changed somewhat," he responded calmly but annoyed they were trying to put the onus on him.

Lady B shifted a little uncomfortably on her chair, re-crossed her long legs and threw her husband a withering look, telling him wordlessly not to capsize.

"I'm sorry you got that impression, Phillip. We just wondered if you'd like to re-apply for your old position, that's all," he replied, catching the glimpse of approval from her.

"In that case, perhaps you can tell me then how the situation has changed, what the salary will be, what my duties will be, what benefits there'll be, the accommodation, how many days vacation and what responsibilities I'd have?" Phillip intoned, still smiling.

Despite Phillip annoying Lady B, she did like how he worked and she admired him standing up for himself, even against her. She didn't like weakness. Probably the biggest thing that annoyed her was that Phillip wouldn't look at her like a desirable woman. It was always eye to eye instead of his eye on her body. How could she manipulate when he wouldn't look?

"Well Phillip," she said taking over from her inept husband, "we have missed you and we would like you back but we also have to consider the other applicants. The position as you knew it has changed in that I'm rarely in that part of the world anymore. This is our home now but his lordship still has his business up there. He has to stay there sometimes and we still have the shooting parties there."

She was speaking very softly, a hint of a smile in her eyes as she remembered previous challenges that Phillip had made.

"The accommodation for the butler is still the same, the salary is still the same, and the vacation time is still the same. There'll be private medical coverage and the duties are the same except that there'll be some cooking. Whoever takes the position will also cover for Tom here during his vacation time. The butler there will obviously be responsible for the house; he'll get petty cash from my secretary for his lordship's groceries and will supervise all the cleaning and the tradesmen. As you see, not very different from when you left except that I'm hardly there anymore. Would you be interested?"

"I'll be interested if there's an increase in the salary and an increase in the vacation time."

"But it's less work than it used to be," she said a little haughtily.

"Maybe so, but I hadn't had an increase for over two years and cooking and shopping are extras from what I used to do."

"Yes, but it's not as if you'll have to do any fancy meals," Lady B stated, implying that Lord B had simple tastes.

"Maybe not milady, but I would require a larger salary and longer vacation time."

"How much longer?"

"Five or six weeks, like your other employees at the company."

"But you wouldn't work for the company," Lady B countered.

"No, but if it's still the same set up, then that's who I'll get paid by."

"Well, we'll have to think about it then, Phillip," she snapped back, standing up to signal this meeting "interview" was over. With that, she breezed out of the room leaving the two men standing, shaking hands goodbye with a little small talk about the period he'd been away.

Phillip then made his own way back toward the kitchen leaving Lord B in the library, who picked up his paper and sat down again to await his lunch.

"Well, are you back?" said Kay excitedly as he stepped into the kitchen.

"I don't know, it's really up to them."

"Oh, I'm sure you will be. We've all really missed you. I've got to run. Lady B has just called down for me but I wanted to see you before you left and just give you another hug," she replied, doing just that before hurrying away.

"She az zey ots for you," smiled Rene as she left.

"Don't be daft. A woman has only to look your way and you think they're after your body. It was just a hug is all."

"It's true, us French are very desirable."

"Only in your dreams, Rene. So Tom", Phillip continued, moving the conversation to the only other person in the kitchen, "how are things with you?"

"Okay. Busy, I suppose."

"Busy?" Rene interposed, "he works like a crazy man."

"It's just a big house and a lot of work, but I'll appreciate your help sometimes if you come back," responded Tom as he began to prepare a lunch tray for Lord B in between doing some dishes.

"This place is friggin huge, it beats me how you know where anybody is?

"Half the time I have to guess or walk round in circles. Sometimes they'll ask for something in one room and when I get back, they've gone to a different one."

"God, that's helpful," Phillip concurred. "So what happened to my replacement?"

"Who? Simon? He couldn't deal with his lordship's clothing. Apparently, he used to hide his shoes in the closets and his suits were just left on hangars. He had no idea how to polish or press so he just didn't bother. He was okay serving, but he had this annoying habit of clicking his heels whenever he entered a room. Lady B liked him though. He was always telling her how wonderful she looked."

"Oh blimey," replied Phillip, "she never got that from me. I sometimes thought about telling her to put her tits away, but that was about it."

"You mean when she puts on those low cut dresses?" laughed Tom.

"That's right, it's almost like they're laying on a shelf."

"Well, I'd better leave you guys to do lunch so I'll say so long."

"I can make you some lunch before you go," Rene said.

"No, that's okay."

"Then go and say hi to my family. The wife will be upset if you don't."

"Okay Rene, I will. Where is your house?"

"Just go to the top of the drive and turn right. Go past the stables on your left and my house is the first one on the right."

"Got it. Great seeing you again, Rene. And a pleasure meeting you, Tom," Phillip replied, going to each in turn and shaking their hands.

"Nice meeting you, Phillip. Are you sure you won't have some lunch? I'd love to chat with you more. Maybe when you come back?"

"We'll see."

Phillip did call in and see Rene's wife and little girl before he left, and as he drove away he took in the sheer size of the property, and how pretty it was in that particular part of England.

It turned out that there were no other applicants, there was more money, but they didn't like giving five or six weeks' vacation, so he settled on four. They kept him waiting before officially asking him back so in return he delayed his answer. But he had a good visit at Stonebridge with his old friends and a couple of new ones, and he did like Lord Baldwin. Although he didn't need to just yet, he went and got his overnight bag ready, put on his shoes and coat, and carrying his bag, he left his tiny house to make the short walk down the lane to Crompton Hall. Lord Baldwin wasn't coming here tonight, it would just be Phillip and the three Yorkshire terriers that'd been brought back by Cathy whose home was still in this neighborhood. So the four of them would sit together on the couch in the family room and watch television, listening to the floorboards creak above them in this old sixteenth century house.

Almost everyone thought the house was haunted, even Phillip did, but if it was it was a friendly presence. Phillip had never been scared in this house. He would quite happily wander around at night turning no lights on. Yet the Baldwin's daughter would not walk alone down the corridor that connected the house to the old chapel which was now the library as it was always freezing. This was true, despite the heating radiators. Even as Phillip and the dogs looked up and followed the footsteps that made the floorboards creak, he had to admit that he could find no reason why that corridor was always cold, nor why it always felt as if someone was always watching you there.

Although the house had been added to over the years, it still had a cobbled courtyard and stable doors that now hid cars instead of horses. It's stone exterior was mostly covered with climbing ivy and boasted a huge front door with a bold brass knocker. All in all, the 16,000 sq. ft. home was quite large for

the family and also included a wine cellar, eight bedrooms, and

two dining rooms . A creepy house in some respects but also

warm and inviting, it overlooked pastures of green fields with

cattle grazing and horses playing, or a helicopter landing or

taking off.

Lady Baldwin was sitting in the helicopter at Battersea Heliport waiting for her pilot to get them in the air and home again. She could have donned the headset and microphone and chatted to the pilot, Ian, but she didn't like him. He was fat and rude so she hardly ever spoke to him, and she was certain that her attitude irked him no end, which amused her greatly.

She'd been in London for a few days now, doing lots of shopping, predominantly at Harrods which was close to her townhouse. She'd also visited with her showbiz friends for lunches and dinners, gone to the theatre, had meetings with her interior designers and of course her liaisons. There was Simon who was always hungry for her and whose bed she'd left not long ago. Then there was Tristan, the long time mate of the movie star, and Lady B's friend, Jane Robins who she couldn't get with as often as she liked. Very often it was with Jane in close proximity which made it even more delicious.

It was only a short flight, thirty-five minutes or so, and she waited for Ian to shut the helicopter down before putting down her magazine. She could just as easily have gotten off without him shutting it down. It wasn't necessary but still she waited, just as Tom and Kay waited on the lawn beside the house. Tom would retrieve her shopping and Kay would welcome her and relay messages and gossip.

"That was a bumpy ride, Ian," she commented as she stepped out the open door he held for her.

"So sorry, Lady Baldwin. Air control wouldn't let me change altitude," he offered as way of excuse.

"Well, don't let it happen again," she uttered, already walking away toward the house gingerly in her stiletto heels on the grass.

"Good evening, milady. Did you have a good trip?" asked Tom who was making his way toward the aircraft.

"Yes, thank you. There are some shopping bags to come in."

"Good evening , milady. You look good tonight and very refreshed. London agrees with you," fawned Kay as Lady Baldwin approached the French doors to the house, one of which Kay was holding open.

"Where are the dogs?" asked Lady Baldwin, looking around.

"Cathy took them to Crompton for a few days as you told her to."

"Well, I like them here meeting me. Tell her to come back and bring the dogs. Is my husband here yet?"

"He got home a couple of hours ago. He's in the library, I think."

They continued on their way. Kay relaying her messages as they made their way toward the master bedroom on the next floor up.

"She couldn't even say thank you for a safe flight," stormed Ian as he retrieved her shopping from the hold, passing the bags to Tom. "She sits right behind me so I can't see her, never talks to me during the flight, always has me shut the engine down, then she always finds something to moan about, the fucking bitch."

"And how do you really feel, Ian?" laughed Tom.

"I tell you, one day I'll really give her a flight to moan about. I'll throw her sorry ass out the door."

"If you do, make sure she's not wearing a parachute."

They both laughed, Ian losing the tension he'd felt since waiting for her at Battersea. Although she thought of him as fat and rude, everyone else quite liked him. He did have a manner about him but then he had been in the armed services for most of his career and was only used to superior officers talking down to him, and he didn't like that either. He was quite large, about 280 pounds, but he was always well dressed. His uniform of blue, officer markings on the sleeves, lighter blue shirt and air regiment tie were impeccably pressed. He even wore a peaked cap most days. Facially he appeared craggy, a couple of small scars on his cheeks, pale blue eyes, good teeth, triple chinned, close cropped beard and moustache.

"I think that's about everything, Tom," he said, closing the hold door and rummaging through the discarded magazines in the passenger compartment.

"Okay. Well have a good night, Ian" he called as he struggled away with all the shopping bags.

"You too, pal. You too."

Tom put all the bags down once inside the house and quickly closed the door. Ian had just started rotors moving so he gave

him a quick wave and picked the bags up again, taking
them into the kitchen. Rene was already cooking something for
dinner and asked Tom what time she wanted it.

"She didn't say."

"Shit," Rene spoke with his accent making it sound more like
'sheet'.

"She's brought some food back," Tom stated, as he looked at
the contents of each bag before picking some of them up
again off the counter and leaving the kitchen.

Rene sighed and lowered the heat under the pans, and taking
the lamb out of the oven before it overcooked. He generally
half cooked the vegetables, waiting to finish for when she
actually sat down for her meal, which could be anytime.
Having stopped cooking he instead began to put away the
shopping, items he himself had ordered which couldn't be
obtained around here, like his favorite French cheeses that were
extremely aromatic.

Kay was running a bath for Lady B. It was hot and liberally
laced with the oils she liked, but the housekeeper hated as
they left hard to dislodge lines. Lady B was sitting by her

marble topped dressing table just to the side of the huge

free standing bath, clipping her hair up and removing her

makeup, wearing just a thick white bath robe.

Hearing a knock on the adjacent bedroom door, Kay turned

off the faucets, closed the bathroom door and opened the

bedroom door for Tom to bring in the bags.

"Just leave them, Tom. I'll sort them out."

"Okay, do you know what time she'd like dinner?"

"I'll ring down when I find out."

Closing the door behind him, she returned to the bathroom.

Lady B always liked either Cathy or Kay in there with her.

She wasn't shy with her nakedness. She felt admired by

everyone, and in here she could gossip and tell her tales

knowing her husband wouldn't intrude.

Although Kay was always embarrassed about having to sit by

the bath with the naked lady, she nevertheless relished the tales

she was told, although having to gossip about the other staff

was sometimes difficult.

The bath was placed directly in front of a huge window.

Sometimes if she bathed during the day, she'd leave the drapes open so she could see outside, even sometimes standing up if someone was out there. It gave her a thrill to think one or more of the estate workers might secretly lust after her. The drapes were down now as she lay back in the hot water with her head on the bath pillow facing them, as the hot water and the oils worked their magic on her sated body.

"So, Kay," she barely mumbled as she sat beside her, " what's been happening around here?"

"Well," she began excitedly, "Lady Entwistle had a dinner party the other night, a big one with a lot of the hunt members like the old Duke, Lord and Lady Salcombe, Sir Robert and Tina Noble, and it was a huge disaster. Some of the wine was corked, most of the meal was cold and she swears she'll never use the same caterers ever again."

"We were invited to that, what fun."

"It's also being said that the owner of that restaurant you go to, Pepe's, was caught with his trousers down with one of the waitresses."

"No, not George!"

"Yes. Apparently his wife wondered why he was late coming home so she went round there without calling. She walked in and he was screwing a waitress on one of the tables."

"Oh my god, I can't imagine," Lady B laughed, "I'll never be able to look him in the face again."

"You might not have to. They're also saying they may have to close if his wife sues for divorce."

"That will be a shame, it's one of the best places around here. I wonder which table they used."

"Does that matter?"

"No, I just wondered is all. So what else?"

Kay noticed the soft smile on her lips, the look in her eyes as she said this and she wondered which table she'd had sex on with George, especially when she imperceptibly touched herself on her breasts.

"It's got the whole town talking."

"Nothing around the house?"

"I think Ann wants to quit."

"Do you mean Tom's wife?"

"Yes."

"Well, she can't . It was part of their terms when they came here. Why does she want to quit?"

"She says she needs more space."

"More space? What does that mean?"

"I think they're having some marital problems and she doesn't want to be around him all the time."

"If she's having marital problems, she should have an affair, but I won't let her quit."

"I think there might be more to the story. I'll let you know."

"Anything else, Kay?"

"I haven't heard anything from any of the children since you were last here, but I think Cathy is having problems at home."

"I haven't heard from the kids either, but I think they hate me.for some unknown reason, and I give them everything. What problems is Cathy having?"

"They don't hate you. They're young adults now and finding their own way is all. Cathy's husband is playing up again about her being here all the time, him having to look after the kids and do all the meals and things."

"He should have moved down here if that's what his problem is. I offered them a house and it's not like he has a job or anything. The kids would get a much better education here and I need her around, no one else knows where all my things are."

"It gets to her, especially with the kids. They treat her like a visitor nowadays. Despite what her husband says it's actually Cathy's mother who looks after them and bringing them here would upset her. I don't think Cathy is bothered anymore as to what her hubby thinks, but her kids are a different matter."

"Get her back down here and I'll talk to her, tell her not to forget the dogs otherwise they'll start pining for Phillip again. He has nothing to do up there apart from spoiling the dogs. Now put some more hot water in the bath."

Kay got up and did as she was told, trying at the same time to avert her eyes from Lady B's naked body. It was almost as if it was flaunted before her, knowing that she struggled with her own figure on a daily basis. She had only to look at some chocolate to gain a few pounds more. It was so unfair.

"That's enough hot water, Kay. Sit back down and I'll tell you what I've been up to."

"Can I tell the kitchen when you'll want dinner first?"

"Don't worry about the kitchen. Let me tell you about the dinner party at Jane Robins house and how Tristan and I snuck away for a few minutes," she whispered, picking up a bar of soap to lather herself with as she told her tale.

Kay sat down, she thought Tristan was gorgeous like no other, but this was as close as she was going to get, she was under no illusions there but she could still dream.

"I'm all ears milady, all ears."

CHAPTER FOUR

Lord Baldwin had been at Crompton for a couple of weeks now, alone and making no visits south to Stonebridge or London which was very unusual. Phillip didn't mind. He was no bother, very appreciative, and even gave him time off at the weekends he'd been here. The dogs had been long gone so it was quiet in the house and with his lordship in residence, Phillip had been able to go home every night, which he was very thankful for.

He knew that his lordship had been suffering the wrath of his wife, he didn't speak of it but Phillip knew she was livid at him for giving him a month off and that she was also angry because he'd objected to her inviting their ex-butler Simon to a dinner party, that was attended by his lordship's friends. He'd caught a few tidbits of some of the stormy telephone calls there'd been and whenever he'd answered the phone to Lady B, she'd been very brusque and cold.

He liked his lordship. He was a nice gentleman who was a good businessman, and a loving father with a good sense of humor. He preferred the simple life, loved his collection of cars and pottering around his country estate. Apparently his wife too had liked this life once, but now she seemed to want excitement and extravagance, partying and column inches..

This morning, Phillip awoke at 6am which was his routine whenever someone was in residence. As was his usual behavior, he went downstairs in just boxers to put his hot water kettle on and then straight back upstairs to pee and to run his bath. He didn't have a shower, just a bath, but at least the water pressure was good and it only took a couple of minutes to fill.

Bath ready, he went back downstairs to make a mug of tea which he took back with him. After brushing his teeth, shaving, bathing and washing his hair which seemed to be turning silver now, he got dressed in his morning suit apart from the black jacket, which remained at the main house. Ready, he returned downstairs to make more tea and picked up his newspaper which had been dropped through his door letter box and sat to read the back sport page. It was still dark, so he had the lights on and he always kept his house warm. He knew it would be chilly outside but at least he couldn't hear any rain. At exactly five minutes to seven he put his overcoat on, turned out the lights, and left for work. It was only a skeleton staff that still worked here at Crompton. There was just Phillip, Maud the housekeeper, Brian the gardener, Susan his assistant gardener, and Gail the groom. If Lady Baldwin came up then invariably Cathy and Kay would accompany her and Rene as well.

Phillip was always the first to arrive and the last to leave and was enjoying his short stroll this morning despite it being quite chilly. The house was situated on a hill overlooking a valley which was fog shrouded today, and the rising sun was beginning to burn it off so it was a very pretty scene. No one else was around so it was very peaceful as he approached the huge wrought iron gates that were the entrance, although the two yard dogs began to bark as he crunched gravel and retrieved the newspapers before tapping in the code for the gates to open. He told them to shush as he walked by. The two male Labradors sniffed around him in recognition but not with the excitement that they showed Brian as he was the one who fed them.

Looking up at the house, he was surprised to see a light on in his lordship's bedroom, maybe he was going to his office soon and wanted an early breakfast. He unlocked the side door and stepped inside, not surprised that the alarm didn't beep as his lordship never activated it. From his routine at home, Phillip then went on another routine here at work, first turning on the lights in the staff/laundry room, hanging up his coat and donning his jacket, turning on the already full water kettle, walking through to the main quarters turning on lights, unlocking the front door, placing the papers on the kitchen table where his lordship would have breakfast and was already set for, then turning on the kettle here in the kitchen in case his lordship rang down for some tea. Phillip hadn't worked last night. He'd been sent home as Lord B had said he was going out for dinner so as Phillip had been turning on the lights he'd been looking to see if anything was amiss, or different. He hadn't noticed anything, apart from an odd smell which he resolved to ask Brian about when he came in at

7:30. He was in the kitchen getting the oranges out to be squeezed when he was shocked to hear his lordship coming down the staircase and into the kitchen.

"Good morning, milord. I'm afraid your breakfast isn't ready yet but would you like some tea?"

His lordship was already fully dressed in a blue business suit and actually looked a little embarrassed.

"That's okay Phillip, I won't require breakfast today, and I forgot you came in at this time so I now need you to do me a huge favor" he sheepishly said.

"Of course, milord."

"I had a guest stay over last night but I can't have it becoming public knowledge. I know I can rely on your discretion. But what of the others?"

"You can rely on Maud, milord. I'll see to that but it may be better if Brian doesn't learn of it. I trust him implicitly but he does get on well with Cathy and may let something slip."

"I understand," he said, visibly relaxing. "Let me introduce you," he continued as the sound of heels on the wooden stairs could be heard and they both stepped out to the hallway to greet the guest. "Victoria, this is my butler Phillip. Phillip, this is Mrs. Harrop."

"Good morning, ma'am Very pleased to meet you." Phillip beamed.

"Good morning, Phillip. It's nice to meet you too. I've heard a lot about you from Alistair but please, call me Victoria or Vicky," she quietly answered in her slight Scottish accent and a little red faced, referring to Lord B by his first name.

"We must dash Phillip, but I hope Mrs. Harrop will be a regular visitor here so you will get to know one another. No dinner tonight but I will come and change before going out." Lord B spoke as he went toward the front door, closely followed by Mrs. Harrop.

Phillip got there before them, opening it for them, then opening the passenger door of Lord B's car for his guest which she thanked him for and also clasped his hands in hers as a personal 'thank you.'

Closing the passenger door, Phillip went around to the driver's side and spoke as Lord B started the engine. "Milord, it may be advisable to turn right out of the gate, otherwise Brian may see you on his way in."

"Good thinking , Phillip. See you this afternoon." With a brief wave from them both, they drove away.

"Well, well, well," Phillip spoke aloud as he watched them leave, "Good for you. Good for you."

He'd taken an immediate shine to Mrs. Harrop. She seemed down to earth and natural. Phillip relied a lot on his first impressions and he was rarely wrong. She was taller than Lady B and about as slim but where Lady B was tits and legs in your face, Mrs. Harrop was more discreet with shorter heels, longer skirt, and a buttoned up blouse. She was pretty too with black shoulder length curly hair and brown eyes. Maybe she was in her late thirties or early forties, homely seeming. Phillip was very happy this morning.

He just had to keep this quiet.

By the time Brian came in, Phillip had already made them both tea and was sitting at the table in the staff room with his jacket off.

"Morning, Phil. Where's the car?"

Brian's first task in the morning was checking over his lordship's car, re-filling it if necessary, de-frosting if that too was needed, and generally having it ready to go.

"Morning, Brian. He's already left. There's some tea here for you."

"Thanks. He's early, isn't he?" commented Brian as he sat down taking a sip of his tea.

"Caught me out as well. Seems he had an early meeting and forgot to tell me."

Brian was a handsome guy, he said that Lady B generally came on to him when she was here, and that he often wondered what he'd do if she took it further. He was tall, muscular, thick dark hair that was short but brushed forward, and always wore his green uniform, which at this time of year also consisted of a thick green sweater and ski jacket

"So how are you this morning?" asked Brian.

"I'm fine thanks, just wondering what the hell I'll give him for dinner tonight." Phillip lied, not wanting Brian to know that Lord B would be going out.

"You should get him some fish and chips."

"That's not a bad idea. I wouldn't mind some for lunch."

"You want me to go?"

"Sure, if you go about 12 I'll ring the order through before you go."

"Sounds good. So any news for me?"

"No, it's fairly quiet here."

"So there's no sign of her coming up?" he asked, referring to Lady B.

"No. I think they're still arguing."

"Is that because of your time off?"

"Maybe, but I don't know why she's getting her knickers in a twist about it because they'll be in Antigua anyway." Every year for the whole month of June and usually July the Baldwin's went and stayed at their house in Antigua, just as they always went there for Christmas and the New Year.

"She doesn't like the staff having fun and time off is why."

"That's true, but she can lump it."

"You know she'll try to scupper your plans. I'd better go feed the dogs. I'll be back in a few minutes." With that, he put down his empty mug of tea and departed the way he came in. .

Phillip didn't see Brian for almost an hour. He'd been checking his lordship's dressing room; taken away a suit and a pair of shoes that needed pressing/polishing, put his shirt and underwear in the laundry for Maud. Then he checked the bedroom to make sure that Mrs. Harrop had left nothing behind. He then checked Lady B's bathroom for the same reason, realized that Mrs. Harrop had used his lordship's bathroom, and then finally checked all the other rooms just to make sure there was no trace of her. Satisfied, he went to the kitchen and cleared up before going back to the staff room for another cup of tea and to do some pressing/polishing.

"Good morning, Phil," welcomed Susan who was in her stocking feet after leaving her boots and coat at the door, "Tea?"

Brian's assistant was Susan, a short blonde haired girl a couple of years younger than Brian who was in his late twenties, and she was very slim, tall, and much stronger than she looked. She dressed in the same uniform as Brian, didn't mind working in cold and wet weather and they looked

quite a team as they worked

"Yes please. Brian's just coming in the door and he'll

probably want one as well."

"I've just made his. I was waiting for you."

"Thanks. So, is it cold enough for you out there?" he asked

her as the three of them took their seats around the table,

which was situated in the middle of the room surrounded by

washing machines, dryers, a machine specifically used for

pressing sheets, and built in cupboards and closets. This room

led directly into another where Phillip did his pressing and

shoe polishing and also where he generally cleaned the

extensive silver from his pantry. There was nearly always

someone in this part of the house as this was where most of

the work was done.

"No, it's not that cold today," Sue replied in her soft , but

only slight, local accent, "the sun is quite warm when you can

actually see it."

"Cathy called me last night" blurted Brian.

"What did she want?" asked the interested Phillip.

"Just a moan really. She says she wants to work here again."

"God, I hope not, I don't feel like I can trust her anymore with all the tales she likes to tell to Lady B. Be like having a spy in the camp with her here. Lady B would never let her do that unless she came back herself and that's not going to happen. So why does she want to come back?"

"She says because her marriage has gone up the Swanee and she misses her kids."

"Well, I don't know why she didn't move them down there at the beginning instead of her leaving them here and visiting once every two weeks or so. That was just asking for trouble."

"Promise you won't say anything, but the reason for that was at the beginning she was having this thing with one of the estate workers down there, and by the time she got bored with it her family up here didn't need her anymore and wouldn't move."

"So then, it's her own fault?"

"Yes, but she blames Lady B."

"Why?"

"Because when she went there, her and Lady B were chatting one day and she mentioned to Lady B that this estate guy was a bit of a hunk and that she liked him looking at her. Fantasizing really. Next thing she knows, she's being taken out to dinner by Lady B who disappears when this same guy shows up. She'd been set up it seems."

"It still takes two to tango. She could have said no."

"Right, that's what I said. Still she blames Lady B because she jumped into bed with him then, and now for her marriage being in tatters."

"So why doesn't she leave?"

"Because she thinks she's too important, she likes the money she gets and all the clothes that Lady B gives her."

"Then I have no sympathy. And it still doesn't explain her being a tittle tattle."

"Her excuse for that is when she gets asked something, she can't lie."

"Yeah, right."

Just at that moment they heard the door open and close and the three of them watched as Maud trundled in, dressed as usual in a short sleeved white blouse, navy blue skirt and flat black shoes. Maud was a big woman in her late fifties now with a round face that seemed perpetually red and permed brown hair. As long as Phillip had known her, which was a few years now, no matter what the weather was like she always left her coat in her car and came into the house like this. The next thing she'd do would be sit down. She didn't disappoint.

After everyone had said good morning, Maud was the first to speak, "What's the news today?" She'd been looking at Phillip when she said this in her strong voice, so naturally it was he who answered.

"Nothing much Maud. His lordship has already gone to his office and said he wouldn't be back until later this afternoon. Just before you came in, Brian was saying that Cathy called him last night to say she wanted to come and work here again. It's to be kept quiet but she has big marriage problems and it will probably end up in a divorce."

"Serves the cow right. She was quite happy when she was dallying around down there but now she's sorry and wants her family back." Maud was always forthright and it seems, intuitive now.

"How did you know about her affair?" asked the amazed Brian.

"A woman knows these things," replied Maud knowingly.

"Well, I didn't know," responded the normally silent Susan.

"You haven't been around as much as I have, duck" continued Maud using a common nickname, "but I'm not sorry for her and I don't want her back here. There used to be four of us cleaning this place and now, whenever she shows her face, she's always telling me it's filthy and just won't do. I don't know who she thinks she is but this house is not filthy." Phillip concurred with that. It wasn't filthy; it was simply some things couldn't be dusted as often as they used to be when there was more help.

"I don't think any of us want her back, Maud," Phillip offered.

"I suppose I'd better go make his bed then," said the rising Maud.

"I need to show you something first," stated Phillip, getting up with her along with the two gardeners who went to rinse out

their empty mugs, " in his bathroom."

As the gardeners left the house, the two remaining went up the service stairs which were just by the laundry/staff room. Reaching the landing on the next floor, Phillip could see out the adjacent window that Brian and Sue were outside and heading toward the greenhouse.

"Maud?"

"Yes."

"I won't beat around the bush because I know you'd guess. His lordship has found another woman."

"Hallelujah!." she exclaimed, "Are they getting divorced?"

"I don't know. I don't think so just yet as he asked me to keep it quiet. She spent the night here."

"Now I know why you're telling me and thank you for doing so. I'd have known within two seconds, especially as I can smell her perfume."

"Exactly. I haven't told Brian or Susan though."

"You did right. He talks to Cathy too much."

"I know he's careful most of the time, but he likes a drink sometimes and that's when stuff slips."

"Well, you know I won't talk to her. It'll be nice knowing something that she won't hear about. I'm so pleased for his lordship but who is she? Do I know her? Is she nice? How old is she? She's not like the other one is she?"

"I only met her on her way out but she seemed really nice and I'm generally good on first impressions."

"I'm glad for him. She's been cheating on him for years and treating him badly. I'd love to be a fly on the wall when he eventually tells her.""Won't that be something? Be a great day when he tells her to go."

"This has made my day, Phillip. I'll go and clean up now." Maud proceeded down the long hallway toward the bedroom, singing a little song in a high pitch that was way higher than her speaking voice.

Phillip knew he didn't need to make her promise to keep it quiet, she wouldn't say anything to anyone, but she would whisper it to one source. Her bulldog, the pride of her life.

"Life was getting interesting" he thought to himself as he went back to the laundry room. "I'm going to the States soon, his lordship will be dumping Lady B, my soccer team is top of the league, and I have a brand new sports car. What else can possibly happen?"

CHAPTER FIVE

The sad figure sitting alone on this almost deserted beach on the island of Antigua was Lord Baldwin. He'd gotten away this early morning because she'd been in a drunken sleep and hadn't even noticed him get out of bed. Not that she ever noticed him in bed anymore; about the only time they had marital relations these days was when they had one of her infernal parties and she'd ride him with her eyes closed, probably pretending he was one of the many guests she'd flirted with that particular night. Up until recently, he'd always loved his wife, had turned a blind eye to her excesses, forgiven her mood swings, chided the two children for staying away from her, let her fire and hire staff at will, tolerated her confiding in Kay and Cathy, and hell, he'd even let her have that dog killed on one of the shoots when she said it was attacking the live birds. But now he was in a real quandary. He was seeing her now for how she really was and he'd fallen for another woman, desperately fallen.

He'd come here to their Caribbean home to see if he could salvage this marriage, not wanting to give up yet, and at the back of his mind not wanting to break up his company that he'd spent years building. Victoria was very understanding. He knew she was uncomfortable being a mistress and the only thing she'd really said was "I'm prepared to wait for you, even prepared for you to make another go of your marriage, but I don't want you to leave everything and then have regrets later. I love you, Alistair, so take your time and sort things out, however long that may take."

As he sat staring at the waves breaking on the white sand and at a middle aged couple walking along the shore with their excited dog, he wondered where it had begun to go wrong, how this, his second marriage, was failing. He'd lost his first wife in a car accident before they'd had chance to start a family, and Charlotte who'd been a friend until then to them both had been so supportive and understanding. He was unsure how they'd eventually began to be romantically involved. It had been a very trying period, but he woke up with her one day and that was it. Two children had come along in quick succession. Then before he'd been ready, they'd been dispatched to boarding school and C, short for Charlotte, had been more and more drawn to these show business types. Since then, he felt like he'd been losing the battle. She didn't like their home in Crompton anymore , she didn't like his friends much, he knew now she was sleeping around, she'd arranged for his vasectomy, she was still taking birth control pills and she was just so spiteful. He knew she'd bought the restaurant in Paris because he'd had to sign the check, he knew she'd spoiled Kay's happiness when the children were younger but wasn't sure how, and she was now making Cathy spend too much time away from her home. Not that he was too bothered about Kay and Cathy because he knew they gossiped and conspired on things with her, but he was bothered that other lives were dallied with for purely selfish and spiteful reasons. Yet still he persevered with her, hoping against hope she'd see sense and that they could return home to their old simple life.

So he comes to Antigua, being told that it will be just the family for this vacation, along with Kay, who the children adore. Yet within three days of arriving here, along comes Jane Robins and her effeminate boyfriend, Tristan who always seems to be whispering and giggling with C. Jane is okay, a bit over the hill he thought for the roles she still wanted, but he didn't really have much in common with her, or with the folk she'd brought with her like the aging pop star and the slimy PR people. So now the children, who also didn't like these people, had more or less vanished, and he was feeling more and more alone although he had made a couple of calls to Victoria. He just didn't know what to do anymore.

In Lady B's dressing room that morning, she was more concerned about how she looked in this new bikini she'd bought than why Charles and Sophie had practically disappeared.

"How do I look, Kay? Is this flattering?"

"Very, milady. You'll stop traffic in this."

"I doubt that but it does look good, doesn't it?" which was more statement than question as she twirled in front of the full length mirror, adjusting her breasts in the bra.

"They won't be able to take their eyes off you," promised Kay.

"John was feeling me up during dinner last night," she smiled, recalling his hand sliding up her thighs under the tabletop.

"John Steele?" "Yes, I think he'll come back for more today. He's very well endowed, you know?"

"You know that?"

"Kay," she said almost indignantly, "If I'm going to let someone feel me up then it's only fair that I can reciprocate."

"Don't let Tristan catch you."

"Oh, him. Jane is hardly leaving his side these days, I can barely get a look in."

"I'm sure you will before long."

"Where are Charles and Sophie?" Lady B realized she hadn't seen her children in some time.

"They went into town a couple of hours ago."

"I've hardly seen them since they came here."

"I think they went shopping," Kay replied, as she kept getting out different sheer bathing gowns for her ladyship to model and to settle on.

"They were as miserable as their father during dinner last night, such bad company. My guests must think they're brats. You must tell them to behave and be more sociable."

"I'll tell them. I think white on white looks good on you" she commented as Lady B twirled some more, admiring her fake tan and the contrast it made with the white bikini, then slipping on some high heels to accentuate the length of her legs.

"Make sure you do. I'm going down to the pool now so tell Winston to get some champagne out there and some appetizers."

With that, she flounced out of the dressing room picking up a racy novel to take with her whilst Kay remained behind to tidy her discarded outfits. Then she called down to the kitchen to tell Winston, the butler, about the champagne.

Kay was secretly very glad about the children's manner. This was what she'd strived for. Although in most instances she was extremely loyal to Lady B, willing to pander to her whims, make excuses for her, tell tales, lie for her and plan trysts. When it came to the children, however, she made sure that they knew how bad their mother was. She did this partly because she felt that she was their true mother, but more so because she knew that Lady B had forced her one true love to leave so many years ago.

Kay wasn't exactly sure how she'd done it although she could make guesses, especially when she'd witnessed many men being seduced. But she'd been extremely hurt losing her boyfriend so had eventually come up with this strategy of slowly taking away the children's affection. It had been nothing overt, just agreeing with them if they thought their mother was being mean or something, letting them accidentally catch their mother flirting with her various men or overhearing her talk badly about their father who they adored.

Lady Baldwin was quite right when she said her children hated her. They did and Kay was very proud of them. As for Lord Baldwin, she knew the children loved him and always would, and she never had reason to try and stop that. She basically just felt sorry for him. He was no match for his wife's wiles and schemes.

"Now," she thought wistfully as she put the unused bikinis away, "if only I could take a leaf out of her book and get someone interested in me."

CHAPTER SIX

Phillip and Ken finally made it to the USA, but not before
a lot of rearranging had taken place. Phillip's primary reason
for taking the trip was to be able to see some World Cup
games and before he started making plans his ideal would have
been to see a couple of games in the first stage and then
some of the later knockout games culminating in the final
itself, which in this particular tournament was being held in
Los Angeles. The competition was being played in major cities
around the country. Rather than travel around trying to fit in
games, he'd just stay in California and catch whatever games
he could in that particular state. Then he discovered how much
the tickets were.

On telling Ken how much they were he wasn't surprised when
Ken declined buying any, and he was very disappointed to
learn that the final would be out of his reach also. He settled
then on seeing three or four games in the first stage, and
then maybe buying a semi-final ticket on the black market,

especially if it was involving an unglamorous team that wouldn't have many supporters there or be attractive enough for the hosts. So he bought the tickets, booked the flights, hired a car and looked into doing some side trips that Ken would enjoy.

Then Lady B stuck her oar into things saying he couldn't go on the date he'd booked as he'd be needed at Stonebridge because she wanted Tom to have some time off and he was supposed to be his relief. He wasn't surprised by this, had been expecting it in fact, but he still thought she was a bitch for doing it, just as he thought Cathy was, as she was her mouthpiece. He was even more angry when he discovered that the house was empty and that it had cost him to rearrange the flight time, not to mention the grief he received from Ken. They finally flew from London to San Francisco for a three week stay. Phillip missed the first game he'd got a ticket for, had managed to avoid paying for it thankfully, but it had been a huge hassle.

Ken was eighty one years old now but refused to act anything like his age, instead he liked to believe he was still a stud in his late twenties and would chat up any woman he saw. The women for their part generally thought of him as a very charming old English gentleman. He was full of tales and would regale any and everyone at every convenience. Phillip had heard them all before, they'd done a previous trip to the US traveling around the whole country and Ken's stories hadn't changed any since then. Phillip tended to take a back seat to Ken and let him enjoy himself. Apart from being a butler, Ken had also worked aboard the old classic liners like the original Queen Mary, had served in the Second World War as a navigator for the RAF, had lived in Australia for a few years, and was also a toastmaster at some of the finest dinners in London. He knew a lot of people, royals, celebrities, politicians' et al, but he didn't have any airs and sometimes when hearing his stories, you could think that he was stretching the truth a little. He did sometimes, but Phillip knew him well enough by now to know that most of them were true because he'd seen his memorabilia and Fran, Ken's friend, had verified most of them.

Within a couple of days of arriving in San Francisco, Phillip had gone along to Stanford Stadium to see Brazil play the host country. He'd never been to an international game though he'd seen plenty on television but had never even gone to Wembley stadium in London to see the English national team play, yet had been there many times to see his club team play. So this was a first for him, his first live international and the most famous country in World Cup history, Brazil, was his introduction. He was very excited. He knew from televised games that the Brazilian fans were a different breed than he was used to, the English fans tended to drink too much and then start fighting, but the Brazilians would rather dance and party. He got to the stadium early, and having parked he wandered around, totally amazed at the music being played, the dancing going on in little impromptu circles by scantily clad women, the atmosphere they created, and the number of fans who recognized the red club shirt he wore as he strolled from band to band. He wondered what the Americans would make of all this, this was all very new to them, but you couldn't help but be drawn into the carnival that was occurring outside Stanford Stadium that day.

Inside was very much the same, but as the American stadiums tend to be open with no roofs, whatever noise is generated is usually lost in the big open space so it wasn't as vibrant as the streets had been. The game itself was no classic, but Phillip did enjoy it and was very sorry that Ken had decided not to get a ticket, he'd have loved it. He said as much when Phillip arrived back at the motel they were staying at.

"Why didn't you get me a ticket?"

"Because you said you didn't want to go."

"You should have known I'd have enjoyed it."

"How the hell would I have known that? For years you've been telling me what a silly game it is."

"I've never watched one before."

"Did you watch this one today?"

"What else was there for me to do?"

"You said you were going for a walk."

"Well I didn't feel like it so I put the TV on."

"Did you understand what was going on?"

"I understand that they have to put that little ball in one of the nets at each end of the field, but I didn't realize there was so much movement involved. I don't understand that offside thing either but it was good. You should have gotten me tickets. I'd at least have liked those Brazilian women dancing"

"I'll know next time Ken. I'm amazed. Not at the women but I thought it was a crap game yet you enjoyed it. Who'd have thought that? So are we going out to eat and to see that willowy barmaid you like so much?

"I hope so, I thought you'd never ask. I'd best get changed then. So tell me about today. Especially the dancing part"

Phillip regaled him with all the happenings that afternoon as they got changed. Phillip put on his normal casual attire of polo shirt and chino's, while Ken got into shirt and slacks with a blazer and hat. No matter how hot it was, Ken always wore a shirt and slacks, it was rare that he'd even wear a short sleeved shirt. Phillip was used to that. What he did find odd was that Ken was the worst packer of a suitcase that'd he ever seen. He just threw things in.

Ken had a friend here in San Francisco. She was a park ranger who was working now at Alcatraz. They'd gone along there yesterday and spent the day with her, and she'd brought along one of the old prison warders who'd very kindly given them a personal tour. He was so interesting that some of the other tourists started following them around as if they had been invited along, even asking questions. He took it all in his stride though, a few tourists after dealing with hardened criminals was easy for him. They had gone out for dinner afterwards and Ken had asked his ranger friend if she wanted to go home with him. No, she didn't, and although she took Ken and Phillip back to their motel, he tried to persuade her inside but she was none too happy with his advances and that would be the last they saw of her.

With Ken being disappointed with her rejection, but never deterred from other women, Phillip suggested they walk over to the bar just down the street and have a little nightcap. That's where they met the 'willowy barmaid'.

The bar itself was very ordinary, even the building it was housed in was mundane and unattractive, certainly not a tourist attraction, which was reflected in the small number of patrons. It did however have a beautiful barmaid. She was tall, slender, a model's shape really, with very long straight black hair, wearing brief shorts and a tiny sleeveless t-shirt that were designed to draw the eye. Both worked admirably. She was very easy to look at. She also had a nice personality, liked to talk to her customers and to listen to them, not minding in the slightest if they also wanted to ogle. Her husband didn't seem to mind either, her built-like-a-brick-house husband, as he sat quietly at the end of the bar.

That didn't affect Ken, he'd found someone who'd listen to his stories and let him look at her, and although she was called Chelsea, for which she got a full description of the region in London where that name is from, he referred to her as the 'willowy' barmaid. So that's where they went for their nightcap that evening. It was as quiet as it had been the previous night but Chelsea had a couple of friends in so as soon as they walked through the door she proclaimed "Hey guys, these are the two English butlers I was telling you about. Pull up a stool gentleman and come join us. What'll be your pleasure?"

"Well, if I may be so bold my dear, my pleasure would be an evening with you." responded Ken with a twinkle in his eye.

They erupted with laughter, setting the scene for Ken to captivate his new audience, which he did for the next couple of hours, as Phillip just listened and quietly sipped a couple of gin and tonics to Ken's small glass of beer.

"I was offering a lady a stirrup cup," Ken was saying.

"What's a stirrup cup?" one of Chelsea's friends interrupted.

"It's a drink we offer to members of the hunt, usually sherry or port, but sometimes whisky, although the 'stirrup cup' itself is actually the vessel that holds the drink. Usually it's a small silver goblet" Ken explained, quite happily before continuing.

"So I was offering her a stirrup cup, holding the silver tray up so she could take one, when this horse lets rip with a mighty fart. Quick as a flash I say 'I do beg your pardon, milady' and she replies 'that's okay Kenneth, I thought the horse had done it'."

Ken continued on with his tales, stewarding on the luxury cruise lines, butlering for royals sometimes, toast mastering at grand occasions, working in Australia and them all calling him a 'pommie bastard' or 'mate' which he didn't like.

"You never worked for any of the royals full time? Or in Buckingham Palace?"

"No my dearest, I never wanted to. I was quite happy to be asked to go and look after someone who perhaps was being a guest somewhere, but I didn't want to work on a full time basis for one of them."

"Not even in Buckingham Palace or at Windsor Castle?" Phillip was smiling at this point, he knew Ken had particular opinions as he'd asked him the same question once, so he wondered how he was going to reply.

"Well, to begin with my dear young lady, the royals don't pay very much and I was better off financially by only working for them through someone else's pocket. For instance, every year I'm asked to go to Vienna by a hotel there, who pay me a considerable sum to look after a royal guest. If I was to go there as a member of his staff, I'd be paid peanuts. Also when I used to work on the liners, it slowly became apparent that it was attracting a lot of the gay community to work on them probably because it entails a lot of time offshore. So I left that life. The same has been happening with the royal staff. By no means are they all gay, but quite a sizeable number are and although I have no ill feeling towards them, I'm not very comfortable being close to that all of the time especially when I'm being paid a pittance."

Phillip was quite impressed with this answer, it was very different to the one he'd got.

"Are you serious?" one of the ladies asked.

"Ooh yes. The royal household has been attracting the gay community for years now. Some of them even have wives and children to mask who they really are, but because they spend a lot of time away especially on the yacht Britannia, they can lead double lives."

"You're joking."

"In fact, I believe there was a gay orgy a few years ago on the yacht, and a few of the crew were fired, but none of the household staff were, they were forgiven shall we say."

"Wow, Ken, that's amazing. You should write a book."

"Funny you should say that," replied Ken, "I've been working on my memoirs just recently."

"Yeah, like for years you have. You're still no nearer finishing" said Phillip.

"I have a lot of memories, son, a lot to write down."

"I thought you had a ghost writer?"

"I do, I just need to get with him more often."

"Then you must do so, Ken."

"I will. Now let me tell these beautiful ladies about the time I did the television game show in England called 'Double Your Money.'"

After all of the rearranging he'd had to do, not to mention the cost, Phillip only had one more game to go and see and that would be in a few days at the same location, but this game would be involving Sweden, who although play in the same colors as Brazil, don't have the same pizzazz. He looked forward to it anyway, sometimes when it's a lesser team then a better game ensues and the Brazil/USA game had been a bit boring. At this early stage of the competition most teams are more interested in not losing, so unless someone scores early then the game can be more tense than exciting.

Once he'd been to the game, he and Ken were going to do some touring. They'd hired a car so a trip to Yosemite and Sequoia National Parks was planned, then a drive up the coastal highway to Hearst Castle, and onwards to Carmel and Monterey. Until then, they pottered around San Francisco riding the cable cars, window shopping in Chinatown, photographing the Golden Gate Bridge, and visiting a winery in Napa Valley. They also took in a mud bath and massage. . Wherever and whenever he could, Phillip would also catch a game on television in one of the various motel rooms they stayed in, and Ken would either watch with him or go and do some laundry. As Phillip did all the driving, he felt it only fair that he should do all the laundry, and he met many interesting people in there. He even got himself a date at one of the stops, having Phillip drop him off at the restaurant and telling

him not to wait up. He didn't in fact show up until almost
lunch time the following day.

"Good afternoon, you randy old beggar. I was beginning to
think I'd lost you."

"Humph."

"What's up with you? I thought you'd have a smile as wide
as the Grand Canyon today."

"I don't want to talk about it."

"Wasn't the old equipment working?"

"Nothing wrong with my equipment, you cheeky sod."

"So what 's up?"

"I'll tell you what's up. I arranged to meet her where you
dropped me off, I had the table booked and everything, but
she was an hour late. Guess what?"

"What?"

"She turns up with her four kids."

"Get out of here." Phillip laughed.

"She did and I had to pay for everyone."

"Serves you right."

"I was a bit miffed at that, especially as her kids were brats, but I thought what the hell, mom's a bit of all right, so she can put them to bed when we get to her place."

"So you thought you were in there?"

"Of course I did. She kept touching me old pecker under the table while her kids shouted and screamed, and after eating me out of house and home she says, okay, let's go to bed. So we all squeezed into her car, get to her tiny trailer home, and she puts the brats to bed and tells me to fix us a drink. So I find some gin in the kitchen, make us a drink, and I'm just getting my leg over her on the couch when I hear the door open. I'm thinking it's another bloody kid but she jumps up like a jack in the box, buttoning herself up, and the next minute I'm being introduced as her old English uncle who's visiting his long lost family. It was her bloody husband who was supposed to be away working somewhere."

Phillip was by now hysterical. This was just too funny. "So what happened then?"

"I had to give him some bullshit about how I'd longed to visit my relatives and had just made a surprise visit. So I had to talk to him for a while, then they went to bed and had me sleep on the couch. Then I had the distinct pleasure of having to listen to this loutish thug of a husband have it away with her. He was still there this morning so I had to have breakfast with them all and now he's just dropped me off."

"So are you having another family reunion tonight?"

"Fuck off."

"I think it's sweet. The kids being able to spend time with their uncle Ken."

"Go fuck yourself."

"How old were the cherubs?"

"Cherubs? Fucking monsters more like. Between 5 and 9. One for every year."

"Aw, I bet they love their new uncle."

"It's the last time they'll ever see him."

"You mean you're not going over tonight?"

"Not fucking likely."

"Poor kids."

"Poor kids, my arse. It's me that's poor after buying them all dinner."

Phillip just couldn't stop laughing about it as he imagined the night that Ken must have had. When the woman called their motel room to ask Ken out for another meal, as her husband had gone again, he was just beside himself as Ken made his excuses. It was all just too much.

After that episode, which Ken very quickly got over, and would form one of his future stories out of, they had very many good days in different locations, lots of laughs and joking around, seeing some great sights. Before they knew it, they were back in the same motel in San Francisco for one last night before flying home to London. They also found themselves back in the same bar with the willowy barmaid.

"Hey guys, I thought you'd gone home without saying goodbye."

"No fear of that, Chelsea. I had to come and see my gorgeous barmaid again before going home," smiled Ken. "I'd almost forgotten how charming you were."

"If that hubby of yours is out of town, I'll show you how charming I can be," Ken continued, climbing onto a bar stool, glad to see she was again attired in shorts and a plunging t-shirt.

"You're such a tease, Ken," she laughed, "Hi Phil, how come you're so quiet compared to him?"

"Hi Chelsea. He has enough stories for both of us and besides, I can never get a word in."

"That's true, but he has some great stories, I've been telling everyone who comes in here about you both."

"Is that why it's almost empty tonight?"

"No, silly. We'll be full tomorrow with a band playing, you'll have to come in."

"We'll ask the pilot to hold the plane. I'm sure he'd like to meet you."

"Oh yes, I forgot. You're going home. Have you had a good vacation?"

"Splendid," chirped Ken, "it's been really nice and while you pour us both a drink, I'll tell you what we've been up to since leaving here."

As Ken, in his usual elaborate style talked about their trip, Phillip sat on the stool next to him and looked around the almost deserted bar, the empty tables and the unused pool table, empty apart from a group of six or seven people sitting around one table, one of the two women in the party sitting on one of the guy's knees as they all laughed and joked around. Phillip was very attracted to her for some reason and disappointed that she was with her boyfriend. He turned back around to return his attention to Ken. He was already about half way through his story when Chelsea interrupted him, asking the approaching party from the table if she could get them another drink. They all wanted refills so as she began to pour the drinks she said, "hey guys, this is Ken and Phillip all the way from England. They're both butlers. Why don't you say hi to them and introduce yourselves?"

They did so and made some small talk, asking the butlers who they worked for and what they were doing there and so on, before the group, having got their drinks, went back to their table and Ken continued with his story to Chelsea.

"Excuse me. Would you like to play a game of pool with us?" asked the woman who Phillip had been looking at previously.

They both turned around.

The woman who'd asked stood about 5'5", had blue eyes and fairly short dark brown hair that she brushed forward at the front to her eyebrows. She was very pretty. Her friend standing with her was dark, a little overweight and not quite as pretty. Both women were dressed as though they'd come here from a casual wearing workplace.

"I've never played before," apologized Ken.

"I have, but not for about 15 years," offered Phillip excitedly

"That's okay, we'll pair up with each other," the first woman who they learned was Natalie spoke, " Jenna is better than me so she can play with Ken, and I'll play with you" she said to Phillip.

"You'd better show me what to do then," Ken spoke as they both got up and all walked toward the pool table. After reintroducing themselves, Jenna racked the balls while trying to explain to Ken what to do and how to do so.

Natalie had a voice to go with her personality and her looks. She and Phillip chatted extensively as they played. She worked at three jobs just to get by and tonight, after finishing work at the third one, her workmates had persuaded her to come

for a drink for the first ever time. She was a year older than

Phillip but looked at least ten years younger. She'd been sitting

on the guy's knee because of some joke. He also learned she

was divorced, had four children and lived with her parents.

Despite of all of this, Phillip was smitten.

"I think she likes you," whispered Ken.

"You think? I think she's great."

"You should take her home."

"I'll ask her but the car is at the motel."

"It's your shot. This is a good game."

"First he likes soccer, now he likes pool. Unbelievable."

They finished the game. Ken and Jenna won. Phillip asked

Natalie if he could take her home which she declined, and

also if he could write to her once he was back home which

she agreed to. Being sure to exchange addresses before a quick

peck on the cheek, and the work party had gone.

Back at the bar, Ken asked if he'd write.

"Yes, I will. She was really nice," and he proceeded to tell

Ken of their conversation.

Some more friends of Chelsea came into the bar so Ken of course flirted outrageously with them and told more tales until he and Phillip decided they had to leave. They shared warm embraces from Chelsea who was sorry they had to go. The next day, they left for home after a very enjoyable vacation.

CHAPTER SEVEN

Lord Baldwin had gone home from Antigua, purportedly to deal with some business matters. Jane Robins, with Tristan, had accompanied him along with the entourage, as Jane wanted a part she'd read so needed to be in London. With their departure Lady Baldwin had quickly invited Simon and her designer Paul over for a few days. This place needed re-decorating so she could discuss that with Paul and Simon could keep her warm at night. She'd also agreed to let the children have a couple of friends over as it was either that or they'd go home and she was already regretting not letting them go. Charles had invited the smuttiest girl he could find and Sophie had a lesbian friend . Lady B was furious.

"Kay, where did Charles find that piece of garbage?" she yelled.

"I have no idea, milady."

"Can't you get rid of her?"

"He'll go with her if I do."

"Then he can go, I'm sick and tired of seeing all that greasy bleached hair of hers and her awful clothes, she looks like a prostitute. Then she opens her mouth and I can't understand her accent and what I do catch is just a torrent of swearing. I blame you for this, Kay. I didn't teach him to like 'commoners'," Lady B takes a break before continuing, "And while we're about it, you can get rid of the lesbians too. Everywhere I go, they're kissing and fondling each other, in front of the staff as well. It was bad enough when she got herself expelled from that school, but then she started sleeping with the grooms like some little tramp. And now she's with this lesbian. It's your fault, Kay. I hope you're happy. And another thing. You can tell this lazy good for nothing staff that they'd better start doing their jobs around here or they'll be fired. It's not clean enough, the cooking is awful, no one is ever around when I need them and they're slow. So tell them to buck up or go!. It's just not good enough!.

Kay was upset, and tears ran down her face after Lady B had stormed out of the laundry room where she'd found Kay doing some ironing. Now she was going to have to arrange for the children to leave and to tell them to go. Not to mention having to threaten the staff with the sack. "Shit, Shit, Shit," she spoke aloud as she re-composed herself.

The kids had gone too far this time, even she would admit that. These kids, both young adults now really. Sophie was a striking slim blonde who turned every man's eye. Charles was another blonde, much taller than his sister but also very handsome. Kay was certain they had conspired together to shock their mother and they'd really succeeded. Too well, for now Kay was getting the blame and she now would have to take it out on the staff. "Shit."

Charles and Sophie were very proud of each other as they had a coffee in town, their friends next door in the department store.

"Where did you find her?" asked Sophie incredulously.

"On a street corner in Liverpool. I offered her an all expenses paid holiday, in the sun, all first class, and she jumped at it. Not to mention a few hundred pounds she gets as a bonus if we get sent home early," smiled Charles, "She said she was praying for me to call."

"You, dog, you. I hope you're using protection?"

"Of course I am, although she assures me she's clean."

"She's perfect."

"I'm very impressed with your lesbianism."

"It's worth it just to see her face."

"Oh, it's a picture. I'm just not sure if I like seeing it."

"I thought all men liked to see lesbians?"

"Only when it's someone else's sister."

They both laughed at themselves. This was going so well.
They wouldn't have done this if their father had still been here
but he'd warned them he'd be leaving early so they made
their plans.

They were still sorry that he was so miserable these days.
They knew whose fault it was, she'd been making life hell for
nearly everyone and disguising it with sudden outbursts of
kindness that would make you forget how bad she could be.
They'd tried as hard as their father to understand her and to
continue loving her, but they hated her now, and her having
that useless Simon here only added fuel.

They were fully aware of why she'd sent for him, yet she

thought she was so discreet about it.

Simon was trying to stay incognito and quiet apart from agreeing

with all her rants. He knew that all you could do with her in

this mood was to let it take its course, don't antagonize her,

and keep her glass full. Sooner or later the alcohol would kick

in, she'd calm down, and then she'd get frisky. Sex was

generally wild after one of these episodes, her husband

generally ran for the hills when she got angry, but Simon

liked her liked this. It was worth waiting for. With any luck,

she'd divorce that husband of hers. He wasn't good enough in

his eyes and she'd take half his money and move him in with

her. He'd be quite happy being a country gentleman.

Kay was on the phone to Cathy:

"Tell me again, Cathy, why the hell I keep working for this

bitch?"

"For the money, the new car every year, first class travel,

gifts, the private health care, and the gorgeous furnished house

she provides you."

"I suppose."

"What's happened?"

Kay told her of Lady B going berserk and then of having to send the kids home. Not that they were the least bit bothered, but she didn't like having to do it all the same. Then having to tell the staff off was worse. She was fed up being enemy number one amongst the staff, not just here it was everywhere, but if she didn't tell tales and Lady B heard it from somewhere else then there was more hell to pay.

"You'll be home in a few days, Kay. If she's still in a mood then, I'll get it. There's something to look forward to."

"I think I'll have to do what Phillip used to do."

"What's that?"

"Go outside and scream my head off."

"Oh god, I remember him doing that. Even Lady B heard the screams and she actually laughed when he told her why."

"I think she was quite proud actually that she could get a grown man to scream."

"That's true."

"Mind you, there'll be another one screaming tonight."

"What do you mean?"

"Simon's here."

"He isn't?"

"As soon as Lord B left he came in on the next flight."

"What's she like?"

"At the moment she's drunk and frisky, I think."

"You'd better stay away then."

"I'll try to."

"Is there anyone else there apart from Simon and the kids?"

"Well, the kids go tomorrow and they're in town now, but Paul is here. You know, the decorator?"

"Oh right, I remember him. The over the top gay?"

"That's him. Loud clothes and lots of arm movement. He's nice though, but I wonder what he makes of all this unrest around here."

"It's a pity he's gay. He's quite handsome."

"I know, I think Lady B thought she could cure him but she's given up now."

"Where is he at the moment? He's not with Lady B, is he?"

"I don't know. I suppose I'd better find out in a minute. How are things with you?"

"Not that good. I thought having a couple of weeks here at home would sort things out but I still feel like a stranger. It's improved a little since getting here but Lady B makes me spend so much time down at Stonebridge that it'll be back to square one again in a couple of days. I keep telling her that I need more time off and she says okay. But then at the last minute says no. If my husband divorces me, then it'll be the last straw."

"Do you think he will?"

"I don't know. I know he had an affair just like I did, but we've been trying to patch things up and it's difficult."

"But why don't you move them down to Stonebridge?"

"I've told you this before, Kay. They don't want to live down there. We have our own house but property prices around Stonebridge are almost double to here, Billy would find it even harder to get a job, and the children would have to go to a new school, not to mention my mother who would never move."

"Then quit."

"I can't. We need the money I earn but if I quit I can't even get social security. Can't you get her to fire me? If I get fired I would get social, but I just can't quit."

"What a mess."

"I know, I'm at my wit's end. But anyway, I have some news for you."

"What's that?" Kay tepidly replied.

"You'll never guess who I bumped into."

"Who?"

"Richard."

"Richard who?"

"You're Richard, that's who."

"You're kidding."

"Nope, I almost walked right by him. He looks good. He asked about you."

"I don't believe you."

"It's true. He wants you to call him, he gave me his number."

"Why would I want to call him? That was a long time ago," said Kay, now remembering clearly her one love and how he'd left, "I don't think there's anything left to say apart from asking why."

"He just said he wants to ask you one question, that's all. It's been bugging him for years."

"He couldn't have asked you?"

"He said it was personal. You want his number?"

"No, maybe I'll call him when I get home. I don't want to speak to him now."

"You're still hurt from him aren't you?" asked Cathy, who knew the story and had been a witness.

"I think I'm over him. It just reopens old wounds is all."

"Well, think about it. I'll bring his number with me to Stonebridge. You don't have to call him."

"I'll think about it. I'd better go now, Cath. See what Paul is up to and try to avoid Lady B. I'll see you in a few days. Bye."

"Bye, Kay."

Kay said she'd gotten over him but wasn't sure now, his name hadn't been mentioned for a long time and no one had seen him to her knowledge, so why now? Still deep in thought she left her room and wandered around, it was quiet,

hopefully Lady B and Simon would be upstairs and she

wouldn't walk in on them, but it was getting dark now so she

began turning lights on as she roamed the house, almost

jumping out of her skin when she suddenly came upon Paul.

"Ooh Kay, you scared me," he cooed.

"You scared me too."

Paul, who was the prototype tall dark and handsome guy that

a lot of girls dream about, was dressed tonight in leather

pants, cowboy boots, denim shirt and all in black, but ruined

the macho look with a flowery bandana. Kay meanwhile wore

a blue summer dress that came to her knees, black loafers,

gold chain around her neck and minimal make-up.

"I suppose we shouldn't creep around in the dark," he

continued.

"Have you seen her ladyship and Simon around?"

"No, I haven't seen them," he said grasping the back of her

hand, his pale blue eyes looking upwards, "but I have heard

them."

She followed his eyes up and toward the room above the
formal dining room that was Lady B's bedroom. Kay could
feel her face turning redder by the second as she listened to
the unmistakable sound of a bed creaking rhythmically, the
couple upon it groaning loudly in unison, not sure why she
should feel embarrassed.

"I guess dinner is going to be late" she offered, breaking the
ice.

"Not for them," Paul giggled, "they're having their oats."
Kay began to laugh, careful to not be loud. She walked
back toward the kitchen, beckoning Paul to come with her.
Shaking her head as she still laughed, amazed at how brazen
Lady B could be even when her children were around.
Luckily they weren't at the moment but she doubted that
would have stopped her tonight. She'd drunk way too much.
Upon reaching the kitchen, Winston was sitting on a chair
reading a newspaper. He looked up when they entered,
probably expecting some news about dinner, but all Kay could
do was shrug her shoulders. Winston was a very slight man, a
native of Antigua, mainly bald but with a shock of white hair,

looked every inch his almost sixty years yet had a very laid back attitude. His wife though, Margo, who did the cooking was a different kettle of fish and Kay was glad she wasn't around at the moment.

"Can we get you anything, Paul. It might be a while before her ladyship asks for dinner."

"Why don't we grab something in town?"

"You mean us two?"

"Yes, I promise not to embarrass you," smiled Paul, making fun of his own campiness.

"Okay. Do you want to go now?"

"Sure. Just give me a second and I'll meet you outside."

Kay grabbed her purse and told Winston she'd see him later and not to make any food for her and Paul. They made their way out to the car, an open top jeep. Kay jumped into the driver's seat and started it up, joined moments later by Paul who had discarded his flowery scarf and was now open necked.

"Where to?" she asked as he buckled up.

"I don't mind, perhaps there's a place that's just simple and friendly?"

"Sure. I think I know just the one," she slipped the car into gear and drove from the house along the coast for about 5 miles until getting to a small fishing village. Kay parked by the harbor, then led Paul up a small alleyway to a nondescript café with a couple of locals sipping rum at one of the two outdoor tables .

It was cozier inside than it had looked from the exterior, with a small bar just inside the door and perhaps a dozen tables for its diners. The tables were set nicely with plain white tablecloths and cloth napkins, small vases of flowers, and oil lamps. The restaurant was quite full.

"If you take a stool, Kay, I'll come and get you a drink. There'll be a table for you in a second" shouted the owner, who was bustling between the tables, chatting and clearing.

"Seems like he knows you," said Paul.

"I come here whenever I can," she motioned to the stools, "that was James. He runs this place with his whole family. They always do good food and make you feel welcome. Sometimes, I just need a place to unwind and this is perfect."

They made themselves comfortable and took in their surroundings. It was nothing fancy, just white painted walls, a few prints of the island scattered around, a stone floor, reggae playing in the background and subdued lighting.

"Let me get you a couple of rums," greeted James as he gave Kay a hug and a kiss, "and we'll see about getting you some food if you're hungry."

"We're hungry, James. It's good to see you. How is the rest of the family?"

"They're good. You'll see them later."

James didn't bother asking them what they wanted to drink. He never asked anybody, just poured them a couple of dark rum and cokes before quickly heading off a couple who'd just vacated their table to say cheerio. Kay explained to Paul about the general procedure here, in that although they did have a menu it was better to just sit and be served whatever they recommended. It was the normal routine here and generally worked out great.

Paul took her advice and they ended up having a fresh garden salad with crab cakes followed by grilled pork chops with a

Creole sauce and yams. They didn't have any wine, just stuck to the rum and cokes.

They'd talked throughout dinner, Kay about how long she'd worked for the Baldwin's and of the places and people she'd met while doing so, and Paul talked of his designing and the years he'd spent in college. James and his family had fussed over them and had talked them into having a dessert, pineapple soufflé tonight which was wonderful. Fully sated, they finished off with a relaxing coffee.

"This has been very nice, Kay. Do you think we could do this again sometime?" asked Paul, putting some cash on the check that had been left on the table.

"Sure, I don't see why not. This has been very enjoyable."

"So if I ask you out for a date, that will be okay?"

"A date?"

"Yes."

"But I thought..." Kay let the sentence trail off.

"That I'm gay?" smiled Paul.

"Well, yes."

"Despite my appearance and manner, I can assure you that I'm not gay. Although I would appreciate it if you didn't tell anyone."

"But why?" asked the stunned Kay.

"It just makes my life easier, is all. You see, in college all the male interior designers were gay and before long, having made many friends there, I found myself talking and dressing like them. Then when I graduated and started working, it seemed almost to be expected that I was gay so I've just gone along with it and I've been successful. So why come clean?"

"But doesn't it make you uncomfortable to be thought of as gay?"

"No. Like I said, my best friends are gay so it's okay. Besides, some of my clients would never have hired me if they'd thought I was straight," he laughed.

"You had me fooled, and Lady B. We often said it was a shame that you preferred men."

"Is that a compliment?" Paul chortled.

Kay blushed, looking around the room until she felt the redness abate from her cheeks.

"You never answered my question, Kay. Will you come on a date with me?"

"Yes, but let's go over to the bar. I think I need another drink now," she smiled, taking his hand quite proudly as they stood and made their way over to the bar.

CHAPTER EIGHT

Phillip had been back many weeks now and was struggling to contain an uncommon emotion for him. He'd written to Natalie almost as soon as he'd gotten back home and since then they'd progressed to telephone calls. At first, it had been one call a week but now it was every morning at 5am, which coincided with her getting home from work at 9pm her time. Despite learning that she not only had been previously married, had four children, and was struggling to keep afloat, he knew he'd fallen for her and had told her so that morning. He was encouraged she'd responded likewise but now he'd soon have to say something to Lord Baldwin. Otherwise questions would be asked about the phone bills. He didn't get any bills directly. They went first to the estate office who would be sure to ask his lordship about all the transatlantic calls from his number. Phillip had used his lordship's line when he'd had to spend the night in the house which had been often as Lady Baldwin had insisted on for some reason.

Now he would have to own up to it. It had been difficult and exciting the past few weeks. Difficult, because when his lordship had stayed the night it had invariably been with Ms Harrop. This was okay but getting harder by the minute to conceal. Today however, his lordship had spent the night alone and was just finishing his breakfast of pink grapefruit, poached eggs on toast, and a pot of tea at the kitchen table whilst reading the morning newspaper.

"Milord, excuse me for interrupting you but I feel I must warn you that your telephone bill will be rather excessive this last month or so."

Lord Baldwin lowered his paper and looked up at Phillip, in uniform but without his jacket as he'd been rustling up his breakfast .

"Why is that, Phillip?"

"Well milord, when I was in America I met someone. Lately I've been making a lot of telephone calls to her. Due to the time difference and our schedules, I've had to use your phone quite substantially."

"That's okay, Phillip. No apology is necessary. In fact, I'm very happy for you. Is this serious?"

"I believe it is, milord, but at the moment we're just talking."

"Anything I can do Phillip, you only have to ask. Now don't worry about the call charges. I'll take care of them. It's the least I can do, especially with all the discretion you've been showing to me."

"Thank you, milord. That's very kind of you but it is getting harder to allay any suspicions, especially from Brian."

"Why is that?"

"Mainly because of the odd hours you keep nowadays, milord. And when he gets in your car to turn it around or to fill it, he sometimes smells perfume."

"I understand, Phillip. Tell him if you have to and if you think he can keep it quiet, but if you can stall him for a couple more weeks then we may be able to come clean with everyone."

"I'll do whatever it takes, milord, and thank you for the phone charges."

"My pleasure, Phillip. Keep me informed, and I hope this works out for you. Ms Harrop will want to convey the same message, I'm sure. Do you have my coat? I think I'll need it today. I won't be home this evening. I'll be going down to Stonebridge tonight."

Phillip got his overcoat from the closet and helped it on for him, then saw him out and into his car before he drove away, breathing a sigh of relief as he watched the car disappear. Closing the door, he walked back into the kitchen and went straight to the telephone to call the estate manager and warn him about the telephone charges.

Phillip had hated disclosing any details of his private life to his lordship. He never spoke to anyone at work about Natalie. The only person who knew of her was Ken, so he was relieved when the estate manager never asked why he'd been calling the USA so much and at such a strange hour. He just wondered how long it would be before Lady B got to hear of it.

"Morning, Phil. Has he gone already?"

"Morning, Brian. Yes, just now. He said he'd be going down to Stonebridge tonight so I expect we won't see him now until next week."

"I'll take out some of the plants then."

The plants were much easier to care for when kept in the greenhouse, so Brian always took them out at the earliest convenience.

"He had me light the fire as well last night, Brian, so if you can see to that as well, I'd appreciate it."

"I was wondering about that. It was a bit chilly last night. I'm surprised he never had you light it the night before. It was even colder then."

"He never asked so I never offered," fibbed Phillip, not telling Brian that he'd actually gone out that night and only got home the following morning.

"Saves me a job when it's not lit, so thank you."

"You're welcome. I'll make some tea in a minute once I finish up in here. Should be ready by the time you fix it up."

Phillip cleaned up in the kitchen while Brian went into the family room to clean the fireplace and set up a new fire that would only need a match to ignite it. Although the house was centrally heated and generally warm, the family room was a little draughty if the wind was blowing and it was always preferable at those times to light the log fire. It made it cozier too. To Phillip, this house was much homier than Stonebridge. It wasn't as much a designers showcase, more a place that you could kick off your shoes and relax. He felt it was too formal there, especially as he was used to the family lounging around here in their pajamas, having casual meals in front of the television like a normal home. The family room, along with the kitchen, was the most used in this house, by the family that is, the other rooms on this floor like the drawing room and the dining rooms being used mainly when they were entertaining or for a Sunday lunch.

Having finished in the kitchen, Phillip made his way down the hall to the laundry room where he found that Susan had already come inside and made tea for the three of them. Two steaming mugs at the empty chairs that Phillip and Brian normally occupied and she was already sitting and sipping.

"Morning, Sue. Thanks for the tea," said Phillip taking his seat.

"Morning, Phil. You're welcome. I see his lordship has already gone. Is he back tonight?"

"No, we shouldn't see him now until Monday. I told Brian he could take all the plants out."

"Where is Brian?"

"He'll be through in a second. He was just making the fire."

"So do you have any plans for the weekend, Phil?"

"Not really. I'll have to stay over here of course, but apart from that I think I'll just go up to Manchester on Saturday for the game."

"Don't you get fed up of staying over here?"

"Yes, I do. It's stupid. If the alarm goes off, they call me at my house if there's no answer here but I think it's because the alarm went off once when no one was around that Lady B makes me stay here. The thing is so loud it's considered a nuisance if it goes off for a prolonged period."

"How long did it go off for?"

"A couple of hours, I believe. The police finally found someone to shut it off but by then I think the whole village had complained."

"But the village is about a mile away."

"Right. I said it was loud."

"Wow, I never realized."

"Yes, but since then we've given the police and the alarm people a whole list of people who can turn it off and also put a limit on how long it can actually make any noise, so I shouldn't have to stay here."

"So why do you?"

"Because Lady B insists on it."

"Oh, I'm sorry."

"What have you been talking about?" asked Brian who'd entered the room and had sat down.

"I was asking Phil what he was doing this weekend," explained Susan.

"Oh really, and I thought you had a boyfriend," suggested Brian.

"I wasn't asking him out," replied the embarrassed Susan, "he was just saying that he was going to the match on Saturday and staying over here."

"There's a surprise," Brian replied sarcastically .

"Hey, it's better going to the football than it is to traipse around town bloody shopping" was Phillip's response.

Before Phillip had even finished his reply there was a knock on the door quickly followed by two men walking in. They were both dressed alike in white overalls and black boots, although the boots and the overalls were liberally smudged with paint.

"Well, good morning," Phillip continued, still sitting, but directing his gaze at the visitors, "if it isn't Laurel and Hardy, our decorator comedians."

"Good morning, everyone," said Bill, the main painter of the pair.

"Morning all," agreed his partner Stan. Seeing Phillip in uniform still, Stan continued, " so the boss is home?"

"No, you're okay. I just haven't got changed yet. Why don't you make yourself a cup of tea?"

"I thought you'd never ask," Stan replied, making his way toward the kettle.

"Well, while you're there, fill ours as well," said Phillip, proffering his empty mug along with Brian and Susan.

"I should have known," grumbled Stan lightheartedly, gathering their mugs as Bill took a seat at the table, "I hope you have some biscuits."

"We'll see what we can find, but what brings you guys here today?" asked Phillip.

"Just a bit of touching up," answered Bill while adjusting his glasses. Bill, who had thick black hair always neatly combed, wore glasses which he continually hitched up his nose.

"Maud will enjoy that," smiled Brian.

"We don't have enough paint to cover Maud," joked Stan from next door.

"I'll tell her that," Brian laughed.

"You'd better not, she'll kill us," Stan again called out."

"Where is Maud?" asked Bill.

"She'll be here in a minute."

"I don't think I've seen you since you went to America," Bill looked at Phillip.

"That was a while ago. You mean you haven't been here since then?"

"I think we were here when you were over there, but not since you got back. I suppose you had a good time?"Bill had always wanted to go to America but had never made it. He was particularly envious of Phillip who'd been several times.

"Yes, a great time. Thanks. Got to see a couple of World Cup games, Yosemite Park, Sequoia Park, San Francisco, the wine country and also the coastal highway. It was a good trip."

"You went to a Brazil game, didn't you?" asked the returning Stan, a balding, ginger haired plump man, handing everyone a steaming mug of fresh tea before sitting down alongside Bill.

"That was a lot of fun," Phillip continued his tale of the game, embellished that story for Bill just to make him even more envious Stan understood this so he continually asked for more detail as Bill got greener and greener.

Susan retrieved the biscuit tin as Phillip regaled his stories. She also put the kettle back on for more tea when Maud finally arrived, breathless from walking quickly from her car and immediately sitting down.

"Well, good morning everyone. I suppose you two are here to splash more paint over my carpets," she greeted.

"Morning, Maud," Phillip interjected, "I think they only come here to eat our biscuits and drink our tea."

But before anyone could add to the conversation, the telephone rang and the room hushed as Phillip got up to answer it. The distinct tone of the main line always making everyone stop.

"Good morning. This is Phillip."

"Good morning, Phillip. So glad you answered. This is Victoria."

"Good morning, ma'am. Nice to hear from you. What can I do for you?"

At this reply, the room relaxed knowing it wasn't any of the bosses or Cathy or Kay. They continued their conversation as Phillip dealt with the caller.

"Are you alone at the moment, Phillip?"

"No, ma'am."

"I understand. I'll try to make this easy for you. I realize this will probably be unusual for you, Phillip, but would it be possible for you to meet with me today, this morning?"

"I'm not sure, ma'am," Phillip was puzzled.

"It's nothing to be worried about, Phillip. I just feel that I can trust you and that you have Alistair's best interests at heart which is all that I want. I just need to talk to someone."

After a moment's hesitation, Phillip agreed, "Yes, I'll be glad to."

"Do you think you could meet me in town at the Lion's Coffee House at about eleven?"

"Yes, ma'am. It'll be no problem."

"Thank you, Phillip. I'll see you there. Bye."

"Bye ma'am."

As Phillip put the handset down, Maud immediately asked who'd called.

"Some woman wanted to make sure that I'd check the mailbox for an invite she's sending to his lordship and to personally hand it to him," Phillip lied.

"Doesn't she know he's not here?"

"Yes, but it seems there's no rush. She just wanted to be certain he'd get it."

"She must think you throw away all the other mail."

"I never thought of it like that. Bloody cheek."

"You'd better have another cup of tea."

"I've a good mind now to friggin lose her invitation."

Everyone laughed and Stan got up to make more tea. Again gathering empty mugs off the table, Phillip heading toward the kitchen for a moment wondering what the hell Victoria Harrop wanted to talk to him about.

Sitting back down at the table on his return he asked Maud if there was anything she needed from the supermarket as he was going to have to do some shopping.

"No, I think I'm fine for now," she replied.

"I may stop off at the chippy on my way back if anyone is interested," commented Phillip, looking at each of them around the table.

Everyone agreed except Maud who never had anything.

"If you write down what everyone wants, Brian, I'll call you when I finish shopping and then you can ring the order through."

"Do you want what you normally have?" he asked.

"Yes. Fish, chips, peas and gravy."

"Okay, I'll wait for your call."

For the next few minutes, they all discussed what they'd be doing this coming weekend. Phillip left them sitting down as he retrieved his cell phone and coat, telling them he was going home to get changed and that he'd see them later.

He remained as perplexed as when he'd received the call as he went about his errands and then walked to the nearby café, finding Ms Harrop already seated as he approached her table.

"Good morning, Ma'am," he somberly intoned, surprising her a little.

Ms Harrop looked behind her. Then she rose, smiling and offering her hand for Phillip to shake .

"Please call me Victoria, Phillip. Thank you so much for coming. Now please sit down and I'll order you a coffee."

She too was dressed casually in brown slacks with matching walking shoes, a beige turtleneck sweater, and a lined white raincoat that was draped over the back of her seat. Phillip did the same with his jacket before sitting down.

"You do want coffee?" she asked.

"Yes please , a latte if they have it. Otherwise just regular coffee with cream please."

"Would you like anything to eat?"

"No thank you, ma'am."

"Please call me Victoria. Otherwise we may attract some attention."

"I'll try, but this is very unusual for me."

Before going any further, the waitress had come over to the table so Victoria ordered a coffee for Phillip and a refill for herself. As they waited for her to return, they made small talk about how the weather seemed to be getting a little warmer and how quiet it appeared to be in town today. When the coffee came, Phillip put some sweetener in his and Victoria hunched down a little so that she could talk softly without being overheard.

"I've asked you here today, Phillip, because I feel I can trust you and because I know you always have Alistair's interests at heart. He doesn't know about this, nor will I ever tell him, so I hope you'll be forthright with me."

"Of course," replied Phillip, wondering what on earth she was going to ask.

She looked at him for a few seconds, no doubt wondering if this was a good idea or not before finally taking a deep breath and blurting it out.

"Do you think I should stop seeing Alistair?"

Phillip hadn't been expecting this question. He thought she'd maybe want to know some personal details about his lordship which would have given her ideas for gifts and such. He rocked back and forth for a moment or two, looking into her eyes for some sign that perhaps she didn't want this question answered but her eyes were focused. She really wanted his opinion.

"No, I don't," he replied simply.

"Not even for the sake of his family?"

"No, but especially for the family's sake."

"What do you mean?"

"If you think they're a happy family then you're very much mistaken. His lordship's two kids would be delighted if they knew how happy their father was at the moment."

"You think so?"

"Most definitely."

"Do you think he's happy?"

"Yes. I haven't seen him this happy since I first came here."

"But don't you think he still loves his wife?"

"I think he still loves her as she used to be, not as she is now."

"So what happened?"

"I don't really know. When I first came here, she was extremely nice. She'd laugh a lot, they didn't socialize that much and everyone liked being around her. Then over time, she started to get temperamental. She wanted to be in London a lot, she got new friends, and it was all very difficult to understand. She can still be extremely charming just like she used to be, but at other times she's downright nasty."

"But why?"

"I don't know, but she doesn't get any easier."

"Alistair says she is having affairs?"

"Yes, she is. I think everybody thought that his lordship
should have divorced her when she started having these mood
swings, but when she started flaunting her lovers in front of
him, no one could understand him staying around."

"But do you think him having an affair with me is his way
of getting back at her?"

"No, because with you I think his lordship has found
happiness again. Lady B doesn't seem to be looking for
happiness. She just seems to be looking for a good time, but it
never seems to be good enough."

"He says it's all going to be resolved soon and that I
shouldn't worry, but I've never been in the middle of
something like this before. I It makes me uncomfortable. Don't
you think that she could be the person she once was again and
that Alistair could fall in love with her again?"

"I think it's gone beyond that point now. This has been going
on for too long. I also don't think that his lordship would

have even looked at you if he'd thought he was still in a marriage, so I don't think you should worry about that."

They both took sips of their coffees, digesting their conversation, silent for a few minutes.

"So you think I should wait for him then, Phillip?"

"If you love him as much as I think you do then yes, I do. He told me this morning that it would all be sorted within a couple of weeks so he seems determined now to finally leave her. I believe that's because he's fallen in love with you and out of love with her."

"Thank you, Phillip. You've made me feel so much better." she smiled.

"My pleasure, but then we never even had this conversation. Right?"

"Right. So tell me about this lady in America you met?"

"You've heard about her already? You must have been talking to his lordship."

"Just before you got here. He was very excited for you."

"Really?"

"Yes, so tell me where you met and what she's like."

So he did, chatting away for many more minutes and having a refill on the coffee before they left their separate ways after Ms Harrop paid the café bill.

"Now that he's left you, Cathy, you can move in to one of the estate houses and bring your children down here. They'll get a much better education in one of the schools around here."

"But they don't want to live down here, milady," replied the sobbing Cathy, "Nor does my mum. Can't you send me back and let me work at Crompton Hall again?"

"No, your place is here, looking after me. There's only you who knows where I keep everything. Now stop your crying and feeling sorry for yourself. It's only a man. There's plenty of them around so damn well get over it. Tell your mother the children have to come down here and if she doesn't like it then too bad. You understand, Cathy? If you go back up there, you'll be out of a job. Now go and get rid of the tears and send me Kay. I can't deal with you today."

Lord Baldwin had already flown off in his helicopter and Lady Baldwin had been glad to see him go, he was such a misery these days and the weekend had been horrid. It seemed to Lady B that they'd had one row after another from disagreeing about cutting the children's allowance, to the guests she wanted to invite over for a weekend in a couple of weeks time. She left her dressing room and went downstairs to the library, sitting herself down in the leather swivel chair behind the desk and taking out invitation cards and envelopes from one of the drawers.

Kay entered the room and was told to shut the door behind her and to sit down.

Lady B was holding a pen and writing names down on a pad of paper, not bothering to look up as Kay sat down and made her wait before speaking again.

"Has she stopped crying yet?"

"No, she's still sobbing her eyes out."

"It's her own fault. I told her a long time ago to move them all down here but she wouldn't listen."

Kay tended to agree with her but could also see Cathy's point. When she worked for her ladyship at Crompton Hall, she used to be home every night to make her kids meals and had every weekend off. Now she was always at

Stonebridge, and instead of getting every weekend off, she'd

get a week off every few weeks or so.

"She'll be okay," Kay offered.

"Don't you agree?"

"Yes I do, but it's never easy breaking up."

"No, but we all go through that. It's not like anyone died."

"I'll have another talk with her, milady."

"Good. There's a lot to be done around here in the next two

weeks. I'm going to have some guests over for a long

weekend so I'll need everyone scrubbing this place clean. We

need some fun people in this house. I'm sick and tired of

miserable faces and the sound of crying. It's bad enough

having to put up with his lordship and all of his moaning, but

it's just too much when Cathy is the same way."

"Who is going to come?"

"I don't know yet. I'm just making up a list but I'll start

with Jane and Tristan and maybe a couple of their friends,

just some fun people."

"Any local people?"

"I suppose, but only those I can tolerate."

"What do you want in the way of flowers?"

"I think you should give my designer a call. You know, Paul. Have him recommend a florist from London, one of his gay pals probably, and tell him to splurge. I want the whole house swimming in flowers. Best champagne as well. Tell Tom to stock up on some Crystal and to make sure we have plenty of great red wine for whoever likes that. I'll talk to Rene but have him put suggestions forward, nothing cheap or tacky. If he thinks Beluga Caviar, then so be it. You can tell Phillip to get down here as well, and if that wife of Tom's still wants to leave, then they can both go after the party and Phillip can damn well stay. He can leave that American girlfriend of his up there."

"Which American girlfriend?"

"Lord Baldwin finally told me last night that Phillip had met some woman in the US and that she was coming over in a couple of weeks. Seems like this has been going on for some time and I'm the last to know. Actually, Cathy must have known about this so have her tell him he has to come down here and that he can't bring any guests with him."

"We don't really need him, milady. Tom can deal with a dinner party."

"Just do it, Kay. It serves them right for keeping secrets from me."

"What shall I tell her to say?"

"Just what I've said. She can tell him that Tom has the weekend off if she wants. Just get him here."

"As you wish, milady. Is there anything else?"

"Not right now. I need to write these invitations. Go and get on with it and tell Tom to bring me some coffee."

A sighing Kay hastily left the room and coming upon Tom, she told him Lady B wanted some coffee and that a long weekend was being planned. She told him to stock up on drinks. When he heard Phillip was being brought down to help, Tom agreed he wasn't really needed.

Kay lost her temper a little, "Look Tom, it's not my bloody idea. I know we can do it without any help but that's what she wants so that's it. Take it up with her if you want.

I'm just the messenger so don't take it out on me!."

Kay walked away, not waiting for a reply but knowing she was probably getting a filthy look from behind her back for raising her voice at him. She found the still sniffling Cathy alone in the laundry room ironing and she slammed the door shut behind her. Sitting down, she leaned her head back for a few moments calming herself down.

"She wants you to call Phillip and have him come down here in a couple of weeks time for a long weekend."

"Has she given Tom some time off?" asked the red eyed Cathy.

"No, she's having house guests and wants Phillip to help. She's annoyed because she's just found out he has a girlfriend and she's coming over to visit him from the US. He can't bring her here either."

"You're kidding. I knew something was going on up there but I couldn't find out anything. So Phillip has a girlfriend?"

"Apparently."

"So why can't he bring her here if she's coming all this way to visit?"

"I don't know. You know how she likes to meddle in our personal lives. It's not as if we even need him here."

"So what am I supposed to tell him?"

"Whatever you like, but you have to get him here."

"Great, I have to do her dirty work again," sniffed Cathy, banging the hot iron on its stand.

"Well if Tom's wife insists on leaving, then I'm going to have to tell him to go with her. And then I'll need to tell Phillip that he has to stay here permanently."

"Do you think he would?"

"Not a chance, girlfriend or not. With any luck, I'll be in the room when he tells her to go fuck herself and to stick her job where it hurts most."

That relieved the tension they both felt and they both laughed, knowing full well that Phillip would do something like that. Leaving Cathy to call Phillip, Kay went to her nearby home to make a couple of calls of her own. First she called Paul who she'd grown fond of since Antigua., She not only told him of the forthcoming weekend but also of her awful

day so far. As always, he was very understanding but he did

have one question.

"Why does Cathy put so much blame on Lady Baldwin for

her marriage failing?"

"Because Paul, Cathy fell for one of the estate workers here

and got pregnant with him. Lady B convinced her that she

shouldn't have another child, that it was just sex and not love,

so she paid for Cathy's abortion and told her to make another

go of it with her husband, who has now gone because Cathy

was hardly ever at home."

"What about the estate worker? Is he still around?"

"No, he left a long while ago and no one has heard from him

since."

"I suppose he left once he heard about the abortion."

"Yes. Now her husband has gone as well."

"Oh god, what tangled webs you all weave there."

"There's more, Paul, I think I should tell you everything

before you hear anything from somebody else."

"Does that mean you like me, Kay, as much as I like you?"

"Yes it does, Paul. I like you a lot."

She proceeded to tell him everything, virtually her whole life story.

The only thing she couldn't tell him was something she found out about in the call she made after this one.

Richard, her old boyfriend, the man she'd wanted her own children with so many years ago, had been told by Lady B that Kay was physically incapable of having her own children. She'd even shown him medical documentation to verify it which was why she'd become a nanny. Although Richard was now happily married with four children, he'd often wondered why she'd never told him this as they had often spoken about starting their own family.

"So why didn't you ask me about this at the time?"

"It was true, wasn't it?"

"No, Richard. It never was and never has been. You were lied to and never even gave me the benefit of questioning me about it. Surely I deserved that?"

"But I had no reason to disbelieve her. She was your boss, like your best friend. You never told me she was a conniving liar."

"At the time, I never thought she was. I thought she just liked having sex with different partners, like you. Once you had sex with her I knew I'd never be able to trust you again and that's why I never wanted to hear from you after you left."

"I never had sex with her, Kay."

"I saw her coming out of our room, wearing just a negligee and a smile and she said never trust any man. When I came into the room, you were still naked in our bed."

" But she had just walked in like that, asked where you were, and I said in the nursery probably. So she told me about your condition and how you ignored it and were too frightened to tell me and then she left. That's what happened. I told you then that she'd just walked in on me."

"Yes you did, but you never told me the other part. If you had, it may have made sense."

"It just seemed like you were stalling on getting married. You knew I was desperate to father your children, yet you kept putting it off and when she said that, it kind of made sense. And I knew that you didn't trust me."

"Because you never told me everything. How could you think I was barren?"

"She was very convincing."

"You know what, Richard? We both got deceived and she got you to leave and me to stay. I've never forgiven her for seducing you, or so I thought, but now you finally tell me this after so much time, letting me think you'd been screwed by her when she'd actually done something far worse. I'm going to go now. I'm glad we've spoken but I can't do so again. It's too painful and we both have separate lives now. Let me just say I'm sorry and that I hope you and your family have a very nice life. Goodbye, Richard."

"Goodbye , Kay. I'm very sorry too. I hope you find the happiness you deserve. "

Putting down the phone, it was obvious that Kay wouldn't be heading back to work anytime soon. She was crying too hard and too uncontrollably.

CHAPTER TEN

Phillip had finally been told by Cathy that his help was needed for the weekend party. She'd told him that Tom was getting the weekend off so he had to cover. She also let him know he couldn't bring his girlfriend down. He knew she was lying about Tom. He'd already spoken to him and he knew it was just spite against he and Natalie.

Brian mentioned that Cathy had been furious with him for not saying anything about Natalie, even though he didn't know anything about her at that time.

Phillip then told Brian about Lord Baldwin. It had gotten to the stage now when it was either tell him the biggest secret, or let him discuss the continuing mystery with whoever would listen, and one of them would be Cathy.

Phillip told Brian he could feed tidbits to her about himself and Natalie and keep his lordship out of it for the time being. That would erupt shortly anyway.

Brian was very happy about this. He actually rubbed his hands with glee at the thought of getting his own back on Cathy.

Phillip did have a more pressing problem though. Natalie was due to arrive and although he'd explained that he was going to have to work down at Stonebridge and she'd fully understood, he wasn't at all happy that he was going to have to leave her on her own for the weekend. He had thought about taking her home and have her stay with his mother or sister which would be okay but she didn't know them, not to mention they didn't know about her.

He had already arranged with Lord B to have a couple of days off so that he could meet her at the airport and then stay in London for a couple of nights. On that thought, he picked up the phone.

"Hey Ken, what are you up to you old fart?"

"Less of the lip, you whipper snapper. You should have more respect for your elders."

"I most humbly apologize. I tend to forget how sensitive the senior citizens get once they reach that certain age."

"Okay, my sarcastic friend, I understand how limited your vocabulary is when it comes to conversing with a person of a far higher intellect. So to what do I deserve the pleasure of hearing from you today?"

"I was wondering if you'd do me a favor."

"You have only to ask, my friend. What may I do for you?"

"Actually, there are two things."

"Fire away."

"First, I want you and Fran to come to dinner on Thursday at the Strand Hotel."

"In London?"

"Yes"

"Of course, we'd love to, but what brings you to the center of civilization when you're most used to the dark forbidding north?"

"Do you remember Natalie from San Francisco?"

"Of course I do. I never forget a beautiful woman. Although I still fail to understand what she saw in you when I was available. What about her?"

"Well Don Juan, she's coming over to see me and I'm meeting her in London."

"Really? I couldn't be happier my friend. Fran and I will be delighted to see you both and it's no favor, it's a pleasure. What else do you require?"

"I need you, if possible, to take care of her for a couple of days because the wicked witch is making me work."

"I'd love to take care of her. I'll give her the grand tour of London but why is she making you work? Surely you told her that you're getting a visitor from San Francisco? Can't you say you won't work?"

"She knows she's coming over, that's why I'm having to work. The bitch is being spiteful. She won't even let her stay there while I work. Natalie understands. I don't think she likes it but what can I do? I can't walk out at the minute because I need the money."

"What does Lord Baldwin think?"

"He's okay. He hates her more than I do but he's still getting up the nerve to tell her he's leaving. I think he wants me there for a friendly face and he's at least sending the

helicopter to pick me up on Friday in London."

"Is he?"

"Yes, I thought that was very kind of him. He wants me to

take as much time as I can for the rest of Natalie's stay.

He'll even send the helicopter for her on Sunday to take her

to my place at Crompton Hall."

"How can he be so nice when she is so nasty?"

"I have no idea. I just want him to tell her he's leaving."

"If he ever does. So what time on Thursday and is Natalie

going to stay in the hotel for the weekend or do you want

her to stay with me?"

"Seven o'clock on Thursday and she'll stay in the hotel if

that's okay."

"That will be fine. It's too cramped here and I can get the

tube into London easily enough. It takes me directly to the

hotel in no time at all. I'm ever so looking forward to seeing

you both."

"Thanks for doing this, Ken. it's a big relief for me. See you

and Fran on Thursday night and send her my love."

"Will do, partner. So how long has this been going on for?"

"Since we got back from the States."

"You devil you. Is she bringing her friend with her, my pool partner?"

"No, she is travelling over with another friend who is going on somewhere but the friend has her paranoid about the I.R.A."

"What do you mean? They haven't set off any bombs for ages."

"I know, but this friend thinks they lurk in all the shadows and that London is about to get blown apart."

"Oh blimey. Tell her not to worry, London is very safe now."

"I have. She'll be okay once she gets here and sees everyone acting normal. Give her your insiders' knowledge."

"Natalie will get the very best tour of London, you can be sure of that. We'll see you Thursday."

"Great. See you, Ken. Bye."

"Bye."

Putting down the telephone, Phillip was slightly relieved but still pissed that he was going to have to work this weekend, especially there at Stonebridge. Yet he was excited as well at Natalie coming over. He'd already told the staff here at Crompton that he was having a couple of days off. Maud was going to come in earlier to see to his lordship's breakfast and Brian was prepared to do anything extra if required. Phillip was going to tell them shortly why he was taking a couple of days off, they knew about Natalie now so he may as well come clean. Besides, this was no fleeting romance. This was serious. Phillip expected now he was finally going to get married so before he went any further he thought he'd better call home. It was time Mum heard about this.

CHAPTER ELEVEN

Phillip was nervous as he waited at Heathrow Airport for Natalie to arrive which wasn't helped by there being a flight delay. He knew she'd gotten on to the flight, he'd called her before she left for the airport. She was also nervous.

"You're not going to run away when you see me, are you?"

"No. Why would I do that?"

"You might not like me anymore."

"Yes I will."

"Do you still love me?"

"Yes I do."

"You sure?"

"I'm sure." After the daily telephone conversations that they'd had with Phillip setting his alarm to wake early just for that reason, there really was no doubt.

"Well, okay. What will you be wearing at the airport?"

"I'll be wearing my beige raincoat and a black fedora,"
Phillip had taken to wearing a hat like Ken always did. "What
will you be wearing?"

"My black woolen coat and a rainbow scarf. You still love
me?"

"I still love you."

It seemed to Phillip that it was an awful long wait from when
the sign said that her flight had landed to when she eventually
appeared at the arrivals gate. He spotted her right away,
waving to her and she waving back, and he actually ran
toward her. So much for butler calmness. Her friend though,
who liked to think of herself as a savvy world traveler, was
struggling with her luggage so after a quick hug with Natalie
he was compelled to help out her friend.

"No, I'm okay" she said, struggling to organize herself, "you
two must go, and I have to get a connecting flight.".
Phillip and Natalie stood staring at her as she bumbled away,
both amused, arrivals moving around them as they also tried
to find the folks they were meeting.

"Let's move from here," Phillip took Natalie's case and headed to a quiet corner with her following.

"Well, you made it," he said, putting down the heavy case.

"Were you waiting long? I was worried that you wouldn't."

"I have patience." Phillip took in her appearance, "You look great. Happy to be here?"

"I am now. I worried all the way over. I was so nervous that you wouldn't be here to meet me. You do love me?"

"Yes, I do. Can we have a proper hug now?"

"Oh yes, I really need one."

They hugged for quite some time in that corner of the airport, both realizing that it was probably the beginning of their life together on a permanent basis and they wanted to get used to it.

Instead of taking a taxi or using the underground, Phillip suggested they take a bus to Victoria Station and get a taxi from there to their hotel. This way, Natalie could see a good part of London from the top of the bus.

Phillip had picked out a nondescript hotel near Charing Cross for them to stay in. It was cheap and central, but also clean and safe which was important as he was going to have to leave her there. He knew she was tired from her flight and the time change. He was also tired from being too nervous to sleep but it didn't stop them from making love for the first time once they got to their room. Clumsy but tender lovemaking that stemmed from all of their conversations, neither disappointing the other.

Then they slept.

Contentendly but not for too long as they were going to have dinner with Ken and Fran, who Natalie hadn't met yet. Phillip knew she and Fran would like each other.

CHAPTER TWELVE

Literally truckloads of flowers had arrived at Stonebridge in the past couple of days. It seemed the whole house had been turned into a fully stocked florist shop with yet another truckload parked outside the rear of the house to replace and replenish the various bouquets and centerpieces. The house smelt beautiful but it didn't prevent the cleaners from cursing. No sooner had they left a room than another petal or leaf would fall. It was a constant to and fro for them.

Apart from all the flowers, the cellar was jammed with wines and various beverages, the freezers and refrigerators were full of food, and all the bedrooms had been aired, re-cleaned, toiletries changed and yet more flowers installed.

Tom had been very busy the last couple of weeks polishing silver and stocking up. He'd already laid the table for tonight's dinner so he wouldn't have to worry about it when the guests were arriving, although he'd probably ask Phillip to take care of them once he got here. Then he could concentrate on doing the drinks and appetizers down here. It was only supposed to be half a dozen for dinner tonight so they were just going to use the breakfast table, but then tomorrow more guests were arriving and there'd be sixteen for dinner which was fairly easy, but still very time consuming.

Four guests were due to arrive, Jane Robbins with Tristan Moore and John Steele with Liz Price. Tom knew the former two but was not familiar with the latter ones, he knew of John Steele and the band he used to front but had no idea who his lady friend was. The interior designer and the florist had already been given a room and although they were working, they were regarded as guests, but they'd already said they were going out this evening. Tom thought that Kay was joining them, that's what he'd heard, but she and Cathy had been so miserable and irritable lately that Tom was wishing they'd both go, permanently. At least Phillip would be good for a laugh, even though he didn't want to be here, he'd no doubt throw a few sarcastic comments Lady B's way with any luck.

As Tom went about his business of checking the wines he'd be serving with dinner, then going around the house turning on lights before it got dark, Lady B was upstairs bathing, with Cathy in close attendance.

"Is everything ready for this weekend?"

"Yes milady."

"You think there are enough flowers, that all the rooms are spotless and we have enough staff?"

"Yes, I think so, milady."

"I think so isn't good enough, Cathy. I want this weekend to be perfect so you and Kay had better make sure it is. Where is Kay by the way?"

"I think she's getting ready to go out. She's having dinner with Paul and Larry, remember?"

"Oh yes, the two faggots. It's a pity they're both gay. Kay has been so moody lately that she really needs to be laid and neither one of them is going to put a smile back on her face. I just hope I get to smile this weekend."

"I think you'll be beaming by Monday, milady" Cathy smiled, though not feeling too jovial.

"If I am, it won't be because of his lordship," Lady

Baldwin said disdainfully, looking upwards toward the noise

the approaching helicopter was making, "now scrub my back,

Cathy, and rub this oil into it. I want my skin silky soft."

She bent forward so that Cathy could do this.

Downstairs, Tom also heard the helicopter approaching. He

stepped outside to greet his lordship and Phillip, a little

surprised to see that Phillip had sat in the back with him

rather than the usual servant position up front with the pilot,

Ian. Phillip waved to Tom and back at Ian as he stooped

needlessly under the still whirring rotor blades, a reflex action

to duck though the blades were high enough not to warrant it.

Then Phillip allowed Lord Baldwin to lead the way up to the

house as he followed carrying his luggage.

"Good evening, milord. Did you have a nice flight?" Tom

shouted above the roar of the copter.

"Yes. Thank you, Tom. Let's get indoors.."

Tom held the door open with a strong grip against the wind

as they entered, closing it rapidly behind Phillip as Ian lifted

off. Normally he'd have gone to the aircraft for the luggage but he knew Phillip wouldn't have let Ian go if there'd been more and it was all probably his.

"Is there anything I may get you, milord?" Tom asked.

"No thank you. I'll go and freshen up. Has anyone arrived yet?"

"Not yet milord, no."

"Good, then I'll be upstairs."

As Lord Baldwin made his way upstairs, Tom welcomed Phillip, offering to take his bag or suit holder as he led him toward the kitchen.

"I'm sorry she's making you work, Phil, but I appreciate you being here."

"It's okay, Tom. I half expected it. As far as I'm concerned, you're the boss here so just tell me what you want me to do. How are you doing anyway?"

Tom was leading him to the room he was going to use which was above the laundry, and looked out over the service entrance.

"I'm fine thanks, but don't ask about Kay and Cathy. They've been a real pain lately."

"Only lately? I thought they were a pain all the time."

"Well yes, they are, but even worse at the moment."

"The weekend gets better by the second, the bitch upstairs and the two pains downstairs."

"Well, this is your room and the bathroom is through there. If it's okay with you, if you'll sort out the guests when they arrive then I'll stay downstairs while you unpack them."

"Sure, no bother. If you can just show me who's going where and how I get there."

"Shall I show you right now?"

"Just give me a second to get in my suit," Phillip said as he took it out of its bag along with a shirt and wash things from his other bag and stepped into the bathroom, leaving the door slightly ajar.

"Is your girlfriend going to be okay on her own?" asked Tom.

"I hope so. I have my best friend looking after her and he'll give her a great tour of London."

"I don't know why she couldn't stay here with you."

"Neither do I. It's probably because the bitch upstairs is unhappy so has to make sure the staff are equally as fed up."

"You may have a point there."

Phillip had gotten ready in record time. He only needed to put on his black shoes as he stepped out of the bathroom, dressed exactly like Tom apart from having a watch chain on his black vest.

"How is your family, Tom?"

"Not so bad, Phil. I think you know that Ann wants to quit working here, she really dislikes Lady Baldwin and doesn't like taking her bad mood home. She says that it's bad enough me going home grumpy but the two of us is too much."

"I suppose the bitch won't let her quit?"

"No, so it's really getting tense now as she keeps threatening to fire me if Ann leaves which we can't afford to let happen at the moment."

"Is that because of the kids?"

"The oldest has to have special schooling at the moment which costs us so we're kind of stuck."

"God Tom, why can't life be simple?"

Tom shrugged with an air of resignation before leading Phillip out of his room and down a different corridor than the one they'd taken from the kitchen, this one led directly to the family's bedrooms and also a couple of guest bedrooms. There were three further guest rooms on the next floor up as well. There was also a couple of doors on this level that led directly into the dressing rooms and bathrooms of Lord and Lady Baldwin and these were located on either side of the bedroom door.

"I'd be grateful if you could do his lordship's valeting over the weekend as well if that's okay, Phillip?"

"Sure, that's fine. In fact, he wants me to take some of his business suits back up to Crompton Hall."

He did in fact want Phillip to take more than a few suits. The reason he'd had him sit in the rear of the helicopter with him was to tell him that this was his final visit to this house and that although he was annoyed that Phillip had been made to work, he was also glad as he could help him move his things out, at least some of them anyway. Phillip didn't mention this to Tom. He'd probably guess when he saw the amount of stuff that was being taken on Monday morning, but it could wait until then as his lordship wanted to get through the weekend and tell her on Monday that he wasn't coming back. It would also give him the opportunity to talk to the children. That was about as much as Lord Baldwin told Phillip which was enough for him to know to keep this quiet, to treat her ladyship and her guests with all due respect, and to give him silent backing for an anticipated difficult weekend. Tom showed Phillip the rooms that tonight's guests would be occupying so Phillip made sure he knew where the clothes closets were, along with the contents of the other closets and drawers before Tom led him down the adjacent main staircase, which led directly to the front door. Tom showed him the elevator if he wanted to use it, then a circular route that took in the drawing room where they'd have drinks, the dining room, the library, a family room, breakfast room, kitchen, staff room, laundry, an office, then back to the front door.

He didn't take him downstairs but Phillip's memory was refreshed a little now, and he recalled that downstairs was dominated by the huge glass , indoor pool area, a hot tub, a sauna, a solarium, a game room, a deck with a built in barbecue, its own bar, tables and chairs, with sun loungers overlooking the lake and the bridge. On weekends especially, this part of the house was used a lot. It was always warm indoors and the pool area was relaxing. The bar was accessible from inside and out, the doors could be opened if it was a nice day and you could sit outside but it was just as comfortable to sit inside and take in the views of the countryside and the lake. If the rooms upstairs felt too formal or uninviting, then it felt very different down there. It was by far the best part of the house.

Tom left Phillip to return to the kitchen. He had to get the champagne in an ice bucket and take it to the drawing room before anyone arrived. The glasses were already there but he'd hear it if the champagne wasn't there when Lady B came down.

Phillip remained by the front door, looking into the guest book as he waited for either the guests to arrive or for someone to come down the stairs.

As it turned out, someone came down the stairs first. Lady B. In Phillip's opinion, this was how she looked best, in a casual attire of figure hugging blue jeans, tanned bare feet enclosed in simple black slippers, a v neck black cashmere sweater,

the mandatory pearl necklace, simple gold studs in her ears

and her blonde hair loose and natural, falling over her eyes as

she swayed down the stairs. She may have had some help

from plastic surgeons but she was still beautiful. Phillip wasn't

going to tell her that though. He never did, it wasn't his place

to and butlers don't do that sort of thing unless they're called

Simon.

"Good evening, Phillip. Has anyone arrived yet?" she asked as

she was half way down.

"Good evening, milady. No one has come yet."

"I'm sure they'll be here shortly," she smiled, "and I'm so

glad you could come and help. We're pleased that you seem

to have found someone to share your life with, it's a pity you

didn't bring her with you, we'd have liked to have met her."

"I was going to bring her, milady, but I was told it wasn't

feasible. Shall I send your guests through to the drawing room

when they arrive?"

"Yes. You know which rooms they're going in? Jane Robbins,

who you know, will be in the blue room. John Steele will

be in the green room. We miss you down here Phillip,
you know us so well and you do things so much better than
Tom does."

Before Phillip could give a suitable reply, a commotion from
the top of the stairs made them both look up. The dogs had
escaped Lady B's dressing room and had spotted Phillip so
were now falling over themselves and each other in their haste
to welcome him. He squatted down to greet them, the terriers
barking and licking him.

"Come on, girls," she motioned as she walked away, "come
with mummy."

The dogs, however, totally ignored her even though she kept
calling them and clapped her hands. Phillip smiled as he
continued playing with them. He was still playing with them
when he heard a car approaching, crunching the gravel on the
driveway, but he waited until he heard it stop before opening
the door. Otherwise one of the dogs may have run out too
soon.

It was a big old American car, a Cadillac he thought, all
white in great condition but a bit big for the narrow roads of

England. The driver had come around the circular driveway so that his passenger was nearest the door. Phillip shushed the dogs as they barked and fussed around his ankles as he went to open the passenger door.

"Good evening, ma'am," he solemnly intoned, holding the door wide open.

This was Liz Price. John Steele had a reputation for always having a model on his arm and this was another one. She too was in jeans, distressed jeans with designer cuts on the thighs, a blue lamb's wool turtleneck, black boots beneath the jeans, a gaunt face surrounded by very short blonde hair, deep blue eyes, very pretty, but also very slim.

"Good evening," she spoke very softly with just a trace of a west country accent, "I'm Liz and this is John. I hope we're not too late," she apologized, offering her long thin hand to be shaken.

"You're not late at all, ma'am," replied Phillip, shaking her hand warmly, "I'm Phillip and I'll be helping look after you." John Steele had gotten out of the car and had come around, he too was in jeans, faded, with white trainers and a white tee shirt under a brown leather air jacket. His hair as black as it was thirty years ago in the same swept style but his features were no longer as smooth as once they'd seemed. Now he looked haggard even though his height made him imposing.

He wasn't as friendly as his passenger ."Two bags in the boot and the keys are in the ignition. Is Lady Baldwin in the drawing room?"

"Yes sir, shall I show you the way?"

"I've been here before. Come , Liz."

With that, he began to walk away.

"Would you like some help with the luggage, Phillip?" she asked, not having moved yet.

"He can handle it. He's the servant. Now come, " he chided, throwing her a look of disgust as he continued away as she went after him, giving Phillip a 'I'm sorry' look.

Phillip muttered an "asshole" in his direction as they walked toward the drawing room, even the dogs seemed disgusted by him and didn't even attempt to follow. They just sniffed around as Phillip got the bags out. He'd barely got the two bags inside the front door when he heard another car

approach so he put them to one side and went back outside to

greet the black range rover and its two occupants, Jane Robins

and Tristan Moore. He whistled at the dogs as they pulled up.

They came to greet the guests. They, like Phillip, knew them

and knew them to be friendly.

"Good evening ma'am, nice to see you again."

"Good evening Phillip, it's nice to see you too. I haven't seen

you for the longest time. You look well." She said this quite

genuinely as she stepped out of the car with a warm smile

and she immediately opened the rear passenger door that

contained within a couple of hanging suit/dress bags and two

small cases. Ms Robins was a famous red headed actress with

a glamorous image who struggled these days to maintain it.

Her once hourglass figure was no more, although she could

still look good and the roles she once got now went to much

younger actresses. Phillip liked her. She was always nice to

him and was an easy to care for guest just as her companion

was. True, he was a bit effeminate and way too good looking

as well as a cheat but he was always very friendly, not the least bit condescending, nor vain. He too was a good guest.

"Good evening Phillip," he smiled from above him, "like Jane said, it's really nice to see you again."

"Thank you sir, it's always a pleasure to look after you both. Don't worry about the luggage. I'll see to it. You're in the blue room and her ladyship is waiting for you in the drawing room."

"Thank you Phillip. Don't worry about unpacking the cases, we can see to them but if you can hang the two bags that will be great. Do you want us to move the car?"

"That won't be necessary, ma'am. Just leave the keys in and I'll move it."

"Thank you, Phillip. We'll catch you later." After playing with the dogs for a couple of minutes, they made their way to the drawing room with dogs close behind. When Phillip had deposited their cases in the hallway and was bringing in their bags, the dogs had already returned probably because of John Steele's presence.

Leaving the cars with the keys in the ignitions, Phillip put the bags and the cases in the elevator, and carrying the garment bags over his shoulder he went up to the next floor to put the luggage in their respective rooms. He retrieved the clothing from the garment bags first, a casual jacket and slacks for Tristan and a couple of cocktail dresses for Jane Robins, which he hung carefully on either side of the closet, letting the lady have the bigger side.

He'd left the cases on the bed and opened the first one he came to. It happened to be Tristan's which had actually been packed well, everything carefully folded with the lighter articles above the heavier ones. If Phillip had packed it he would have put scrunched tissue inside the folds to prevent any creases but this was pretty good. He put the shirts and the sweaters, still folded, on different shelves and the underwear and socks in one of the drawers. He'd also brought some swim shorts which went into another drawer, a couple of tee shirts that went into another, brown cords that he unfolded and hung up, toiletries that he placed on one side of the sink, shoes at the bottom of the closet, a book and a travel alarm that went to one side of the bed (nearest the door) on the nightstand and finally a pair of pajamas that he placed directly on the same side of the bed. The empty case with the garment bags inside he placed in a corner of the bedroom. The second case was locked, he hadn't been given any keys nor had come across any so he left it untouched on 'her' side of the bed.

He left the room and went to unpack the two bags in the green room. Both had been left on the bed and he went to the nearest one, a flowery bag and presumably Liz Price's. Her bag too had been packed well, someone had taught her the rolling method whereby if you're short of space but want to take as much as possible without having to iron everything when you get there, then carefully roll up your clothing. It did work but Phillip preferred his method because it didn't take him as long and folded clothes look better. But obviously she traveled a lot and doing things this way she probably didn't need to put her bag in the hold which would save her a lot of time. Phillip went through the same procedure as he'd done with Tristan except he had to shake everything loose. Then he opened his bag, instantly realizing that John Steele probably didn't expect his bag to be actually opened. he probably thought it would just be left in his room. Or he was shameless. The top of the bag's contents was sex toys, from a vibrator to a whip, from videos to a leather thong, condoms to a camcorder. Phillip smiled, although he was a little surprised that she was into this, but then, one never knows. Beneath all the 'goodies' lay his regular clothing, haphazardly thrown in however they were found, and although Phillip could have taken it all and pressed them, he didn't. He just hung and refolded where necessary and if John Steele wanted anything ironed then he could damn well ask. With everything put away or placed in a relevant position, there was only one thing more that Phillip would do before leaving this room and it was something he would never have done if Mr. Steele hadn't been rude to him. He displayed all the toys and paraphernalia all over the top of the bed so it would be the first thing they saw when coming into the room.

"Asshole" he muttered, closing the bedroom door before going to move the cars around to the back of the house.

CHAPTER THIRTEEN

"Hi Phil. How are you?"

Phillip bumped into Cathy as she came down the back stairs.

"Hi Cath. I'm fine thanks and you?"

"I'm okay," she said none too convincingly, "do I need to go and unpack the ladies?"

Lady B preferred it when someone of the same sex unpacked a guest's luggage but Phillip had been doing this sort of thing for years so he wasn't going to wait around for a maid if they were busy doing other things.

"I've taken care of John Steele's girlfriend and I would have done Jane Robins if I'd had her key. I just left her case on the bed."

"She always leaves it locked. I think she prefers to do it herself. I'll check it later when I turn the bed down during dinner."

"Hopefully they'll eat soon. I don't fancy a late night."

"Don't count on it. So how is your girlfriend?"

"She's fine thanks but none too happy that she couldn't come here with me. Being told that I had to come because Tom was off was one thing. Now I have Lady B saying I should have brought her."

"She said that?"

"Just a few minutes ago but that was just another lie. I'm sure she thinks I'm as stupid as I look."

Cathy really didn't want to go any further with this conversation, it was beginning to hurt.

"I'd better go do some ironing. Tell me when they have dinner, will you?"

"Okay," Phillip stared at her back as she walked away with a look of contempt.

"Hey, Rene."

"Hey, Phillip."

Both men shook hands in the middle of the hot kitchen, genuinely glad to see each other.

"So you have an American girlfriend?"

"Yes, I tried to get a French one but they don't understand me in that poxy country."

"That's because French women have class."

"But your wife likes me."

"I think she must be Belgian."

They both laughed.

"Oh Phillip, don't go saying anything but I think I've found another restaurant just outside Paris. You and your Cherie will have to come and visit us," Rene whispered.

"That's great, Rene. Have you given your notice in?"

"Not yet, but I don't think I will be doing. I found out who gazzumped me."

"You're kidding? Who was it?"

Before he could tell him, Tom came into the kitchen to say they'd be ready for dinner in a few minutes so Rene got busy again.

"Phil, do you think you could clear up the drinks in the drawing room please while I get things ready here?"

"Sure Tom, be happy to."

Phillip made his way to the drawing room to tidy it up and to retrieve the empty glasses and drink tray that Tom had previously taken in. The room was empty apart from Lord Baldwin standing with his back to the fireplace, holding an almost empty glass of champagne which Phillip replenished with the bottle in the wine bucket.

"Anything else I may get you, milord?"

"No thank you, Phillip, I'm ready for dinner. But remind me never to upset you," he smiled.

"Why's that, milord?"

"Because I've just had the distinct pleasure of showing our pop star friend his bedroom."

Phillip nodded his head, he didn't need to reply. He wasn't being admonished or anything so he just cleaned up and with the drink tray fully laden he made his way back to the kitchen where he emptied the ice bucket, filled one side of the sink with hot soapy water and began to wash the glasses, rinsing them under running water before putting them on the rack.

"Phil, if you can help me serve. They're just having it plated tonight. I'll sit them down and go round with drinks, and then you can just follow me around the table. Wait here, I'll be right back."

Rene was getting hot soup bowls out of the plate warmer and was putting them on the waiting saucers. Then he got some bread rolls out of the oven and put them in the basket that was by the saucers side, covering them with a napkin.

Tom came back into the kitchen and told them both he was ready so Rene took a pan over to the bowls and ladled the soup in.

"Is this minestrone?" asked Phillip.

"Yes," replied Rene, sprinkling a little parmesan cheese on top of each bowl.

Tom took the first three, closely followed by Phillip with the second three. He'd started to the left of his lordship and was just putting a bowl in front of Lady B who was directly opposite Lord B, so Phillip continued on from there, finishing with Lord B. Tom had gone back into the kitchen so Phillip got some more parmesan which was in a gravy boat on the sideboard with a spoon. He began offering round, starting again at Lord B's left, followed now by Tom who had returned with the bread basket. It only took them two minutes to do all of this and Phillip was back in the kitchen. Tom remained topping up drinks.

Within a few minutes, Tom opened the door to signal he was ready to clear and keeping to the same order, he did the first three and Phillip cleared the second. Rene plated up the entrée plates as they did this so he was almost finished by the time they were depositing the used plates. It was fresh sea salmon tonight with just a hollandaise sauce, new potatoes, courgettes and roasted parsnips. As before, Phillip returned to the kitchen while Tom stayed in the room.

He'd almost forgotten about Cathy so called on the intercom to the laundry to tell her they were down, then rinsed the plates and put them in the dishwasher and washed the cutlery by hand.

Polishing the silver ware in a tea towel, Phillip wandered over to Rene who was using another sink washing his pans. "So who was it, Rene?"

He looked around before answering, making sure no one else was within earshot.

"That fuckin bitch in there."

"Lady B?"

"Who else?"

"Jesus Rene, that's stooping low even for her. Are you sure?"

"Yes, without a doubt. I'll get my revenge on her, you'll see."

"What are you going to do?"

"I don't know yet but something. As soon as it's legally mine, I'll take my revenge."

"Do you know when it will be yours?"

"Not yet but it could literally be any minute. I just wait for the telephone to ring."

"Well, tell me before you go. We can have a celebration."

"Yes, of course. Are you ready for dessert, Tom?"

Tom had come back into the kitchen, turned on the coffee machine and was putting some cream in the jug that was on the already prepared tray.

"Almost Rene, about two minutes."

Rene began preparing the dessert which tonight was individual strawberry meringues with ice cream.

"After they leave, Phillip, can you clear the table and begin to set it up for breakfast?"

"Okay, for six again?"

"Lay it up for six. We may have a rolling breakfast with everyone coming down at different times and there's eight really if we count the florist and Paul. Let's go and clear the table."

"Do you want everything off?"

Phillip normally took as much off the table before dessert as he could, but as this was Tom's 'house' he felt bound to follow his rules just as Tom would when going to Crompton.

"Yes, as much as you can."

With that, they cleared the table of virtually everything apart from glasses they were still using, before again, in the same order, serving dessert. Tom replenished the drinks while Phillip did dishes before Tom came back into the kitchen, filled the coffee pot and took the whole tray to the family room where Lady B would serve coffee and Tom would do drinks before leaving them to it.

It was all very much a routine. Tonight was easier because it was fairly casual but tomorrow would be more formal. The main course and dessert served butler style, which meant that everything would be offered to each guest individually from a silver salver. They would have to serve themselves with a spoon and fork as the salver was held to their left. For the servers, it was back breaking and hot work as they bent over at each setting and the speed was determined by how slow or fast the guests were.

As was customary both in this house and at Crompton Hall, the staff ate after everything was finished with which they preferred as then they could relax a little and enjoy their meal. Rene, being the chef, also was more agreeable to this as it was far easier this way for him. Besides, he liked a glass of wine or two.

Cathy, having turned all the beds down came back and set up the silverware for the four of them tonight while Tom and Phillip quickly cleared the breakfast table once they'd all left and Phillip got it ready for breakfast.

Tom told Phillip he didn't need him for the rest of the evening so once they'd all finished their dinner, Phillip got himself a mug of sweet tea and went to his room, immediately calling Natalie in her hotel room.

"Hi hon, how are you?"

"I'm missing you, Phillip."

"I'm missing you too. I'm so sorry I'm not there with you."

"I know you are but it doesn't make it any easier."

He could hear the beginning of a little sob so quickly changed the subject,

"What did you do in London today?"

"We went and saw Buckingham Palace. Ken said she was home because the flag was flying. We saw another palace on the way there but I forget its name, the house where the Queen's mom lives, Westminster Abbey, and then the Houses of Parliament."

"You must mean St. James's Palace and Clarence House."

"That's them. Everything is so old."

"They sure are," Phillip giggled.

"I saw where your prime minister lives and then we went to Trafalgar Square and then Oxford Street before coming back and having dinner. "

"Sounds like you had quite a day?"

"It was wonderful but I do wish you'd been with me."

"So do I. Where is he taking you tomorrow?"

"Tower Bridge, the Tower of London, St. Paul's Cathedral, Harrods and Covent Garden I think."

"Don't wear him out."

"I'll try not to but he says he's okay and having so much fun that he doesn't feel tired at all."

"He's probably having a blast telling you all the history."

"Oh yes, he knows so much. It's like having my own tourist guide."

"Wait till he gets you in the Tower. He'll be in his element there."

"So how are things there, Phillip?"

"As expected. Pretty tense between Lord and Lady B but he has told me to pack his clothes."

"Really?"

"Yes. I don't think he's going to say anything, at least not until the weekend is over, so you can feel the tension here."

"Has she spoken to you?"

"A little. She told me that you should have come with me and that she prefers me to the butler here."

"She said that?"

"More or less. Tom is a way better butler than I am but he's just more serious about things. Considering how much walking you have to do around this place, I think they're lucky to have him."

"What do you mean by all the walking?"

"Well, because this place is so big it means that doing a simple job takes forever because of the time it takes to get there and back. And trying to find someone is practically impossible. So you combine that with Lady B's penchant for not eating on time and being late, it means that the work day gets longer."

"I understand now. So why won't she eat on time?"

"Because she's a bitch . She doesn't care or even think that's it any hindrance to anybody. Even the guests wonder sometimes when they're going to eat."

"What are the guests like this weekend?"

"There were only four I had to deal with tonight. Jane Robins and Tristan I already knew and they're always nice, as was the girlfriend of John Steele but he was a prat."

"You're kidding? He always looks so amiable. What did he do?"

Phillip proceeded to tell Natalie of his arrival and his behavior, especially toward his girlfriend which was Phillip's biggest gripe. He went on to tell her of what he found in his luggage, how he arranged it all over his bed, and the subsequent look of new respect he imagined he'd received from him during dinner. Natalie took some convincing that he'd actually done this to a pop star, was quite shocked really, amazed he had the nerve.

Although they were both tired, it was very hard for them to say good night so they both talked for a while more before the yawns yielded to sleep. Declaring their love for each other and wishing each pleasant dreams and good days tomorrow, they finally said good night.

To have listened to the conversation at tonight's dinner party, a casual observer may not have guessed that the hosts were barely talking to each other these days, nor have guessed that John Steele and Liz Price had a very heated discussion after they had been shown their room. Liz thought of herself as a liberated, adventurous woman who had come for this weekend fully aware that she'd be expected to share Steele's bed. That was okay with her. True, he was older than she preferred but he'd been very charming when he'd asked her. But he'd been very different traveling here and to sleep with him was one thing but she sure as hell wasn't going to be handcuffed, whipped or videotaped. She almost left but he apologized, promising not to compromise her in any way or embarrass her further. So she agreed to stay.

He, along with Jane , had been very entertaining during dinner. He told stories of his 'glory' years when teenagers would scream so loud that he and his band couldn't even hear what they were playing, about the endless road trips that took him all over the world but saw very little, the bitter breakup of the band, and his new recordings as a solo performer. Jane had talked of her career as well, the good parts and the bad, and now she too was trying to revive her career so she was doing auditions for 'older' parts.

Once dinner was over and they moved into the family room for coffee and drinks, the conversation flowed as it had before, each contributing with something before Liz made her apologies and said good night. She'd had a long day and was exhausted, imploring Steele to stay awhile and finish his drink. Politely, he said he would but should first escort her upstairs. Upon returning, Steele explained she'd been on a shoot at the crack of dawn which Jane Robins related to, saying it was funny how the photographers always wanted to shoot film at the most 'ungodly' hours.

It wasn't that much longer before Lord Baldwin was making his excuses and placing a peck on the cheek of Lady B as he said goodnight. Then, with much protestation from

Lady B, Jane and Tristan departed with a hug and a kiss, leaving just Lady B and John Steele.

Tom, on a customary round, was told he could clear away the coffee things and to go home. Lady B replenished the drinks, champagne for her and malt whisky for him, kicking off her shoes as she sat on the couch and then swinging her legs up so she could stretch out. Steele stood with his back to the still glowing fire.

"Where did you meet Liz?"

"Awards show a couple of weeks ago. She had been invited and I was doing a little gig. We got introduced and I invited her here for the weekend after I received your invitation."

"Just like that?"

"Just like that. I know it sounds preposterous to invite someone for a weekend after basically just an introduction but that's my world."

"You didn't even go on a date or anything?"

"No, nothing. I didn't even have her phone number, I got my agent to call her."

"I'm surprised she agreed to come. She doesn't come across as a roadie or anything."

"She isn't, I think it's our images that are to blame. We're always being told it's important to keep in the public eye so the likes of me and models like Liz get together and then the press will take photos of us and we'll be in the news."

"But there's no press here."

"No, but there was outside her flat when I picked her up and they'll be there again when I take her home. So it will look like I've still got it and her fee will probably go up. It's a win for both of us."

"So, why aren't you upstairs with her now?"

"I screwed up big time. I treated her badly on the way here, for some reason I thought she was going to be another brainless bimbo and I spoke to her as such. I also thought I'd need a few things to make the sex at least a little interesting and she freaked when she saw that."

"Oh God, how funny. What on earth did you bring?"

"I suppose it is funny now but at the time it wasn't. I'd brought handcuffs, whips, a video camera, some clothing and what have you. Very embarrassing."

"How delicious," Lady B laughed, standing up and going over to the door which she opened and then let close, making sure the kitchen light was off to let her know Tom had left, "it's way too bright in here. Let's just have firelight." She switched off the lights, making her way to the ice bucket to top up her glass then going over and standing directly in front of him. She took a sip of her drink with her right hand, placing her left on his chest and looked up into his eyes.

"So, you don't have a woman tonight?"

"It seems not," he replied.

"Then John," she whispered, reaching around him to deposit her glass on the mantelpiece, standing on tiptoe as she wrapped her arms around his neck, "why don't you have me?"

"But what about Alistair?" he responded, letting her take his drink and place it with hers on the mantel, her breasts pushing onto him as she did so.

His hands went to her bare waist. "Never mind about

Alistair. Don't we have some unfinished business to take care

of?" she eyed his lips.

"You mean Antigua?" he crushed his lips to hers, their

tongues violently colliding.

"I seem to recall a certain excitement in this particular area"

she broke off the deep kiss momentarily and stroked his

crotch.

"The excitement only grows," he gasped, his hands having

found her naked cheeks under her jeans, "you didn't wear any

underwear tonight?"

"No, I was hoping for this."

"But what if I hadn't upset Liz?" He found her bare breasts

and erect nipples beneath her sweater, his breathing heavier

now between the kisses.

"Then I'd have found an excuse to take you into a closet or

a bathroom for a quickie. But now dear, we have time and

the space," she pulled him down to their knees, pulling up his

tee shirt then taking it off him, letting him do likewise with

her sweater before rolling him onto his back, "now" she

smiled unbuttoning his jeans, "let's see what all the

excitement is about."

CHAPTER FIFTEEN

Phillip didn't sleep well that night, whether it was being in a strange bed, a different locality or more likely because he'd left Natalie in London, he felt like he was awake for most of the night. At least he had the satellite television and could make himself some tea to while away the hours. He did though learn one useful piece of information from his vantage point above the service entrance. The designer, Paul, spent the night with Kay. "Good for her," he spoke aloud as he watched her open the door for him and then kiss him on the lips as she went back to her house, "but I wonder why he pretends to be such a queer?"

He'd called Natalie a few minutes ago which didn't exactly make him feel better, she'd been a little tearful again at the prospect of another day without his company so hopefully Ken would give her a great day and she'd feel better. Checking his appearance again, he turned off the television and went downstairs.

The dogs, who slept in their own little room close to the kitchen and staff room signaled his arrival first by their barks and general excitement. Tom had let them out of their room when he'd come in and the door would stay open now until they were put to bed again, so they'd probably follow Phillip around as was their want. Unless there was food available elsewhere. One of the gardeners had come in to feed them so they went to him temporarily, he fed them from a room across the courtyard so they all followed him, taking the opportunity to relieve themselves before bounding back after him. Phillip went into the kitchen.

"Morning Tom, how are you today?"

"Morning Phil, I'm fine thanks and you?"

"I'm okay, thanks."

"You're down soon. I didn't expect to see you for another hour or so."

"I was awake so what the hell. Anything you need doing?"

"You could make some tea if you don't mind?"

"A man after my own heart."

As Phillip put the kettle on, Tom went through into the house to 'open' it, letting the dawn permeate each room as he pulled the cords on the drapes, unlocking the front door and tidying up as he walked around. Finally, with the two glasses and the ice bucket from the family room, he came back into the kitchen.

"Do you take sugar, Tom?"

"No thanks."

"Have the newspapers arrived yet?" asked Phillip, passing the mug of hot tea to Tom.

"Thank you," he acknowledged. "They'll probably be here in about ten minutes."

"So what's the agenda?"

"Well, I doubt if anyone will be down for breakfast for another hour or so. No one has asked for a breakfast tray so once you finish your tea, you could sort out his lordships dressing room. It's not my favorite job at the best of times and I know you're good with his stuff.

It would be a huge favor for me, is that okay with you?"

"That's fine with me. Good morning, Rene."

"Good morning, Rene," chorused Tom.

"Morning gentlemen. Have you made any coffee yet?"

"Not yet, but I will in a second," responded Tom.

"What time did you guys get away last night?" asked Rene as he turned on the ovens and a couple of gas rings, putting a large wooden chopping board on the island worktop.

"It was about ten or just after for me I think."

"About eleven for me," added Tom.

Rene snorted his disapproval. If there was one thing that staff hated, it was late nights especially on a regular basis. In this house Lady B was regularly late.

"I'll be upstairs then or in the laundry room if you need me," said Phillip, rinsing out his empty mug and setting off up the stairs closely followed by the dogs who'd just come back in. Finding Lord B's dressing room with only a little uncertainty, Phillip was quite happy to hear him say 'Yes?" when he knocked on the door.

"Good Morning, milord. I was just going to pick up some of your things."

"Good Morning, Phillip," he opened the door, amused at seeing him with the dogs like a pied piper, "Glad you came. I was just sorting out a few things."

Phillip closed the door behind him.

"What can I help you with, milord?"

"Well, I can't take everything but I can't decide on what to leave. What do you suggest, Phillip?"

"I think that if you sort out your personal things like jewelry, certificates and what not, items that you can't replace, then you can restrict your clothing to items that you've worn during the last year. It looks like everything is sorted at the moment with its color," he deemed, looking around, "so if we change it to have this side as 'take' and the other as 'leave', it might be easier."

Lord Baldwin contemplated for a moment, looking around the room.

"That's a good idea, Phillip. Why don't you go and get a bag and we can start with my watches and cufflinks and shoes? I'll start moving things around."

"Very good, milord. I'll take your suit from yesterday with me and I'll be right back."

Phillip and the dogs left the room for the laundry where Kay was already at work putting some laundry in one of the machines.

"Good morning, Kay."

"Good morning, Phillip. I was wondering where these little blighters were."

She got down on her knees as they fussed around her, trying to lick her.

"Where did you go for dinner last night?"

"We just went to an Indian restaurant. It was pretty good though."

"Can you keep the dogs here for a minute? Lord B wants me to help him sort something out in his dressing room. I'll be right back."

"Sure, just close the door so they can't follow you."

"Okay, be back in a sec."

Phillip left the room, leaving the suit on a hanger and going to his room first for one of the bags he'd brought before entering Lord B's dressing room again.

"Right Phillip, all the stuff on the floor can go as well as everything on the right, but don't take the clothes on the end. I'll need them for this weekend. If there's any room left, just take pot luck."

Phillip looked around, rather impressed with Lord B's decisiveness, he'd practically halved the contents and very quickly too.

"I'll take it out in stages, milord, and I'll rearrange things in case someone comes in here and wonders why half the room is empty."

"Good thinking, Phillip. I'll go down for breakfast now and leave you to it."

He left by the same door Phillip had used as Phillip began to fill the bag he'd brought quickly without using his usual meticulousness as he didn't want to be seen . As it was, the bag was in his room within a couple of minutes and he was in the laundry room again.

Phillip went to one of the ironing boards and turned the iron on after making sure it had water in it, then doing the same with the steamer. Taking the pants off the hanger he laid them lengthways on the board, folding the uppermost leg back.

"Is there a pressing cloth in here, Kay?"

"Look in that drawer there," she pointed.

Phillip found it. Then he carefully arranged it over the pant leg he was going to iron, he didn't think the material he was ironing merited using a damp cloth, these particular pants would be okay with just the dry cloth and then the steam from the iron. He set to work, making sure he kept to the original crease as he pressed the steaming iron down, knowing full well that if he created a double crease then he'd have to wet the material to rectify it, but he was used to doing this and it was rare when he messed up.

"Tom hates doing that," said the watching Kay.

"I know, but that's okay. I hate polishing brass."

"Don't you like brass?"

"No, but that's because it tarnishes so quickly. You can almost see it begin to tarnish as soon as you polish it. At least silver lasts a while before it needs re-polishing."

"Tom always seems to be polishing the silver."

"It's probably the silver that comes into contact with food. There are certain foods that cause a chemical reaction , like spinach and broccoli for example, and it only has to touch the silver and it turns it black. I think Rene does it on purpose sometimes" he smiled.

"So how's this girlfriend of yours?"

"She's fine, thank you."

"What does she think of you having to work?"

"Same as me."

"Which is?"

"It sucks. I don't mind coming and helping Tom but I didn't need lying to and I don't know why I couldn't have brought Natalie. That was spiteful."

Kay smiled. Phillip was never afraid to speak his mind which was refreshing as everyone else, including herself, bottled too much up.

"I don't think she intended being spiteful," Kay lied,

defending Lady B again.

"Of course she did, it's a natural occurrence for her these

days but you should know that with all the time you spend

with her."

Kay contemplated for a minute or two. She knew he was

right, recent events had only confirmed that. Her long term

plan of taking the children's affection away seemed pretty

lame now. But what else could she do to exact a more fitting

revenge?

"I don't think I notice it as much as you do," she confided,

"I'm so used to her asking about everyone and she can be

really kind and considerate sometimes. Yet at other times like

you said, spiteful."

Phillip had finished pressing the pants which he'd left on the

ironing board as he began to steam out the creases on the

jacket while careful to avoid putting lines on the sleeves.

"I think it's time you moved on, Kay. Now that the kids have

left there's nothing to hold you. I think you'd walk into

another job."

"I don't know, Phil. I don't know whether I'd want to do this job for somebody else for a lot less pay. I just don't know what to do anymore."

"You need a life away from here, Kay. Now do you fancy a cup of tea? I'm finished here so I'm putting the kettle on."

"I'd love one. I'll follow you into the kitchen once I finish this button."

Phillip however made a detour before going to the kitchen. Along with the one he'd just pressed, he took a few other suits out of Lord Baldwin's dressing room and lay them all on his bed to tend to later.

Only his lordship had been down for breakfast so far and he was still in there reading the newspapers. Cathy was having a cup of tea. She was expecting Lady B to call down as she usually did for some juice and coffee, maybe a boiled egg and some toast which she'd take up for her.

Breakfast was traditionally buffet service, but as the meal was so staggered in this household it was easier for Rene and better for the guests if the hot dishes were done to order, so although the juices, fruits, cereals and beverages were on the sideboard, Tom was going to ask each person what they required.

As the staff stood around in the kitchen drinking tea, Tom would periodically come in and ask Rene for two poached eggs on whole-wheat toast, or a full English breakfast or just toast. Phillip took his jacket off and rolled up his sleeves to do dishes while Kay and Cathy disappeared into the laundry room.

Various people came back and forth through the kitchen and staff area. Ann, Tom's wife, not looking at all happy, a couple of other cleaners, the gardener from before who had been designated to help Larry with his flowers, Paul came wandering through as camp as ever which really made Phillip smile. Before breakfast was over, Tom began to lay up the dining table for the dinner this evening.

He looked outside,. Phillip had been finishing breakfast off and asked if he needed to lay the breakfast table for lunch. It was beautiful outside, an Indian Summer day and by all accounts, the same was forecast for tomorrow. It wasn't hot enough to sunbathe, but it was certainly warm enough to sit outside in so Lady B would probably want lunch out there.

He told Phillip to lay it up for breakfast again tomorrow

morning, and once he finished to start putting silverware on

the dining room table from the trays that Tom had previously

prepared during the week. Tom meanwhile would go

downstairs and begin to prepare things for lunch.

CHAPTER SIXTEEN

"Is it cold outside, Cathy?" asked Lady Baldwin between mouthfuls of boiled egg and toast.

She was sitting at her dressing table in just a thick white toweling robe after a hot and steamy shower. Cathy was making the bed just a few yards away.

"No milady. It's quite warm and they say it's going to stay like this until late on Monday."

"Well, that's good. I was afraid the whole weekend would be rainy and we'd all be shut inside getting on each other's nerves. That reminds me, have you seen my husband?"

"He was downstairs a few minutes ago. He'd just asked Phillip to bring one of his cars around, I think he was taking Liz out for a spin."

"Really? Well maybe she'll cheer him up. What is wrong with him these days? Is there something going on that I don't know about?"

"Not that I've heard, milady. Perhaps he's having some business problems. He never talks much about his work."

"You've heard nothing from Phillip or Brian?"

"Nothing at all. Whatever is bothering his lordship, it isn't something that they know about. Otherwise I'd have found out."

"It's probably work, like you said then. He does get moody when his profits go down a little."

"I'm positive it is, milady."

"Is everything ready for tonight?"

"All the bedrooms are being aired and Larry is doing flowers for them as well as for the dining table. Tom and Phillip are setting the table now."

"You all know which rooms tonight's guests are going in?"

"Yes milady."

"I'm hoping that Simon will hit it off with Suzy Walker. He's getting so possessive about me these days, it would be good for him to have someone else."

"You wouldn't mind that, milady?"

"Not at all. She might even teach him a few tricks.

Besides, he'd still be mine."

"Do you think she'll go for him?"

"Oh yes, he's just her type. I've already spoken to her about

him and she can barely wait. She told her husband that it's

all girls here this weekend. She's a bit like me - Suzy, she

likes to have fun."

"Is she anything like the character she plays on television?"

"Oh no, she's much more glamorous than that dowdy person

she portrays but she's very down to earth, funny and great

company. Her husband has had medical problems but she

won't leave him, so she relies on discreet liaisons. Simon

would be good for her."

Cathy was finished in the bedroom and was now in the

dressing room folding clothes and putting them away. Lady B

was drinking her coffee.

"What are you wearing today, milady?"

"I think, seeing as it's warm, a skirt and a cotton top, maybe

a light sweater on my shoulders and flat shoes, so I can take

a walk. Tonight, seeing as we're not doing too formal,
maybe that red dress I brought home the other day."

"You mean the short one?"

"Yes, I only brought one."

"I'll get it out later. Which underwear today?"

"I'll wear white this morning. But here, let me take a look."
Lady B rummaged through her underwear drawers as Cathy
got a selection of skirts out, Lady B pointing out the flowery
one amongst them which Cathy paired up with a sleeveless v
necked white top and a sweater the same color as the skirt.
Black slip on shoes finished the outfit, as Lady B had found
the underwear she wanted which she placed on top of the
hanging skirt.

"Have you moved into that house I gave you yet?" Lady B
asked as she sat back down at her dressing table, brushing out
her damp hair.

"Not yet, milady. I'm still not sure I'm doing the right thing
by making the kids come down here, they barely talk to me
these days."

"You can't reason with kids, Cathy. They have to be told. Why don't you get me the key to it and I'll go and see if there's anything I can do to make it nicer for you?"

"Thank you, milady, that's very kind of you. The key is in my purse. I'll be right back with it."

"Bring Kay back with you. I'll tell you both about last night and John Steele while I put my make-up on."

"He was my idol growing up. I had his pictures all over my bedroom walls. I still drool when I see him."

"You do? Go and get Kay," she commanded, "and tell Tom we'll have a barbecue lunch outside," turning on her hair dryer as she watched the door close in the mirror.

CHAPTER SEVENTEEN

It was a beautiful day for late autumn. Jane Robins, Tristan, John Steele and Paul were all lounging around, reading the newspapers and magazines while Tom tended the bar. He'd already laid up a couple of tables for their lunch. There wasn't a big table down here but then it was never formal here either and as no one knew how many there'd be for lunch it was no real problem. Tom had left Phillip upstairs laying the dining table and he would also take care of any arrivals. No one had taken a drink yet, not alcohol anyway, but that would change once Lady B came down.

At that moment, she was actually in the dining room messing around with Phillip's placement of the silverware which drove him crazy. He felt like giving her hand a slap as she moved various forks and knives, spoiling the alignment. She was a cutlery fiddler. When she sat down at a table she'd immediately move everything in front of her away and to the side, same with the glasses. Phillip came across many people like her, he thought there must be some psychological reason why they did it, but he didn't know what it was, all he knew was that he wanted to slap their hands no. Funny thing was, if he set a table with everything askew she'd go barmy.

"You do lay the table nicely," she offered, still moving things.

"Thank you milady," he replied, following her around the table putting everything back.

"I like that you always get it done ahead of time. Tom tends to leave things until the last minute."

This was partly true but not completely. Phillip kept his mouth shut.

"He doesn't understand us as well as you do, Phillip."

Again, he kept quiet but his thoughts were racing.

"You know which rooms the guests are using tonight?"

"Yes milady, Tom showed me earlier. Do you know what time they'll be arriving?"

"I told them to come whenever they wished, so they may arrive for lunch or later this afternoon. Is Rene in the kitchen?"

"Yes milady."

Satisfied with how the table was looking, she headed toward the kitchen where she'd talk to Rene about the progress of tonight's dinner, then find Larry and see how he was doing with the flowers, especially the centerpiece.

Phillip began to fold the first napkin as she walked away, he was doing a rose which entails a lot of folding in on itself before turning the whole thing over for another fold inward before pulling all the folds out. It was an effective decorative napkin but very time consuming to do. He'd almost finished the first one when the front doorbell rang, but he didn't just discard it, he finished it off and placed it on one of the cover plates as he headed to the door.

"Good afternoon sir," he said to the back of the gentleman's head as he opened the door, wondering what he was looking at away from the house. He turned slowly around.

"Good afternoon, Phillip," he smiled.

"How are you, sir?" Phillip opened the door wide for him to enter.

"There's no need to call me sir. You know me, just call me Simon."

"Away from here I can do that, but when you're here as a guest I'm duty bound to call you sir as you know. Now, can I get your luggage, sir?"

"I understand, Phillip, but you don't need to show me to my room, just point it out and I can manage the rest." He went to retrieve his small suitcase from the back seat of his range rover which no doubt belonged to his boss.

"Ah ah ah, sir. You know full well I'd be in big trouble if her ladyship saw me pointing you to your room carrying your own luggage. Now why don't you just relax and go and say hello to the other guests downstairs? Let me take care of your luggage and your car."

"Okay Phillip, will do. Thank you. Maybe we can have a cup of tea together before I go back?"

"Of course sir, that'll be nice," he lied, taking his small case and closing the rear door, "Tom is downstairs waiting to pour you a drink."

"See you later then, Phillip," he waved as he strode purposely toward the stairs, looking every inch the young country gentleman in his brown corduroys and check shirt.

He didn't get a reply. Phillip didn't even watch him go down the stairs, he just shut the front door and made his way past the staircase to the elevator which took him and the suitcase up to the top floor and to Simon's bedroom where he unpacked the case quickly and without any surprises although he wasn't too impressed with the packing, another reason maybe that his lordship didn't like his work.

Simon had said hello to Jane, Tristan and Paul who he already knew. It was Jane who introduced him to John Steele, telling him he was the personal attaché to Mr. Byron James of the famed American banking family. Tom couldn't help but giggle at this new job description, he had to duck under the bar to stifle his snickering and wipe the amusement off his face.

"Good afternoon, darlings!" called out Lady B as she breezed through past the bar where Tom was still crouching.

"Good afternoon, C," replied Simon who was nearest her, exchanging a kiss on their cheeks.

Everyone else did the same, Jane and Paul getting a gentle hug whilst the others got more of a squeeze.

"Let's have some champagne," she looked at the empty appearing bar, slightly startled when Tom popped up from behind it.

"You can tell Rene to start the barbecue as well, Tom. I don't know about the others," she looked around, " but I'm starving."

They all concurred and as Simon was the new guest he was asked if he had a good journey and if he'd met everyone, especially John Steele. As Tom poured the drinks and brought them around on a tray, they all chatted about how glorious the weather was, the morning they'd had, how they'd slept and where on earth had Alistair and Liz gone. That was answered within a couple of minutes as they came down looking a little windswept, Alistair telling everyone how he'd got his favorite Aston Martin out and taken Liz for a spin around the back roads of Oxfordshire which she really enjoyed as she was nearly always cooped up in a city somewhere.

Rene arrived with a couple of aluminum trays covered with foil which he placed down to the side of the barbecue before lighting it, not speaking to anyone but casting envious glances at the rear of Liz before heading back to the kitchen for some more food and tools. Tom meanwhile was getting the plates out of the cupboard after making sure they all had ample liquid in their glasses.

Rene had another tray ready in the kitchen which contained a big wooden bowl of salad, his barbecue tools, sauces for the meats and dressing for salad.

"Hey Phillip," he looked around making sure the kitchen only contained the two of them, "she has the finest ass this side of Paris."

"I never thought you coveted Lady B. You should tell her that, she'll probably let you have it."

"I don't want her slimy ass. I was talking about that Liz Price."

"She is a stunner. She seems like a nice person as well."

"What is she doing with that old pop star?"

"Actually, she's probably not doing anything. I don't think she was too happy with him once I displayed the contents of his luggage."

Phillip went on to explain what had happened the previous night.

"He must be crazy," laughed Rene, "It's no wonder she was making eyes at me."

"Only in your dreams, Rene. Besides, you're happily married to your own model."

"But we French, we're allowed to have mistresses."

"Then I'll have your wife as mine."

"French wives stay loyal to their husbands, but they realize that us men need to play around. They encourage us to find a mistress."

"You're so full of shit, Rene," Phillip laughed. "Your wife would castrate you with your own knife if you got a mistress."

"On my own chopping block too," he agreed, " but you'll have to send this Liz Price through to give me her autograph."

"Do you want it on tonight's menu card?"

"No, she can sign my dick."

"The only thing I can say to that Rene, is," laughing still, "it's a good job she has a very short name."

Phillip went back to folding napkins as Rene returned downstairs to cook. He would finish off the dining room table and then see if the flowers were ready to be put on, or at least be ready to put on later.

"Hi Phil," smiled Cathy as she walked into the room, "The table looks nice."

"Hi, Cathy. Thank you."

"Does Lady B know that the dogs are here?" Cathy clapped her hands to get their attention and knelt down to greet them.

"I don't know. They disappeared a while ago so I thought she'd taken them downstairs. But then they came back while I was having a cup of tea."

"So what's wrong with his lordship at the moment? He doesn't seem as chirpy as normal," she looked up from the floor.

"I've no idea, he's been okay with me, just a little quiet is all."

"He looks like the whole world is on his shoulders."

"He's probably pissed because he's got to watch Simon drool over his wife all weekend."

"He doesn't drool, he's just a good friend to her is all," she objected.

"I don't know why you defend her all the time. You know damn well that Simon worships the water he thinks she walks on."

"So you think his lordship is okay?" she asked, ignoring his previous statement.

"Yes, he's fine. He's just been spending a lot of time at work lately."

"Right, that's what I thought. Come on girls, I think you're all needed downstairs," Cathy called to them as she got to her feet, making the dogs follow her out of the dining room after learning nothing whatsoever from Phillip.

His eyes followed her as she left, slightly amused at her fishing attempt and her misplaced loyalty.

As soon as the dogs smelled the food cooking on the barbecue, they needed no further encouragement. Although they knew Rene wouldn't feed them, the same wasn't true of Lady B, and with this being outside she'd encourage everyone else to feed them as well. The dogs sprinted toward the smell at which point Cathy turned on her heels to make her way to the laundry room until lunch was ready.

Kay and Ann were inside. Ann was running a sheet through the steam roller and Kay was hand washing a wool sweater.

"Hi," said Cathy as she entered.

"Hi," the two chorused back, not breaking off from what they were doing.

"Is everything ready?" asked Cathy to no one in particular.

"They're finishing off upstairs at the moment" replied Kay, referring to the other maids who worked here generally on a part time basis, but for this weekend they were getting more hours.

"I'll go and check on them in a minute, make sure they're doing it right."

"They know how to clean, Cathy. They've been here long enough now to understand how her ladyship is."

"Well it's me that gets told off if something isn't right."

"Calm down, Cathy, everything is okay."

"No, it isn't. Lord Baldwin is in a mood about something and Phil won't tell me what it is, probably because I had to lie to him. My kids don't want to live down here or my mother, and I can't go back home."

"You can go home. Just quit and find another job."

"That's easier said than done. How many times have you threatened to leave?"

"That's true," admitted Kay, ruefully.

"Well, I can't work here much longer," chimed in the so far quiet Ann, "it's bad enough that Tom is always in a bad mood when he comes home but both us in a mood after work is destroying our life."

"You know she won't let you quit," stated Cathy.

"Too bad, I see everybody's life being ruined around here and I can't go on like this."

"If you walk out, you know she'll fire Tom."

"That's what we've been fighting about lately. He doesn't want to live at my parents house which is what we'll have to do if he gets fired, but I think that's the only way to save our marriage now."

"You're serious?" asked the concerned Kay.

"Deadly."

Cathy left the room after that disclosure. She couldn't fault Ann because she knew that she herself should have quit a long time ago before her marriage crumbled. Now she felt trapped.

"You don't think that living with your parents will break up your marriage?" continued Kay.

"It might, but it's worth a shot at least because it won't last here."

"It's that bad?"

"Yes."

"I'm sorry, Ann. I knew you were having problems but not this bad."

"I'll stick at it for the weekend but not much longer."

"Oh god. I'm so sorry."

As Kay said this she was also looking out the window as she'd heard a car approaching and she recognized the car immediately.

"Oh good," she exclaimed, "it's the children." She ran out to greet them.

"Hi Kay," greeted Sophie as she jumped out of the passenger seat of the battered looking Land Rover which was Charles's best ever present from his father that had been given him on passing his driving test when he was seventeen.

"Sophie." Kay beckoned her to her open arms for a kiss and a warm hug.

"Is there one for me too?" Charles asked once he got out of the car.

"Come here," Kay said, breaking off from Sophie, "and let me have a look at you both"

After hugging and kissing them, Kay took a step back to admire them. She adored them as they did her and she was ever so proud of them.

She was probably most proud because although both had the ability to stop traffic with their looks, neither of them was vain or snobbish. They were dressed similarly today in jeans, trainers and tee shirts except Charles's outfit was much baggier than his sister's.

"You'll do," gushed Kay. "And I see you're still driving around in this tank."

"You know I can't let this go, Kay. Besides, it still runs great and it's ideal in the country."

"They're all downstairs having lunch if you're both hungry," said Kay changing the subject.

"Can't we just have something in the kitchen?" asked Sophie.

"No, you'll have to go down I'm afraid. You can talk to your father."

"How is he lately?"

"He's okay, I think. He's been busy at work by all accounts and didn't really want to be here this weekend."

"Neither do we," chimed Charles.

"I know you don't, but try to make the most of it. I'm glad to see you here so you can always keep me company if you get bored."

"I'll take you up on that, Kay. Come on, Charles. Let's get this over with and go say hello."

"Do you have anything to come in?" asked Kay as they began to make their way downstairs.

"No Kay, we traveled light today," smiled back Charles.

In actual fact, they both had everything they needed in their bedrooms so didn't need to bring any luggage. They'd traveled here from London and their adjoining apartments in Chelsea. Both were attending college, he for land management and she for drama though real love was horses. She'd ridden a lot in her teens and still did whenever she came here but her mother had pushed her into drama when she stopped riding for a while. So reluctantly, like her brother, she was living in London.

Both kids had started riding at Crompton Hall, had entered and won many competitions for young riders around the UK, but it was while doing that they began to learn of their mother's indiscretions with other men. That's when they began to lose their love of riding. Sophie had always been the more naturally talented with horses. Charles had to work for any success but he just loved being outside. he'd have been as happy riding a tractor around a field.

Kay watched their backs as they headed downstairs, hoping they'd stay quiet this weekend so that she wouldn't be blamed by Lady B for their 'horrible' behavior.

CHAPTER EIGHTEEN

To a casual observer, the barbecue would have looked like just a gathering of a few friends and family gathered around eating and drinking. A little ostentatious perhaps with a personal chef and butler in attendance but otherwise fairly normal.

What would have been missed by the observer were the private conversations, the knowing looks, intimate touches, barbed comments and an insider's eye.

Lord Baldwin kept well away from his wife, played genial host with much politeness, but mostly kept company with his daughter. Charles, much to his delight, found a wonderful person in Liz Price who was also well liked by his sister. Simon was eager to get his hands on the enticing Lady B, his eyes hardly straying from her. John Steele was lustful too. He wondered if Sophie was as good as her Mom or if he could just have another night like the previous one. Jane Robins was wishing she could bottle some of Lady B's allure but in the meantime she'd keep a reign on Tristan. He too was hoping. He'd flirted outrageously with Lady B recently on the telephone but hadn't actually been intimate for quite a while.

Lady B was in her element, she knew she was getting these looks although she tried to play innocent. She didn't want Sophie to think she was encouraging them. Sophie didn't like John Steele looking at her but was delighted that his 'girlfriend' didn't seem to like him either. She would be a good match for Charles if she could arrange it. Paul had a twinkle in his eye; Kay had told him many things recently and he was no longer a casual observer. He could see what was going on now.

Sophie thought it would be a good idea to go riding and mentioned this to her brother and Liz who both agreed, although Liz wanted to be sure she would get the most gentle and slowest horse. Sophie also asked her father along and was amazed and delighted when he agreed. Without asking anyone else, the four excused themselves and disappeared.

Lady B made an excuse as well, she said she had to go see her estate manager for a few minutes but for everyone else to make themselves at home and that she'd be back very quickly to do some swimming.

After a while, Tristan said he needed a little walk to revitalize but was actually secretly meeting Lady B in Cathy's house.

"Oh Tristan," she sighed, pulling him by the hand inside as he came to the door, "I've been wet all week thinking of you,"

"I can't stay long, C. Jane is already suspicious, but I do need you, darling," he whispered, pressing her against the wall of the musty smelling lounge before they frantically kissed.

"Then take me, Tristan. Now."

He raised her skirt and took her panties in both hands, dropping to his knees as he pulled them down and lifted each foot in turn to remove them as she held her own skirt up. As soon as he'd removed them she parted her legs, she wanted an extra.

"Lick me first," she told him, grasping the back of his head before burying it into her vagina, gasping as his lips then his tongue found her swollen clitoris.

She came soon, convulsing onto his face before she quickly tasted herself on his mouth as he stood up and kissed her lips while dropping his pants. She took his manhood in her hand guiding it as she felt his hands on her ass, lifting her. Both her arms went around his neck as he began to enter her. Her legs straddling him as she fully took him, thrusting into her as he pressed her against the wall, both gasping loudly as they screwed, letting it all go without care until they both came but not together.

"Thank you, Tristan. That was wonderful," she murmured, smiling as she caught their reflection in the mirror above the fireplace.

He kissed her long and passionately as he pulsed inside of her, only letting go once he was slipping out.

"I have missed you, C."

"I'd never have guessed," she smiled, bending down to pick up her discarded panties, "let's go and wash up."

She led him by the hand again as he held up his pants and underpants as they walked, letting them go again as she washed him. He found himself getting hard again when he washed her and she was quick to notice.

"There's a bed we can use."

"If we get into bed, darling, you'll need to cancel dinner."

"I'll have dinner sent over," she enticed, licking her lips.

"I imagine you would, darling, I really do."

CHAPTER NINETEEN

Tristan went straight up to his room to join Jane for a nap when he got back, not even waiting to see Lady B on her return a few minutes after he. She immediately suggested a swim for everyone and hastened upstairs to change into a swim suit.

The riders still hadn't returned and wouldn't for a long time yet, they'd been gently moseying around the estate enjoying the weather, scenery and each other so were in no rush to return home. Charles and Liz had been leading the way, quite obviously attracted to each other physically but finding they were also attracted mentally as well. Charles, despite his privileged upbringing was really just a country boy at heart. He wasn't comfortable with his London-loving, rich friends. Liz was much the same. She had to live in cities for her career but her heart belonged in the countryside.

Lord Baldwin and Sophie trailed behind. It had been a long time since they'd had chance to spend any time together so were catching up on one another and were realizing how much they missed each other. It was almost when they'd got back to the stables before anything really important was said.

"Dad?"

"Yes, sweetheart?"

"Can I ask you something?"

Lord Baldwin caught the tone and saw the seriousness in his daughter's eyes so he brought his horse to a stop, letting it's head drop to graze. Sophie drew up beside him and did the same, Charles and Liz not noticing as they continued.

"What is it, sweetheart?"

242

It took her a moment or two, this wasn't a question that hadn't been repeatedly thought about.

"Dad, why don't you leave Mother?"

Now it was Lord B's time to take a moment or two.

"Do you think I should?"

"We both think so, Dad, me and Charles. We realize you must still love her but you look so miserable these days that it breaks our hearts."

Tears broke from Sophie's eyes as she said this and Lord B took a few more moments to consider his reply.

"I don't love your mother anymore, sweetheart. I thought I did but there's nothing left anymore. I met someone else a while ago who told me that I must be absolutely sure there's no love left before leaving and that's why I'm here this weekend. Now I'm sure. I may lose my business over this, sweetheart, but I don't want to lose you and Charles. If either of you want me to stay then that's what I'll do."

"We've been miserable too, Daddy. We just can't stand Mother's behavior anymore."

"So you'll be okay if I leave?"

"Yes Daddy, we will."

With tears still coursing down her face, Sophie leaped off her horse and half ran the couple of paces to her father who was more slowly getting off his. He took her in a big bear of an embrace.

"So you've met someone else, Daddy?"

"Yes sweetheart, just recently."

"Is she nice?"

"Very. I think you and Charles will like her very much. You must understand that she is not forcing me to leave, the only thing she's done is make me open my eyes to what's going on, all the things I used to ignore but just can't live with anymore."

"You mean like all Mommy's affairs?"

"Yes, and her mood swings and the spitefulness."

"Is something wrong?" asked a concerned Charles who'd seen his sister and father embracing from the stables and had walked back, leaving Liz tending to their horses with the groom.

Sophie let go of her father and placed both her hands on her brother's shoulders, "It's finally happened, Charles," she beamed, "Daddy is leaving Mummy."

It took a moment for the news to register with Charles as his eyes darted from his sister to her father and back again.

"Are you serious?"

They didn't need to reply, he could see it was true in their faces and his face slowly turned into a huge smile as his eyes began to water and he held his left arm out for his father until all three were hugging each other.

"Are you leaving now?" he suddenly thought aloud.

"I've been trying to find the courage to tell you both but when Sophie flat out asked me, there was no point avoiding it. I was going to leave on Monday morning. I don't want to ruin your mother's dinner party which I've been dreading, but now I think I'll go tomorrow afternoon when everyone else leaves as well."

"Can we leave with you?" asked Charles.

"It might be best if you leave as intended. She's still your mother and I don't want her to hate you both as well. Let's just see out tonight and lunch tomorrow and then maybe you can both come up to Crompton Hall next week."

"Does anyone else know about this?" asked a concerned Sophie.

"Only Phillip."

"What does he think about it?" she asked.

"I haven't asked him but I don't think your mother is too popular with him at the moment as she made him work this weekend and wouldn't let him bring his girlfriend who's visiting from America."

"Kay told us about that," continued Sophie, "it's just so mean of Mummy."

"I know but you two must be careful. I don't want to ruin your relationship with your mother and despite everything, she still loves you two and you must never forget that."

"We know that, Daddy. Our biggest concern has been you but if you're happy then we will be as well. So who is this other lady? Can we meet her? Is she nice?"

"Well, her name is Victoria and I'm just beginning to

realize just how much I love her and how much that you two

are going to like her."

Phillip had taken a nap after lunch and was now sitting in the staff room with a cup of tea and of course the dogs.

Everything was more or less ready for dinner. Tom had also got a trolley ready for some afternoon tea if needed, and Phillip was waiting for the overnight guests, Suzy Walker and Robert and Mandy Mills to arrive.

He'd come across the Mills' before. They were a famous equestrian couple who still rode a couple of Lady B's horses in competition, but they weren't as young anymore and were gradually curtailing their competitive riding. They used to be frequent visitors when Sophie was still riding a lot, but they hadn't been here for a while. They were always nice though when Phillip had previously seen them, so he knew they were no problem.

Phillip didn't know Suzy Walker, only by reputation, she was another older actress who by all accounts loved life and having a good time. Tom liked her so that was good enough for Phillip. He was worried though about Tom. He was looking like he had the whole world on his shoulders and seemed totally exhausted.

"Are you okay, Tom?" he asked when he came in to have a sip of the tea he'd made him.

"Yeah, I'm fine, thanks."

"Why don't you sit down for five minutes? They'll be okay on their own down there for a while," Phillip said, referring to Lady B and whoever else was swimming with her.

"I suppose you're right. I think they'll need a nap before dinner with the amount they've drunk."

"They've had a lot?"

"They've gone through about a bottle each."

"Wow. Who's down there now?"

"Just Lady B, John Steele and bloody Simon." Tom sat down at the table, "Jane Robins and Tristan came back down but they've gone off for a little walk now."

"They're swimming?"

"Swimming and larking about."

Phillip could well imagine.

"So what's wrong, Tom? You don't look too well."

"Thanks for the compliment."

"You know what I mean."

"I know, I'm just worried is all. Ann hates working here and wants to leave but if she does then I'll have to go as well. If that happens we'll be forced to go and live with her parents until I can find something and we don't exactly get along. They're here now looking after the kids while we work, and all they seem to do is tell Ann that she wouldn't be miserable now if she'd married her old boyfriend instead of me."

"Charming."

"Exactly. They haven't forgiven me for taking her to Australia when we got married. They don't realize that I only took this job and came back to England because she was homesick and worried about them."

"So Ann wants to live with her parents again?"

"No, it was her idea in the first place to emigrate and now she feels like she's neglecting the kids so has to leave this job. Which means I'll get fired and we'll have to go and live with her parents."

"Lady B won't let her leave and keep you on?"

"Apparently not. I've been told in no uncertain tones that if Ann quits after this weekend then I'm not to come in either."

"Fuck's sake. Who's going to do your job if you get fired?"

"You, I suppose."

"If that's what the cow thinks, she can think again. I'll be on that helicopter with his lordship on Monday morning and if she doesn't like that, she can fire me as well."

"That makes me feel a little better that you don't want this job, but I still think I'll be living with the in-laws come next weekend."

"I'm sorry, Tom. I don't understand why Lady B has to be such a bitch toward you because you do a great job around here."

"Thanks, Phil. I'd best go and check on things downstairs, but keep your ears peeled for the Mills' and Suzy Walker, will you? You know which rooms they're in?"

"I know."

"And watch out for Suzy Walker. She's a huge flirt."

251

Tom got up from the table and went to the sink to wash out his empty cup leaving it to dry on the drainer, and as he left the room Phillip heard him say to someone, "He's in there."

It was Lord Baldwin, looking as happy as Phillip had probably ever seen him, and he closed the door behind him. Phillip stood up.

"Don't get up, Phillip, I just want you to call Ian and ask him if he can pick us up tomorrow after lunch. Maybe he can take us home after going down to London?"

"Very good, milord, I'll call him straight away," Phillip replied,

smiling.

With that he left the room so Phillip made his comment to the dogs,

"Sorry girls, I have to go earlier than I promised you."

Right on cue, the front doorbell rang and Phillip laughed a little at the irony.

The dogs were already barking and heading toward the door, and Phillip followed behind them.

The Mills' were standing by the door as he opened it, and before he could greet them they had both said, "Good Afternoon, Phillip. Great to see you again."

He struggled to convince them to let him take their luggage, but he managed to do so but they wouldn't let him unpack them, and they said they would probably take a short nap before venturing downstairs.

Phillip was smiling as he and the dogs made their way back downstairs. The Mills' were absolutely no bother to look after, yet they would leave a generous tip.

Suzy Walker arrived shortly afterward. Phillip saw her car approaching and was waiting at the door with the dogs as soon as she pulled up. She was driving a little two seated sports car, with the top down, he thought it was an MGB GT, in a British racing green. It wasn't a new car, but it was in great shape. Just like its owner.

As Tom had warned him, she did flirt. She was wearing almost the obligatory jeans, but tight and form fitting, with a white blouse that was practically open to her waist. Her bra was in full view, displaying her breasts to best effect. It was very difficult for Phillip to his eyes averted, and she purposely kept bending in front of him and kept touching his arm or back as he retrieved her luggage.

Even following her up the stairs, she swayed her hips invitingly, knowing he was right behind her.

"Do you ever get into London?" she asked him softly, as he strode in front of her to lead her into her bedroom.

"Sometimes ma'am, but only if I have to."

"You should call me next time," she purred, "we could have a nibble or two."

"I'll keep it mind ma'am" he answered as calmly as he could, trying hard not to look as she decided to stretch out on the queen sized bed.

"This is very comfortable," she spoke in just above a whisper, "do you do room service, Phillip?"

"Yes ma'am, whatever you require. Would you like me to unpack your luggage?"

"As much as I'd like you to rummage through my smalls, it's not necessary," she smiled.

"Very well then, ma'am, I'll let you get comfortable. Her ladyship is swimming I believe in the indoor pool which is located in the basement. Your bathroom is just through here," he signaled, "and is there anything further you require?"

"No, not right now Phillip. I think C has plans for me but she never told me about you. I may have made my own if I'd known," She gave him another enticing look as she watched him make a hasty exit.

"Holy shit," he said to no one in particular as he hurried away with his trusty dogs in tow, "why did no-one warn me about her?"

CHAPTER TWENTY ONE

Kay and Paul had gone for a walk when the frolicking around the pool had started and were now having some tea of their own in Kay's house, resting before Kay helped with the dinner service and Paul took his place with the other guests.

"So what do you think that was all about?" asked Paul.

"You mean the children and their father?"

They'd seen the group hug from a distance but hadn't approached.

"Yes."

"I don't know. I'll have to ask one of them later. I haven't seen them do that for years. It was very strange."

"No ideas at all?"

"The rumor is that Lord B has been having some business problems, maybe that's it. Phillip probably knows what it was all about although he hasn't been saying anything."

"Have you asked him?"

"Yes, but I don't think he trusts me and Cathy anymore. He just tells us what he wants to and nothing else."

"That isn't very helpful."

"No, but it's a taste of our own medicine really. He knows that Lady B pushes us all the time for information from up there and then she makes me and Cathy lie for her and not give the whole story to him."

"What do you mean?"

"Like this weekend. Instead of being able to tell Phillip that Lady B wanted him working because she hadn't been told his girlfriend was visiting, she made Cathy tell him that Tom was off and it was part of his job to cover for him."

"So if Phillip had told her about his girlfriend, she wouldn't have made him come?"

"Of course she would. She's spiteful, remember."

They both laughed.

"How have you put up with this for so long, Kay?"

"I don't know. I've told you about Richard and I'm over him now. The children are grown and rarely here. I suppose I'm just afraid of starting afresh. I earn a lot of money here, I travel a lot, I have this house and a new car every year, and although Lady B can be really nasty to me, she can also be extremely nice. It's hard to explain."

"I was talking to Larry earlier. He is totally intrigued with this place, he thinks he's in his own real life soap opera."

"He probably is."

"I had to laugh though. He said half the men here had the hots for Lady B and the other half hated her. He wanted to know how he could get the same reaction."

"I'll have to tell her that, she'll crack up."

"He thinks she's a nymphomaniac."

"Not quite, Paul," Kay laughed, "but almost. Actually, she's very selective and most of the time it's only her and Lord B who are in the house and she isn't throwing herself at the gardeners or anything. I think she feeds on jealousy mostly, she flirts and likes men coming on to her but it doesn't seem to turn her on unless she thinks that it's behind someone's back. Even then, she won't sleep with them. It's just sex, another game to her really."

"I don't think I could cope with her like Alistair seems to do. He must know."

"You'd think, but I have never heard him say anything to her in all these years. It's almost like he blanks it out."

"Hmmm. Interesting. Going back to earlier, Kay, let me ask you another question. What would it take to get you to leave here?"

"I don't know , Paul. I wish I did.   Why do you ask?"

"I'm not sure , I just thought it might be worth knowing."

They looked at each other for a long time wondering about this and possible consequences with different answers. It was amazing how one simple question could make you think of so many answers.

CHAPTER TWENTY TWO

It was noticeable that night, if you were looking, that Lord Baldwin, Charles and Sophie were in a good happy mood. Lady B and Kay certainly noticed and every time that Kay served her, Lady B was asking why? All Kay could get from the children was a whispered, "I'll tell you later."

Lady B was already regretting her table plan, she'd put Lord Entwistle to her right knowing he was a huge bore, thinking he'd have been enamored with Liz Price to his right, but she was ignoring him to talk to Charles who was on her other side. So Lord Entwistle (Edgar) had gained Robert Mills' attention who was to the left of Lady B, and they were discussing hunting, which bored Lady B no end. She looked down the table on her left side. Suzy was all over Simon, her hand kept disappearing under the table so maybe she was seducing him. He looked quite consternated, she thought. There seemed to be quite a conversation going with the next two, Larry and Mandy, which also involved the two opposite

Tristan and Sophie. John Steele was no doubt charming

Lady Entwistle, who was sitting by Lord Baldwin. He was in

conversation with Jane and Paul to his left.

It looked like a successful dinner party except Lady B was

bored. She thought of earlier as she feigned interest in the

joys of hunting which she hated. She'd had way too much to

drink, and if she hadn't had a nap and a long shower she'd

have struggled to have made it tonight. Most of the afternoon

was a bit of a blur but it had been fun. The servers were

coming round again, maybe Kay would find something out, but

why was Cathy looking so miserable? How could she be so

ungrateful? She'd fixed her up for tonight, she'd have a man

later, and yet she was miserable.

Her eyes went round the table again. Robert Mills, who

she'd had sex with once, just once because it was terrible,

finished before he started really and she'd never encouraged

him since. He was quite good looking though he smelled too

much of horse. He still had a good figure and his own hair,

and still won the odd competition for her which was fun.

Suzy, poor Suzy with the invalid husband. Small and petite, attractive, short black hair, just wanted discreet good wild sex once in a while to keep her going without her husband reading about it in a tabloid. Simon would be perfect for her. Mandy Mills, Miss Dowdy really, a good horsewoman but nothing much else about her. If she made some effort she could look good, but she does nothing with her mousy hair, wears badly fitting clothes and almost no makeup.

Lady Entwistle, or Margo, was the opposite of Mandy in that she spent a fortune on clothing and make up yet still looked terrible. A typical country lady, a pillar of the community, and very good at small talk. She wasn't sure what John Steele would be talking to her about. Maybe she was a fan of his once, you never know.

Tristan looked delicious as usual. Jane was lucky there to have him but was keeping him on a short leash these days. Maybe she was getting suspicious? Mmm, I should go and grab him.

It looks like he's keeping Larry entertained, camp Larry who's done a wonderful job with the flowers and for what he charges he should have done.

What is wrong with Sophie? I haven't seen her smile so much for ever. Even her miserable father is happy. What is wrong with them?

Charles is totally dominating Liz. I wish he'd let Edgar talk to her, it would give me chance to talk to Suzy with Robert.

"What was that you said, Edgar? I didn't quite catch it."

It was going   smoothly in the kitchen, putting the food on silver platters was easier for Rene than having to plate each individual plate and one of the part time cleaners had come in to wash his pans and generally help him where needed. Kay and Cathy were helping Tom and Phillip with the serving, and doing dishes in between, while Ann had gone upstairs to turn the beds down and tidy things up. It was quite an operation. Tonight was a simple menu for a Lady B dinner party, all it consisted of was a smoked salmon salad, noisettes of lamb with a redcurrant wine sauce, Parisian potatoes, glazed carrots and green cabbage, a cheese board, then crème caramel with a compote of fresh fruit.

"It looks like Simon has caught Suzy's eye," joked Kay as she began to wash some glasses one by one before rinsing them under running water and placing them on the draining board.

"He's caught more than her eye. I swear her hand was in his lap when last I looked," replied Phillip as he began to dry and polish a glass.

"He didn't look too comfortable to me, or hungry. He hardly touched his salad," Kay continued.

"I suppose it's difficult to eat when someone's rubbing your pecker." laughed Phillip.

"Depends what you're eating," joined in Rene.

"Well, I hope he gets some of his main course. He's going to need his strength later I think," giggled Kay.

"I think she wants to be his main course, not to mention his dessert as well," Phillip added.

"What is she like, this Suzy Walker? Maybe she prefers French food," said Rene, never slow to offer his own services.

"She's an attractive woman, Rene. She's flirty, small and cheerful and probably a lot of fun. I don't know what she sees in Simon but then I don't know why Lady B likes him either."

"It's because he looks good, dresses well and acts well," offered Kay, ignoring Phillip's reference to Lady B.

"Not to mention his young loins," Rene came back, emphasizing the loins.

"You're so bad, Rene," laughed Kay some more.

"Liz Price is looking good, I think Charles is smitten with her," Phillip observed.

"So am I," offered Rene, "even though I don't know what smitten means"

"It means in love with," explained the educated Kay.

"I thought it sounded right. I bet that pop star is loving Charles being all over his girlfriend," responded Rene.

"I don't think he cares," said the sullen Cathy.

"Lady Entwistle seems to be interested in whatever he's saying to her. Maybe he recalls her being one of his groupies 20 years ago," smirked Phillip.

"I can just imagine Lady Entwistle waiting around in a hotel lobby in a twin set and pearls, being summoned to a pop star's room for a sex and drug party," laughed Kay some more as she watched Cathy storm off somewhere.

"I think you've upset her," Phillip said to Kay, referring to the departed Cathy, "you know she's a big fan of Mr. Steele, maybe she recalls her ladyship hanging around."

"Who knows? So anyway, Phil, why does Lord B look so happy all of a sudden?"

"I have no idea. He doesn't look any different to me," lied Phillip.

"You know damn well he's been miserable since coming here," pursued Kay.

"Aren't we all miserable when we come here? He looks the same as he normally does at Crompton Hall."

"You know what I mean."

"He's probably just realized that he's going home on Monday is all."

"But the kids are looking happier as well."

"Charles has every right to look happy when he's sitting next to a gorgeous model who obviously likes him, and Sophie is on a promise from the chef which amuses her and makes her look happy."

"What promise did I make her?" asked the perplexed chef.

"You promised her a bath full of whipped cream along with a lifetime of her favorite dessert."

"What's her favorite?" inquired Rene.

Just then, Tom came in to tell everyone it was time to clear the main course dishes and Phillip followed him back out, stopping momentarily at the door to say, "Kay will tell you." Rene turned to her, "Well?"

"Spotted Dick!"

CHAPTER TWENTY FOUR

If this dinner party had been at Crompton Hall then it would invariably have preceded a pheasant shoot, so the normal occurrence there was for the men to remain in the dining room after dinner, to drink port and smoke a cigar. However, this was Stonebridge and Lady B didn't have to follow that tradition here so once dinner was over she wasted no time in leading everyone back into the drawing room.

Tom had already deposited a large silver tray that held a coffee service and after dinner mints, just as he'd already prepared a small bar with brandy, whisky, liqueurs and champagne. Although Lady B had dropped the customary port practice, she hadn't dropped the typical after dinner role of pouring coffee for those that wanted it, just as Lord B was on hand to offer the alcohol. This gave the staff chance to clear and clean up and also eat their meals.

The drawing room was large so it gave everyone enough seats and room to stretch out and mingle, but mainly it was Lord B talking to Lord Entwistle, Charles, Sophie, and Liz chatting with the Mills', Lady Entwistle discussing fabrics and floral arrangements with Paul and Larry, while Lady B was holding court with Jane, Tristan, Simon, Suzy and John.

Lord B had taken up the hunting theme in his conversation, the Mills' were arranging a horse ride with Sophie and Charles and Liz if she wanted, and the bigger group were talking about their favorite restaurants in London and the fashionable places to see and be seen.

Occasionally there would be chance to have a quiet word with someone, so Lady B was able to clear things up with John.

"So you'll be able to make Cathy's dreams come true?" she asked, trying to make sure they were out of earshot.

"Sure, she was the slim blonde right? I'll do it if only you promise me yourself again, and not just once."

"I have a place in London we can meet. It's small and very private and I won't forget this favor. She's been so miserable lately and I really need her around but with a smile on her face."

"I'll see what I can do, but do you think she'd mind if I brought something along?"

"What are you thinking?"

"Maybe a camera?"

"A video?"

"Yes."

"You're so bad , John. If you do then hide it, I don't think she'd like it if she knew about it."

"I'll put it in a bag or something. Maybe we could watch it later?"

"Maybe John," she said with a glint in her eye, "you remember where her room is?"

"Yes, I'll go there in another hour or so."

"Then go and sit down and I'll get you another drink, a weak one," she laughed.

As John sat down again and Lady B poured a drink, it was Liz who quietly asked Charles a question.

"Would you mind, Charles, if I slept in your room tonight, or maybe I could sleep in Sophie's?"

"That would be okay. Can I ask why?"

"John gives me the creeps," she explained, casting a quick glance to where he was sitting, "and I'm kind of hoping that you might want to see me again after this weekend?"

"Are you serious? I'd love to," Charles beamed.

"I don't want to rush into anything though, Charles. I'd like to spend more time with you first, so if it's okay, I don't want to have sex with you just yet."

"That's okay, Liz. I think I'll ask Sophie if you can sleep in her room. She won't mind, and it would be too difficult for me to leave you alone if you slept with me."

"That goes for me too, Charles, but I really like you and I want to know you some more. You really don't mind?"

"No, not at all. In fact, I'm flattered."

"I'll get my things later."

Simon was also looking for a quiet word and he was constantly glancing in Lady B's direction to gain her attention. He thought he'd got it a few minutes ago but then John Steele had stepped in, but he saw her get up again and was quickly at her side as she poured herself some more champagne.

"Suzy won't leave me alone, C," he apologized.

"That's okay, Simon, she needs some company. Don't you like her?"

"She's nice enough, C, but I was hoping we could spend some time together."

"If the opportunity arises, we will, Simon. So is Suzy coming on to you?"

"I'll say. All through dinner she was touching me and now she keeps whispering to me to about how wet she is and how quickly she needs me to make love to her."

"You can never accuse Suzy of being shy," Lady B laughed, "is she turning you on, darling?"

"Yes she is, but all the time I'm thinking and looking at you."

"It's only sex, darling, you mustn't worry about upsetting

me. It's actually quite a turn on for me to think of you with

another woman. Now get yourself a drink and go and have

some fun."

With that, Lady B went and sat down again, winking and

smiling at Suzy as she did so.

CHAPTER TWENTY FIVE

All the staff had eaten, and with the exception of Tom who was just checking doors and windows before he too left, had gone to their homes or rooms.

Phillip was already on the phone talking to Natalie.

" Did you have a good day?"

"Oh yes, I loved the Tower and the bridge. I even got a photo with one of those beefeater guys."

"That's great, so you got to see the Crown Jewels?"

"Yes, and the cottage they let one of Henry VIII's wives stay at before she was beheaded."

"I think that was Ann Hathaway but I'm not sure."

"Ken told me who it was but he tells me so much I forget most of it."

"I'm the same way, it goes in one ear and flies out the other."

"I wish you'd been with us."

"I do too but I do have some good news."

"What's that?"

"I'll be seeing you tomorrow."

"Are you coming to London? What's happened?"

"Lord B told me to rearrange the helicopter so you must have Ken get you to the heliport by 1pm, once you get back to Crompton Hall the helicopter will fly down for us.

"Okay, I think he's taking me to a market in the morning. So why are you leaving early?"

"That must be Portobello market. His lordship must be telling her he's leaving so there's no reason to stay on."

"What do you think will happen when she finds out?"

"I don't know, I really don't."

"You have no idea?"

"Not really. She'll either raise the roof I suppose or take it out on the staff."

"Be careful then."

"Oh, I'll be okay. I'm leaving with him so I should escape most of it."

"Well, make sure you do. So what's been happening there today?"

Phillip told her of the day at Stonebridge and found out more about her day in London before they both called it a night, said they loved each other, and looked forward to Sunday afternoon and meeting up again.

CHAPTER TWENTY SIX

Lady B had gone to bed alone and woke up alone as well. Everyone had gradually disappeared after dinner except her, the Mills', Jane and Tristan. Once they left, she even went looking for Lord B who was busy in his office and so she'd gone to bed, smiling as she passed Suzy's room who it seemed liked loud sex.

"It's no wonder she has to be discreet," mumbled Lady B as she walked by, "she'd wake the dead."

She called down on the intercom for Cathy to bring her breakfast up along with a newspaper while she went to the bathroom and then sat at her dressing table to think about what she'd wear today. Cathy was there shortly after and actually smiling as she put the tray and paper down in front of her.

"Good morning, milady."

"Morning, Cathy. It's nice to see a smile on your face for once. I take it you had a good night?" she asked mischievously, pouring herself some coffee.

"Despite my reservations, milady, I had a wonderful night. Thank you."

"You mean you weren't looking forward to it?"

"No I wasn't, milady. I felt obligated in a way but he put me at ease and I had a great night."

"I knew he'd be good for you, Cathy. You see how I look after you? I hope you gave him a good time?"

"I think so, milady, he seemed to have a good time and didn't seem disappointed. He even gave me an autograph."

"It sounds like he gave you more than an autograph," laughed Lady B to the now embarrassed Cathy.

"Yes, that's right," she giggled back.

"So is anyone down and having breakfast yet?"

"Nearly everyone I think, milady. The children are already riding with the Mills' and the only ones that haven't been seen are Simon and Ms Walker."

"He might need oxygen more than breakfast, Cathy. Suzy was ravaging him last night and is probably at him again this morning."

"I know how that feels now, milady," muttered the red faced Cathy.

"I bet you do. Now run my bath, Cathy, while I eat. Then we can decide what I'll wear today and you can tell me more about your night with John."

"Yes, milady. And remember your secretary from Crompton Hall will be here today to help you with a few things".

As Cathy made the bath ready, her smile was turning into a frown as she wondered how she was going to tell Lady B that Ann hadn't come into work this morning.

Kay was also facing a dilemma. She'd caught Sophie before she'd gone riding and had been told that Lord B was leaving this afternoon, for good. So now she was looking for Paul, she had to talk to him about this. She found him by the lake reading a newspaper.

"How am I going to tell her?"

"Is he really going to leave her?"

"I don't think he'd have told the children if he wasn't serious."

"How have they taken it, are they upset?"

"On the contrary, I think they're more relieved than anything else."

"So how do you think Lady B is going to react when she finds out?"

"I have no idea."

"So don't tell her."

"But if I don't, you can bet your life she'll ask me later if I knew he was leaving."

"Then lie and pretend you had no idea."

"She won't believe that, I'm sure she won't."

"Well, if she gives you a bad time with it then tell her you're going as well."

"Where on earth could I go?"

"You could always come with me."

"Are you serious?" asked the shocked Kay, sitting down now.

"Yes, I am," he replied, taking her hand, "lets walk a little." They rose and walked away.

So it was that this particular Sunday at Stonebridge, would be a definitive day for most of its occupants in one way or another.

CHAPTER TWENTY SEVEN

The call came in very early that evening to the detached cottage not very far away from Stonebridge, and the lady who answered the telephone was dressed comfortably in white sweats and white sport tee shirt, barefooted, minimal make-up, and her thick brown hair only loosely combed. She and her husband had enjoyed a lazy Sunday alone so there had been no need to 'dress'. She was attractive, blue eyed with high cheek bones, a ready smile, quite tall and almost slender now that she and her husband had begun to get fit again, they'd even turned one of the two children's bedrooms' into a gym of sorts. Both kids were married now, had their own homes nearby, so having their own gym was a godsend to her as she worked from home, and knew full well that she wouldn't go to a regular gym, at least not on a regular basis.

"Hello," she answered the phone simply, with a hint of a Welsh accent.

"Hello, Meg," responded the caller in his deep baritone, shortening her name from Megan, "how are you tonight?"

"Hello, Steve," she replied almost resignedly, knowing his voice well and it's normal implications, "I'm fine thanks. How about you? I take it that this is a social call?"

"Err, not really Meg I'm sorry to say. Work is rearing its ugly head again and I need to speak to Chris. Janet sends her best though, and she was wondering when we could have a meal out again. It seems ages since we did that."

"Send her my regards, Steve, and tell her I'll give her a call this week sometime. We'll see if we can arrange something."

"Okay Meg, is Chris there?"

"Yes, hang on a minute, I'll go and get him" and she put the receiver down while she found him.

"Chris," she shouted, "Steve's on the phone for you."

"What does he want?" he commented in his usual soft voice as he made his way into the lounge from the kitchen, "do I have to go in?"

Meg just raised her eyebrows and shrugged her shoulders in reply, making her way back to her armchair and the crossword she'd been attempting to finish.

Chris was dressed fairly similarly to Meg in that he too was in sweat pants. Although his graying black hair was a little unkempt, he had showered and shaved just a little while ago, his blue eyes were fully awake, and despite his attire, he still had the ever imposing presence that he normally had.

"Hello Steve, I suppose you're just calling to remind me that you're picking me up at 7:45 am tomorrow? Or do I have the day off like today?"

"Hi Chris. No, I'm sorry. We've been called in and I need to come and pick you up now. Can you be ready in five minutes?"

"Give me ten and I will be. So what's the situation?"

"I don't know much apart from that we have a body. We also have a suspect in custody and our Inspector wants us, or namely you, to handle it."

"Okay, Steve," he replied resignedly, "then let's make sure we have all the angles covered. Make sure the crime scene is sealed, get forensics out there, and don't let anyone leave. Where is the crime scene anyway?"

"It's actually not that far from you. It's one of those private estates that I often think of buying, you know, one of them with a bloody big house, it's own village, and a couple of farms thrown in."

"I always suspected you had money, Steve, you're an eccentric millionaire who just pretends to be broke all the time."

"Don't tell Janet that or she might believe you."

"I'll be ready in ten minutes. Wait for me outside."

"Yes sir."

Chris put the phone down and saw Megan looking his way. She already knew his Sunday off had come to a halt, but she just wanted confirmation.

"I have to go in" was all he said.

"I gathered that. I'll leave a sandwich in the fridge for you if I go to bed, but call me anyway."

"Will do. I'll just go and get changed." He made his way upstairs taking the stairs two steps at a time.

Megan knew better than to ask him anything much now, he'd tell her later, but for now he always liked to approach jobs in an open mind, to see things for himself.

He dressed quickly and conservatory in a dark gray suit , and seeing the car waiting for him after peering through the laced windows, he kissed Megan on the lips as she sat.

"I shouldn't be too long," he stated, making his way out.

"Be careful" was Megan's goodbye.

"So what do we have, Detective?" Chris asked as he climbed into the car, an unmarked saloon.

As always, once work commenced Chris and Steve slipped into their work rank. Steve was a detective sergeant who's immediate boss was Chris, the detective inspector.

"We have a dead body , sir. Shot it seems, a suspect being held, a house full of staff, but we also have a lot of folk missing and family flying in sometime soon."

"Flying in?"

"Yes, sir. It seems they have their own helicopter."

"As one does. What do you mean about there being folk 'missing'?"

"They had a party there this weekend but all the guests

left

some time ago."

"Who allowed that to happen?"

"That happened before we were called, nobody knew or was

saying that anyone had been killed so they all went home."

"Great, I suppose we'll be chasing about all over the place

now to interview."

"Afraid so, sir, unless this suspect actually did do it."

"Let's hope so, sergeant, but is everything sealed off?"

"Tighter than a duck's ass."

"Which estate is it?"

"It's the Stonebridge estate and it's owned by Lord and Lady

Baldwin. The entrance should just be further up this lane."

"I've heard of them but I've never met them. I don't think

they've been here that long, I think a foreign prince used to

live here and the area used to be swarming with his secret

service guys."

"Oh that's right, I think I remember now the patrol guys complaining that they could never give them speeding tickets because of diplomatic immunity."

"They didn't complain as much as the locals did, sergeant, everybody used to complain around here, and that included me. They used to literally fly along these tiny lanes. It was a wonder no one was ever killed."

"Here we are, sir," said Steve, slowing the car down to a crawl as they approached the gate, and the two police officers who were stopping a couple of reporters and a few milling people from attempting to go up to the house. Steve acknowledged one of the policemen who had recognized them both and let them through. The detectives did not stop to talk to the obvious pressmen. That would come later. Instead, they pressed on, a quiet, early summer country evening only spoiled by several flashing lights from emergency vehicles.

Pulling up to stop in the crowded driveway by the front entrance, they were met immediately by Constable Johnston, who they both knew.

"Evening constable," spoke Chris warmly as he exited the car while the constable held the door open.

"Good evening, sir."

The constable was tall and rakish, he had a brain and would progress.

"Good evening, constable," Steve smiled, walking around from his driving side, his size wholly appropriate for his deep voice. He was a big man yet his short fair hair framed a boyish face.

"Good evening, sir."

"You were the first on the scene?" asked Chris, straight down to business.

"Yes sir, I'd just pulled over a motorist down the road a ways for a faulty taillight when I got the call to come here."

"Had the motorist been here previously?"

"I don't know, sir, I don't think so but I didn't ask."

"Check on it. Now when you arrived here, who met you?"

"That would have been the nanny sir, Kay Morgan", replied the constable who was consulting his notes.

"Was it her that discovered the body?"

"Yes sir."

Steve was jotting all this down in his notebook.

"Did you see anyone else on your way here?"

"No sir."

"Was the nanny upset?"

"She seemed more in shock than upset, sir."

"How do you mean, constable?"

"Well, she was shaking a little and was pale, but she didn't look like she'd been crying."

"Okay, then what happened?"

"She took me to where the body is, downstairs on the patio by the pool."

"Did either of you touch anything on the way?"

"I didn't, sir, but she may have. I'm not sure," offered the apologetic constable.

"That's okay, don't worry about it. Now, did either of you touch the body?"

"I did, sir."

"Why's that, constable, and where?"

"To make sure there was no pulse, I touched her right wrist."

"And there was no pulse?"

"No sir."

"Did you try any CPR?"

"No sir. Despite it being quite warm still, the body was quite cold and the lips were purple. Besides," the constable began, but was unable to finish the sentence.

"Besides what, constable," Chris pressed.

"There was a bloody big hole on the side of the head."

"Which side ?"

"On the far side to me. It was a lot of blood."

"Did you step in any of it?"

"No sir. Once I established the body was dead, I escorted the nanny away and called in the details."

"Then what happened?"

The constable took a moment, re-living finding the body was no easy task.

"My sergeant told me to get all the people in the house into one location, get their names, and tell them to stay. Then back up arrived to secure the crime scene and block the entrances."

"So since you've arrived, no one has left or arrived?"

"No sir, not since I arrived."

"Has your sergeant taken over now?"

"Yes sir. He's downstairs."

"What time did you arrive here, constable?"

"It was six fifteen, sir."

"Very good, constable, good job. Now why don't you go to the kitchen for a cup of tea and a sit down? Don't talk with anyone, but you can keep your ears open. That's all for now, just show us how to get to the patio will you?"

The constable led the detectives inside and pointed the way down, Steve gave him a pat on the back before he headed off.

"Oh constable," Chris called after him, "do we happen to have a name for the body?"

"Yes sir," Constable Johnston replied, turning around to face them, "it's Lady Baldwin."

CHAPTER TWENTY EIGHT

Phillip, Lord Baldwin, and a veritable mountain of luggage had taken a very subdued flight back to Crompton Hall that afternoon, each had been immersed in their own thoughts and his lordship hadn't even put on the headset to chat with Ian which was very unusual. Phillip did have his on. He was flying up front with Ian so he couldn't very well ignore him, but it had only been small talk apart from Phillip informing Ian that Lord B had now left his wife. Not that it bothered Ian, he couldn't stand her anyway but he would have liked to have known more than Phillip was telling him.

Lord B went out almost as soon as they got back, telling Phillip not to worry about putting away his things. He could do it tomorrow. He wouldn't require anything more for the night. Phillip still checked out everything, turning down his lordship's bed and putting some lights on for later. Satisfied that all was in order, he went home with his own luggage.

Natalie had been back for some time and it was she who welcomed him home, almost scaring him half to death as he was still not used to coming home to anyone.

"Hi Phil," she blurted as she went and hugged him as soon as he opened the door, "I've missed you so much!"

"Hi Hon, thanks for the big welcome," he hugged back, dropping his luggage to the floor, "it's so good to see you."

"What's wrong?" she asked, a look of concern on her face when she had expected a kiss but received only the embrace.

"Nothing, why do you think something's wrong?" he said too hurriedly.

"I can see it in your face. What's happened?" her arms dropped to her side and he closed the front door behind him before facing her again

"Oh, it's just been a horrible day is all and I'm worn out. I'll be okay in a while." He sat down on the armchair, undoing his shoelaces and taking his shoes off.

"Can I get you some tea or something? Did he tell her he was leaving? Did she take it out on you? Will you talk to me?" Natalie demanded in a worried tone.

"Some tea would be nice. I'll tell you about it later if that's okay. I just need to unwind a little first. Why don't you tell me about your day instead?"

"I'm worried about you. I've never seen you like this."

"I'm okay, Hon, really. It's just been a really long weekend, a bad day, and I just need to relax a bit. How about that tea and then you can tell me about London?"

"Okay, but only if you're sure?"

"I'm sure. Now what was the market like this morning and how was Ken?"

Natalie, after determining that all was okay, proceeded to tell him of her day in London and Ken's knowledge and kindness. She really couldn't have had a better guide. He'd even taken her on the buses rather than the underground because it gave a better perspective. And now, she just loved London.

Phillip got changed eventually and unpacked, putting on a more casual attire of jeans and tee shirt before he took Natalie to the local supermarket for a few groceries. There was no food for dinner and the milk was souring so they went and bought a few things. They were about to sit down to dinner when Phillip heard an unmistakable sound and he went to the living room window to go see.

"Well, I'll be damned," he commented.

Natalie joined him and they both watched as the helicopter landed in the field opposite, keeping its revs going as they watched someone dash under the spinning rotor blades and climb in.

"Does this mean you have to go back to work, honey?"

The helicopter slowly rose from the ground, hovered , then turned around so it was facing away from them, then the cockpit seemed to dip down and it flew away very quickly, directly south, slowly ascending.

"Apparently not"

"Was that Lord Baldwin getting on?"

"It looked like him but I have no idea why. I heard him tell Ian that he'd see him tomorrow and Ian would have told me if he was coming back."

"That's odd."

Phillip was about to comment further on this strange occurrence but the telephone rang before he could. Then he found out just why Lord Baldwin had indeed climbed

aboard his helicopter again, why it was heading south, and

why his two children were already on board.

It was an emotional scene in the staff room at Stonebridge .

They'd been sitting and standing around in here since soon

after the first policeman had come. The only time they'd

gotten away was for bathroom trips which with the copious

amounts of tea and coffee they were consuming was at regular

intervals. Tom had been able to persuade the policeman

outside the room that the dogs needed relief as well but he'd

only allowed them five minutes in the immediate courtyard

and watched them intently as they went about their business.

Even the dogs seemed disconcerted.

"How long do you think they're going to keep us here?" Rene

asked to no one in particular.

"I suppose until we've all made statements," answered Kay.

"We could be here for hours," grumbled Tom.

"I'd never seen anyone dead before," stated the still teary eyed

Cathy.

"I saw my grandma when she died," remembered Kay.

"What happened to Lady B's secretary, Mrs. Roberts? Did

she go home?"

wondered Tom aloud.

"I don't know, I suppose so. I can't remember if I saw her

when all these police arrived and I don't see her car in the

courtyard," Kay said, standing up to look out the window.

"She never parks there anyway," Tom went on, "not unless it's

raining. Whenever she comes here she usually parks up at the

stables so she can visit with the horses, then walks down."

"I bet she left," commented Rene, "if I'd known we'd have

been hanging around like this, I'd have left too. Lord Baldwin

will be back I suppose soon so he'll want dinner. These cops

will have to let me back in the kitchen then I expect."

"I still can't believe he packed up and left today," stated Kay.

"I still can't believe it took him this long. But I never thought

he'd be back this quick," Rene continued.

"I never had any notion he'd actually leave her," commented

Kay, still shocked, "did you know about it, Tom?"

"I had no idea, it was a complete surprise."

"I still can't believe that any of this is true. First he leaves, then she gets killed, and what happens next? It doesn't seem real. I keep expecting her to call down for me to go run her bath or something." Cathy was still white with the shock .

"I know, it's weird," Kay grasped Cathy's hand for support, "and even though we all saw her body, I still expect her to walk through the door and say something."

"Bitch about something, more like," said Rene.

"So is his lordship coming back alone?" asked Tom.

"No, the children should be with him. When I finally got hold of him, he said he'd call them and they'd come together, but I'll tell you one thing, I never ever want to have to tell anyone that someone has been killed again."

"Rather you than me, Kay, I couldn't have done it," sniffed Cathy.

"How did he take it?" Tom enquired.

"Better than expected I suppose, but it was still difficult to do."

"Is anyone else coming back?" Tom further enquired, his mind reverting to work details.

"Not that I know of, but I think there's only Phillip who knows."

"How did he find out?"

"I was calling to find out if his lordship had left and he sensed something was wrong so I told him. He'd have found out sooner or later anyway."

"There will be someone else who already knows," Rene surmised.

"Who's that?" Kay wanted to know.

"Whoever killed her."

"That's true, but then there's something else we need to realize."

"What?"

"That person may still be in this house and this room."

Nothing more was said in that room for some time. Each went back to sitting quietly, deep in their own thoughts.

No matter how often you came across a crime scene it still didn't make the job easier. There was a lifeless body, intact most times, but sometimes not, disarray or absolute neatness, a crowded street or an empty room, grief stricken family or no one who cares, many variations, yet there was always one common thread. Someone was dead.

Lady B was still sitting on her chair and if it wasn't for the tell tale pool of blood around her and the stained hair, you would think how unperturbed she looked. Chris could see she was a good looking woman, a lot of sex appeal to her, her whole demeanor from the perfect make up to the pedicured toes telling you she had money and liked to take care of herself. It looked like she'd come out here to enjoy a few rays of unexpected hot sunshine, taking off her dark blue blouse and thin light blue denim skirt without having to get up off the chaise lounge, she was sitting on the skirt which had simply been unzipped and she'd basically just released her arms from the unbuttoned blouse. Her tanned long legs were still crossed as they stretched out and her black bikinied torso was unblemished by any of her blood. Chris couldn't see her eyes, she still wore sunglasses, but he rightly imagined they'd blend in perfectly with the rest of her.

"Good evening , Detectives. I don't think I'm going to have much for you on this one," welcomed the always cheerful, always smiling pathologist, Dr. Susan McBride. She was a striking redheaded Scotswoman who was usually matter of fact and nearly always in a rush to get home to her three youngsters and devoted house husband.

"Good evening, doctor, I suppose you're finished here and are off back home?" he asked, smiling.

Much to the disgust of some of the policemen who'd been sent here tonight and had actually seen her on occasion in normal wear, she was wearing non-descript overalls tonight that matched her white surgical gloves and the hat that covered her hair.

"Not quite yet, detective, but not much longer I don't think," she smiled back, not at all perturbed with Chris's sarcasm, "there doesn't seem to be much evidence I can collect. You can come under the tapes now. Let me show you what we have."

"You can always just tell us rather than show us, doctor" pleaded the stricken looking Steve.

"How can a big lug like yourself be so squeamish, Sergeant? She's not going to bite. Come on, I'll protect you," she smiled knowing full well about Steve's discomfort around corpses. Chris led the way over, still smiling but understanding Steve's plight. Even he was never entirely comfortable.

"So what do we have, doctor?" asked Steve, making sure to not stand in any of the blood.

"Fairly simple really, our victim was in this exact position when someone came around to here," the doctor demonstrated the killer coming to her right side, "held a cushion to the right side of her head, presumably to muffle the noise, and shot her once through the temple right here with the bullet exiting here," she demonstrated again, "killing her instantly and very cleanly. But you're going to have to earn your money on this one, detectives."

"Let me guess, doctor. There's no evidence?" asked Steve.

"That's about the sum of it. We have the evidence she was shot and we have the cushion, but I don't have the gun. If I could get prints off the cushion it would no doubt contain a hundred others and unfortunately she didn't write down who it was that did it. But," she paused a moment, "we do have someone who says they did it."

"So I heard. I just want to make sure everything is watertight. You didn't mention if you found the bullet, nor did you give me a time of death."

"I've got one of the techs looking for the bullet, but with the angle that the gun was fired, which was probably a 38mm by the way, I'm not too hopeful of finding it. She died some time ago, probably around 3pm, but I might be more specific once I've done the autopsy."

"Sergeant?" Chris called out to the uniformed officer who had taken over from Constable Johnston. He'd been standing off to the right when the detectives had met up with the pathologist, and as Chris and Steve knew him well they'd given each other a barely imperceptible nod in each others direction.

He joined the threesome as they stood beside the body.

"Yes sir?"

Sergeant Highton was a tall man in his late twenties, his dark features highlighted by prominent dimples when he smiled, and as a lot of women seemed to like this feature, he was prone to smiling a lot.

"Sergeant, I need you to go and find out who was in and around this house this afternoon and where they are now, also if possible, the actual time they left. I think Constable Johnston was met by someone here, go and talk to her."

"Yes sir, but you do realize we have a suspect who has confessed?" The sergeant, who had a local accent, was no doubt trying to impress the doctor who he perpetually hoped would dump her husband and take up with him if she had any sense.

Chris smiled with his lips only.

"I'm very aware of that sergeant but thank you for pointing it out to me. It makes it even more imperative that you get me these details as soon as possible. I also need you to assign a couple of constables to assist our good doctor here in

accumulating any of the victims belongings that may be useful

as evidence. Okay?"

"Yes sir, I'll get right to it." With a beaming smile in

Doctor McBride's direction, he strode purposely away.

"I think our good sergeant is in love with you, Doc," laughed

Steve to a slightly blushing doctor.

"I don't encourage him," she half protested.

"But you don't stop him either," Steve laughed some more,

quickly stifling it at the unmistakable sound of an approaching

helicopter, "Who the hell is this? You think our inspector is

checking in on us?"

"It's probably Lord Baldwin. Whoever it is, go and meet

them and keep them away from here," ordered Chris.

As Steve moved away, Chris told the Doctor what he

wanted."Bag any of her possessions, but in particular things

she'd have used over this weekend like her clothing, diary,

notes and medication. It might be a good idea to move the

body if you're done with it, at least put it in the ambulance, and I'll see if Lord Baldwin can make a formal identification."

The helicopter was getting louder now, it was coming in to land so they were having to shout.

"You want me to search the whole house?"

"It should be enough to do around here, her office if she has one, bedroom and bathroom. Have a general look around the other places, see if you can find the gun."

"Is there something in particular you're looking for?"

"Not really, apart from the gun that is. Have you done a powder test on our suspect?"

"Yes, but both hands looked clean. I took scrapings and swabs and I'll know more when I get back to my lab. I also took the clothing for blood tests."

"Good. Are you done with the body?"

"Until I get back, I am, yes. I'll have them move it into the ambulance, but I can't clean her up yet."

"That's okay. He can still identify her. You'll need to do gun shot powder tests on everyone still here as well. I'll leave you to it, doctor, I'd better go and introduce myself to the

grieving husband."

CHAPTER THIRTY ONE

As Chris uncertainly made his way back upstairs, hoping he was going in the right direction, he was intercepted by Steve. "Glad I ran into you, Sergeant. I have no idea where I'm going."

"If it's any consolation, Sir, I got lost before. It's all very well having these big houses but how on earth do you find anyone?"

"Maybe that's the idea. So how is the husband doing? That was him arriving, wasn't it?"

"Yes sir, along with the two children, Charles and Sophie Baldwin. They seem to be okay, the young lady was a bit red eyed but the two gentlemen seem quite calm."

"Keeping a stiff upper lip?"

"Maybe Sir, but I don't think they're too upset. You'll see for yourself soon enough."

"Only if you show me the way, Sergeant. While I go and introduce myself, see if there's an office or a small room we can use to have a small interview with everyone, but check it out first for any belongings of the victim. Once you have that sorted, take the suspect there and check with the Doc if we can have the body formally identified, then come and tell me. Got that?"

"Yes sir, are we going to take statements from everyone?"

"I think we'll have them all make a written statement about their day, while their memories are fresh just in case, and then we can follow up later if need be."

"Very good, Sir. I'll have someone find some pens and paper."

They'd already begun walking and had reached the door behind which Lord Baldwin and his two children were waiting. Steve told Chris this and left him to introduce himself, finding his way eventually to the staff room where he found out that there was indeed an office he could use, it was directly across the courtyard and normally used by the estate manager. He checked it out carefully, nothing of Lady Baldwin's that he could see was in there so he called over one of the plentiful policeman to tell him to get the suspect in there and make sure it was all secure.

Having done that, he took a little tour around, to get his bearings better acquainted, then found Doctor McBride who told him that the body could be formally identified and she waited for him as he went into the drawing room to inform D.I. Shaw. Both detectives came back out almost immediately and Chris asked her to wait a second, the sergeant was just going to show him where the suspect was.

"Well, that was different," Chris commented as they made their way to the commandeered office.

"How do you mean, Sir?"

"I may be wrong but I got the distinct impression that although they're upset that she has been killed, they don't seem at all perturbed that she's gone from their lives."

"I thought they seemed calm when I met them. You don't think she'll be missed then?"

"Not by those three, I don't. Or maybe I'm just reading them wrong."

"You don't normally, Sir, but here is the office we're

going to

use."

"So who is this suspect that seems to have done the rest of

the family a favor?"

"The suspects name is Mrs. Roberts. She's the secretary, or

was the secretary to Lady Baldwin."

"You don't say. This gets more interesting by the minute.

Take Lord Baldwin to identify his wife and then come back

here. I'd like you to hear what this Mrs. Roberts has to say

and then maybe we can wrap this up with any luck."

"I'll be right back, Sir."

There was a constable outside the office and another one

inside, both standing to attention as they guarded Mrs. Roberts,

which Chris thought was a little over the top when he finally

met her. She was sitting quietly in her chair facing the neat

mahogany desk which looked like it was seldom used in this

very plain room. There was nothing remarkable about Mrs.

Roberts, she was a fairly average elderly woman with gray hair

who looked odd only because she was wearing overalls. It was like seeing your grandmother dressed for a painting contract. She was fairly small, wore black framed glasses, and looked like she was ready to take some notes as Chris introduced himself and sat down behind the desk facing her. Chris knew enough to know appearances didn't preclude one being guilty or innocent. Sometimes the worst offenders looked like angels and the most innocent could look like thugs. He sat there for a few moments weighing her up silently, trying to see if this would make her uncomfortable or irritable but she remained very still, not even tapping a finger or looking around when Steve came into the room and sat down to Chris's right.

"It's Mrs. Roberts, is it?"

"Yes," she spoke quite elegantly, "Mrs. Agnes Roberts."

"This is just an informal interview, Mrs. Roberts, but if you would like some legal advice then I will fully understand. I'm not charging you just yet but I will be holding you in custody for a period not exceeding 72 hours, at which time I must formally charge you or let you go. Do you understand?"

"Yes, Inspector. I don't want any legal advice."

"Tell me what you know about Lady Baldwin's death."

"It's quite simple, Inspector. I shot her."

"Where did you get the gun, Mrs. Roberts?"

"It was my husband's."

"You say was, does it not belong to him anymore?"

"I said was because my husband died."

"I'm sorry, I didn't realize. Did he have a
license for it?"

"I don't think so. No."

"Do you know what caliber it is?"

"No."

"Do you know where it is now?"

"In the lake, that's where I threw it."

"Where on Lady Baldwin's body did you shoot her?"

"On the right side of her head. I shot her through a cushion
and then I threw the gun away, and my gloves."

"You were wearing gloves as well? Where are they now?"

"In the lake, with the gun."

"Why did you shoot her?"

"Because she broke my husband's heart, killed him really, and everyone is better off without her."

"How did she break your husband's heart?"

"He had cancer, but he always loved to help flush out the birds at the Baldwin's pheasant shoots. It kept him going really and got him out with Brandy, enjoying the countryside."

"Who's Brandy?"

"Brandy was our Labrador."

"Was?"

"Yes. She was as frail as Bill, that's Mr. Roberts, but going beating seemed to perk them both up, almost as if it gave them new hope."

"Mr. Roberts was dying?"

"The doctors said there was nothing more they could do, but whenever he went shooting he seemed to come back better somehow much to everyone's amazement."

"So what happened?"

"Bill and Brandy went beating and Lady Baldwin had Brandy shot. Bill gave up after that and died not long after."

"Why did she have your dog shot?"

"Because she saw her pick a bird up that was still alive, and she wrongly assumed that Brandy had attacked it on the ground. The bird had been shot, winged more like, and Brandy went to retrieve it which was her job but Lady B insisted it was a rogue dog and she had one of her friends shoot her."

"I'm sorry."

"Yes, but it broke Bill's heart. She didn't even apologize or ask who's dog it was. Bill didn't last long after that, he just gave in."

"I'm sorry, Mrs. Roberts, really I am. You came here today with the gun and with the sole intention of killing Lady Baldwin?"

"I came with the gun, yes, but I didn't know I was going to shoot her today."

"So why today?"

"Because she still didn't apologize to me for what she did and then she had me wait around for her, this after driving all the way down here on a Sunday."

"Where do you live ?"

"In a small village near their other home in Derbyshire."

"So it's quite a drive for you?"

"Yes it is, and I'm not getting any younger."

"I understand. We'll have to impound your car as well. Is it in the courtyard?"

"It's at the stables, but you've already got the keys, they are in my purse."

"Okay. Why did you throw the gun and gloves away when you were going to confess anyway?"

"I don't know."

"I think that will do for now. The constable will take you down to the station where you'll be informed of your rights, and like I previously told you, we have to formally charge you within 72 hours. You'll be asked to make a written statement once you get there in which I'd like you to detail as much as possible all the events of today, and then I'll probably want to ask you some more questions. Do you have any questions of me and is there someone I can contact on your behalf?

"No Inspector, but thank you for asking."

"In that case, I'll be seeing you at the station." He stood up as the policemen came over to take her by the elbow and lead her away, sitting down again as soon as the door closed behind her.

"What do you think, sir?" Steve asked.

"I think we'll get a conviction. How about you?"

"Seems very straight forward. What do you want me to do with the family members and the staff who are still here?"

"I'd like to meet them all and then I expect they'll all want to go home or just be left alone. We can go through their statements in the morning and question them later."

"I'll make sure we get all the statements." Steve got up to approach the door.

"Have the divers search the lake, impound Mrs. Roberts car and start the ball rolling for a search warrant for her house. Also arrange for some legal counsel for her and find out if she has any family we can call," instructed Chris, his fingers stroking his chin as he thought.

"I thought she said she didn't want legal help or to call anyone?"

"She's trying to make it easy for us, Sergeant, but there's one big problem. I don't think Mrs. Roberts killed Lady Baldwin."

CHAPTER THIRTY TWO

Phillip took Natalie into work the next day. She was quite shocked about the murder of Lady Baldwin, especially as this was England and death by bullet was more prevalent in her native land. She was also seeing a different side to Phillip than the one she knew. He didn't seem at all shocked or upset about this, at least not on the surface. He appeared as calm as normal and not at all excitable.

Phillip introduced Natalie to everyone at Crompton Hall before mentioning the big news from Stonebridge. He wanted everyone together before doing that as he didn't know how they'd react, it was never easy talking about the death of someone, especially when she was the boss.

Brian, Susan and Maud made a big fuss of Natalie, wanting to know about her, about her sightseeing in London, her life and family in San Francisco, what she thought about Phillip having to work when she'd just arrived, her thoughts on Crompton Hall and the surrounding area, everything. They'd barely mentioned the fact that his lordship should have been in residence, that had been the plan, but then it had also been planned that he and Phillip would be arriving back today yet Phillip was already here. When Maud eventually got around to asking Phillip about this, she knew something was up when he had her sit down along with Brian, Susan, Bill, Stan and Gail.

"What's happened, Phil?" Maud spoke up, the seriousness in her voice grabbing everyone's attention, silencing all the chatter, their gazes following Maud's to the now standing Phillip.

"Well, as most of you are aware, I should have been returning here this morning with his lordship, but he decided to bring his plans forward so we came back yesterday afternoon. Unfortunately, he had to go back to Stonebridge last night because after we left there, Lady B was found dead." Everybody looked at each other as if to say "is he joking?" Natalie's head was down, she was quite upset and this was noted by the others, answering their silent question.

"Bloody hell," stated Bill, simply.

"What do you mean by 'found dead'?" asked Maud.

"It seems that late yesterday afternoon, or early evening, Kay found Lady B on a sun lounger out on the patio. She'd been shot through the head and was already dead. They called his lordship, who went back down there, and I was told just after he'd flown off."

"Who did it?" asked Brian.

"I'm not sure for certain but Tom told me this morning that Mrs. Roberts has gone missing. Her car was towed away by the police so presumably they're holding her."

"Mrs. Roberts? Get out of here, you can't be serious? She couldn't hurt a fly," protested Maud.

"I agree, Maud, she's the last person I'd think of but the police must think otherwise."

"That can't be right," commented Bill, "I've seen her around and she's just a sweet old lady. She couldn't have shot her."

"Isn't there anyone else who could have done it?" asked Gail.

"It depends, I suppose, on when she died. If it happened just before she was found then it would be just the staff down there under suspicion. If it happened earlier, although that would be hard to believe, then there was a full house to choose from."

"Why would that be hard to believe?" Stan questioned.

"Because Lady B nearly always has someone around her. It's unthinkable that she'd be alone for a couple of minutes, never mind a couple of hours."

"Unless it was Kay or Cathy that did it," reasoned Maud, playing lady detective..

"I don't know, Maud, but somebody killed her. We'll have to see what happens."

"So what will this mean for us here? Will his lordship move down there now and fire us all, or will he live here?" Susan directed at Phillip.

"I can't see him going to live there. This has always been his home so there's no reason to think otherwise."

"Do you think he's upset about losing her?' Stan wanted to know.

"I'm sure he is. He may not have loved her anymore but she was still his wife, he's probably shocked more than anything, just like we are."

"I still don't believe it," Brian shook his head.

"It's difficult to comprehend, maybe we'll begin to after Stan makes us all a cup of tea."

"I was wondering when you'd ask me to brew up, I hope you have some biscuits," Stan grumbled as he got up to make it.

"I'll have one as well," called out Maud, which was the first time she'd ever asked, "I think I need one today."

CHAPTER THIRTY THREE

Chris was in his office . He had a window to the outside world, not much of a view but at least he could see the weather which today was pleasant again. There were a few clouds and a breeze but still quite warm. He sat with his back to the window in his reclining black leather chair facing his big pine desk. His office door was in the opaque glassed wall facing him, which although it prevented him from seeing who was coming in, he could at least see the outline of everyone, not many that were bigger than Steve who was just approaching.

Steve, as was his normal practice, was bearing two mugs of steaming sweet coffee in one of his huge hands, as he lightly tapped on the glass door with the other and turned the handle, not waiting for the reply before making his way into the office, placing both mugs on the desk, and himself on one of the chairs facing it.

"Good morning, sir," he said cheerfully.

"Morning, Sergeant. I've been glancing at some of these statements," Chris signified with a wave of one he was holding toward the pile.

"Did you notice the same thing I did, sir?"

"What was that?"

"They all seemed to have been with the victim around the time of her death."

"Has our lovely doc come up with a definite time of death?"

"I'm just going off what she said last night, I haven't had an update yet."

"Yes, I did notice, and not one of them gives an exact time."

"Hopefully we won't need them to. Maybe Mrs. Roberts's story

will pan out."

"Maybe, but the more I think about it, the more I think she didn't do it. I just don't believe if she did it, she'd throw the gun away or wear gloves, then just sit around for three hours waiting for someone to discover the body. She may as well have gone home."

"You don't think that she planned doing it and then figured on getting away with it?"

"It's possible but not likely. She's trying to take the blame because she's alone now and wishes she could have done it."

"The divers are out there now. Once we find the gun and gloves, it could nail her case."

"Is her home being searched ?"

"Yes sir, as we speak, and her car as well."

"Do you think she did it sergeant?"

"I think her story is plausible and if we convict her, I don't think we'll hear her pleading her innocence to the court. She'll take the sentence with a smile. But do I think she did it? No, I don't."

"So who's got your vote?"

"I'll go with the tried and trusted. The butler did it," Steve smiled in triumph as he indulged in the cliché

"What makes you say that?" Chris asked, putting down the file he was still holding..

"I don't know, I probably watch too many mysteries I suppose. Who do you think did it , sir?"

"I think we should look at the husband first and go on from there, but we need the doc's report first. Maybe she has proof that Mrs. Roberts actually did it. In the meantime, what's happening in our other cases?"

Like detectives everywhere, they always had several cases on the go but as they'd just been put on a murder case, then that took precedence. They discussed other cases until the doctor came walking in, bringing along the items she'd collected in the evidence bags.

"Good morning, doc, it's not often we see you up here. What do you have for us?"

Neither of the detectives got up when Dr. McBride tapped then entered the room. It looked like she was on her way somewhere as she was wearing a light jacket and slacks rather than the normal white surgical coat.

"Good morning to you both, gentlemen. I don't think this case is going to be cut and dried, I'm afraid," she replied, placing a folder and the bags on Chris's desk, before seating herself down.

"Morning doc, can I get you some coffee or something?" asked Steve.

"Why don't you get us all one , Sergeant," Chris looked up, opening the folder that the doctor had just deposited, "so what do have for us ?"

Steve caught a constable outside the office who'd lingered too long after ogling the doctor and had him get the coffees. He was seated again before the doctor had replied to Chris's question.

"The victim died officially of brain trauma which was caused by a gunshot to the head, a 38mm as I thought, and death was instantaneous. There was no sign of a struggle on the part of the victim. She wasn't in a fight or have any abrasions to indicate she was held down, nor did she have any gunpowder residue on her hands so I rule out suicide. The best I can estimate the time of death is approximately 3pm, I can't be any more definite because she was outside and not in a constant temperature but several minutes either side of 3pm is my best estimate.

The victim was sexually active, she'd had sex prior to being killed, and I have taken sperm and saliva samples. I also found some almost imperceptible bruising on her thighs, probably caused by someone's hands, although I can't get any fingerprints from them. My guess is that they belong to whoever she had sex with."

"Her husband?" asked Steve.

"Probably, but I'll know when I take a saliva sample from him and measure the span of his hands."

"It didn't look like she was in the middle of a sex act when she was killed, do you think her body was rearranged in any way?" asked Chris.

"No, she wasn't rearranged. The sex probably occurred earlier that day."

"You said she wasn't held down, doc, but now you say her thighs were held?" Chris inquired, confirming this from her report in the folder.

"That's right, Inspector, she wasn't held when she was shot. Her thighs were held no doubt during the sex she had, and the way and the direction of the markings indicate they were employing a wheelbarrow, or a doggy style position."

"Huh?" Steve pretended to be puzzled.

"She laid down on her stomach and he lifted her legs to his waist by placing his hands on her thighs. As the bruising was barely visible, she no doubt helped by taking the weight on her hands, so that when he entered her it resembled someone pushing a wheelbarrow. Doggy style I think you're aware of" she smiled, not at all embarrassed about making this clear to Steve.

"I've got the picture now," he smiled, much to Chris's amusement as a policeman entered the room with their coffees. "So what else did you find out?" Chris asked.

"She drank too much, her liver was in a poor shape although not life threatening. She'd had cosmetic surgery on her face, her neck, her breasts, waist, bottom and thighs. Her dental work was of the highest order. She was on birth control pills, her other vital organs were in pretty good shape and there were no illegal substances in her. Her diary was kind of cryptic, a lot of initials combined with engagements, some of it in her writing and the rest in somebody else's. You'll see. I found a couple of door keys in her purse, a video cassette, and what I found most interesting, was that her husband's closet was almost empty."

"Now there's an interesting thing. What was on the video cassette?" Chris asked as he found the bag that contained it.

"I was hoping that the killer may have left us a movie of his or her work but that's not the case, although I was able to get a couple different sets of fingerprints off it. The cassette is actually from a camcorder, it has one of those little inserts to enable it to be played on a regular video machine, but you may want to view it once I leave."

"Why's that?"

"It may embarrass our sergeant here," she smiled again, "it's a sex video, very amateurish and possibly filmed without one of the participants knowledge."

"I didn't realize you were an expert in this field, doc" Chris devilishly replied.

It was her turn to be embarrassed.

"I'm no expert Inspector but the woman in the video seems oblivious to the camera. I don't know who she is but the man looks very familiar. I know I've seen him before."

"Was that in another movie?" He asked in a teasing tone.

"No , Inspector, it wasn't and before you embarrass me even more, I'll take my leave, I need to go back to the house."

"How are the divers doing?"

"Not very well by all accounts. It seems the lake has a very thick mud bottom and they haven't found anything yet so I want to go see for myself. We can't find the bullet either."

"We'll be making our way out there as well in a few minutes, but just do what you can. Thank you for the quick report."

"You're welcome, but there is more bad news I'm afraid."

Chris and Steve didn't reply, just looked expectantly for her to finish.

"Mrs. Roberts was totally clean, no gunpowder residue on her or on anyone else there we tested, no blood spatters, nothing. If she changes her story, there's nothing I could present in the way of evidence to convict her but I'll keep looking and maybe something will come up." With that she got up to leave, taking her coffee with her.

"It looks like we've got some work to do, Sergeant. Let's see who's on this tape first and then we'll go back to Stonebridge and see if we can make any sense of all this. The Chief Inspector called me this morning congratulating me on wrapping this up so quick. He was non too impressed when I told him I didn't believe the confession, so I'm going to have to explain to him why not later."

"Rather you than me, sir, but at least it will keep him in front of the cameras."

"That's true, he'd probably enjoy being in his home movie as well. He might get ideas if we show him this one. Put it in Sergeant, lets see if we recognize them." Chris said, hopefully.

CHAPTER THIRTY FOUR

By this time the media had gotten a full hold of the story, and although it would have garnered their interest anyway, the fact that Jane Robins, John Steele, Liz Price, Suzy Walker, and Robert and Mandy Mills had been there, just escalated their coverage. Headlines in the tabloids had ranged from "Stars in Bloodbath!" to "Murder at the Mansion!" to even naming names like "John Steele in Murder Quiz"

Extra police had to be deployed to protect the perimeter of Stonebridge from journalists and cameramen. A couple of helicopters had been deployed to at least get some aerial shots of the house. They didn't seem to know yet that there was somebody in custody, that would surely come, so for now they were able to speculate at will.

Obviously, someone had leaked the guest list, probably one of the PR people who worked for one of the stars, so when Detective Inspector Shaw and Detective Sergeant Green arrived back at the house, it was through a jostling throng of press with flashing cameras and shouted questions which the detectives totally ignored.

It didn't come as any real surprise that the Chief Inspector was waiting at the door when Steve crunched the car over the gravel and parked. Normally the two detectives only ever saw him at the police station but after seeing the morning papers it was only expected that he'd show up here, he couldn't resist the lure of the cameras.

"Good morning, Sir," said Chris very properly as he stepped out of the car.

"Good morning, Sir," echoed Steve, immediately after.

"Good morning, Inspector and Sergeant. Any update on what you told me earlier on the phone?"The Chief Inspector, despite his fondness for media attention, was actually well liked by his staff as he allowed them to do their jobs, providing they were always honest to him. "Well Sir," replied Chris, glancing up at the partially clouded sky and the circling helicopters, "as you know, we have Mrs. Roberts in custody and she has confessed to the murder, but I just can't believe her story. I think somebody else did it."

"Why don't you think she did it and who do you think did?"

"Mainly because there is no physical evidence of her doing it when she'd have no reason to hide anything. As for your second question, I have no idea yet but I plan to find out."

"So what's your next step ?"

"I need to interview everybody who was here for the weekend, find a motive, and hopefully find some evidence."

"Are you sure that Mrs. Roberts didn't commit the murder?"

"Not yet, and who knows, stranger things have happened."

"If I tell the press we have someone in custody, are you going to embarrass me by releasing her in a couple of days?" Chris looked at Steve, up at the sky again and back to Steve and then the Inspector again. "Do you think you could tell them that we have someone in custody but that the investigation is ongoing?"

"So you want me to stall them?"

"Yes. Sorry but I really need some time to talk to everyone and if they all think that we have our killer then they may be less than careful with their interviews."

"You realize that will keep the pressure on until we charge someone?"

"Sorry, Sir."

The Chief Inspector then took a few moments to digest this, looking to the sky like Chris did, thinking before deciding.

"Very well, Inspector, I'll stall them for a couple of days but keep me closely informed on this one. I don't want any surprises. I also don't want to convict someone who would prove their innocence later."

With that he strode off to his car, his driver starting the car before he climbed into the back seat and away to the press conference.

"What did that last comment mean?" asked Steve as they both watched their boss leave.

"It meant that if we don't find some proof of somebody doing this, then we can't convict anybody even if they confess."

"Then let's hope that our gorgeous Dr. McBride can find something then."

"Amen to that, Sergeant."

CHAPTER THIRTY FIVE

Inside Stonebridge it was almost surreal with the staff trying to do their regular jobs as they had family in residence, but with the police and the forensic technicians being here there and everywhere, it made it difficult for them. They had been allowed to go home or to their rooms and his lordship and the two children were being very discreet, not asking for anything or expecting things, and even sitting around the kitchen with everybody as if they were staff themselves. After the police had arrived yesterday, they'd systematically searched all the rooms they were allowing everyone to use and were slowly and surely giving the house back to the occupants, but didn't want anyone cleaning until they were given the all clear. They weren't stopping Rene or Tom from cooking or offering refreshments though.

The divers were still scrambling around in the lake hoping to find the murder weapon but they didn't hold much more hope. They should have found it by now despite all of the mud, the lake wasn't that big. No bullet had been found either, despite one of Dr. McBride's technicians coming up with the bright idea of shining a laser on the estimated trajectory. The search area had been narrowed down though to about a dozen trees.

Susan McBride wanted to go home. Knowing this was a big case, she'd worked late yesterday, and had come in very early this morning and hadn't spoken in person to any of her family since yesterday breakfast. As the pathologist, she not only determined the cause of death but was also in charge of collecting evidence, and so far they had squat apart from the cushion that was used as a silencer. Maybe when she and her technicians processed the body and the DNA samples they were slowly collecting, they might begin to put the jigsaw together but that was a long process. As she was leaving to go back to the lab, she bumped into the two detectives again. "Have you found the bullet yet, doc?" asked Chris.

"They're still looking. I'm going back to my lab, there's nothing more for me here."

"Our eagle eyed sergeant recognized the participants in the tape. One was the pop star, John Steele, the other was Cathy Jones, the personal maid to Lady Baldwin"

"You don't say. It seems unusual for a maid to sleep with a guest, wouldn't you think?"

"You'd think, and also unusual for the tape to be in her boss's possession, but let's check their rooms first and see if they actually filmed this here first. Have you got the room list and map sergeant?"

"Yes, sir. His room is closest so we can check that first."

The sergeant led the way, frequently checking his directions. John Steele's room was very quickly ruled out so they proceeded on to Cathy's room. As they walked, Chris asked his sergeant if John Steele had come with a partner.

"He came with Liz Price, the model," replied Steve, consulting his notes.

"So he brings his girlfriend and goes and has sex with the maid?"

"It looks like the room to me, Inspector," opinioned the Doctor as they entered, "and the camera was probably placed on this dresser," she pointed.

"Did you take samples from this room, Doctor?" asked Chris, silently agreeing that this was indeed the tape room.

"We took them from every room but we were hoping to narrow down the list as it's a lot of lab work that takes a long time to process."

"Understood, but the deceased was in possession of this tape for some reason and I'd like to find out why. It might give us a motive. I also need to know who had sex with her and the more you can find out while we have Mrs. Roberts in custody, the better it will be."

"Then I'd better go and get the ball rolling."

"You still have technicians here?"

"In the lake and the woods."

"Well, if they haven't found anything by now in the lake then it's doubtful they ever will so abandon that search. Leave a tech for the woods though and I'll get the uniforms to help out there. Sergeant, organize those uniforms for the woods and while you're about it, get another uniform to try and find

some locks that those keys will fit, the keys that were in the

deceased's purse."

CHAPTER THIRTY SIX

At Crompton Hall, Phillip and Natalie were walking through the Baldwin's home. Phillip was giving her a guided tour of his workplace "So can you tell me now, Phillip? Why were you so upset when you got back yesterday, you know, before we heard about Lady Baldwin's death? You didn't have anything to do with her murder, did you?"

Natalie gave Phillip a worried look as she asked, watching as they moved inside the warm library and he sank into one of the many armchairs in this very masculine room.

"No, hon. I didn't kill her, but I must admit that I'm not sorry to hear she's gone. I won't miss her."

"So why were you so upset?"

"Well, not only did the cow fire me yesterday. She also said she'd do her damnedest to ruin our lives by any means possible. Whether it was convincing you that she and I were lovers or by accusing me of theft or something, she was going to do something. She believed it was my fault His Lordship was leaving her as I had influenced him in some way."

"Do you think I'd have believed her?"

"No but the police may have, especially if she'd gotten Kay and Cathy to back up her story which would have been very likely. Well, not so much on the part of Kay, but Cathy would have ."

"God, that's nasty."

"Well in her mind, I betrayed her by not telling her His Lordship had found someone else. I'd conspired with him, so she was going to ruin him and me also."

"But Lord Baldwin wouldn't have let her fire you, would he?"

"No, but if she could have threatened to take his business away or something, then who knows?"

"So he did tell her he was leaving her?"

"Yes, and she went ballistic in front of all the guests apparently. I missed it because I was getting all his stuff ready to throw onto the helicopter."

"So when did you see her?"

"After he told her, she demanded to see me along with Tom, Kay and Cathy."

"So what did you say when she fired you?"

Phillip laughed, remembering, "I told her to fuck off and while she was about it, to go fuck herself for a change, in the apartment she bought in London purely for her and her men friends."

"What?"

"It's one of her biggest secrets. It's her little hideaway in London that she thinks no one knows about. She only uses her old bank account so his Lordship never sees anything on their account and any invoices she gets goes to a private box number."

"You're kidding! How did you find out about it?"

"By piecing the puzzle together. I'd hear snippets of conversations, meetings being arranged, a careless piece of paper here and there, an odd phone call, even a key once."

"What was her reaction?"

"Shock for a moment, then she told me to get out, collect my Yankee girlfriend, and that she was going to get me."

"I'm not a Yankee," said the indignant Natalie. "You really told her to fuck off?"

"I sure did," smiled Phillip.

"Do you think the police will want to question you?"

"I suppose so. I was there and I don't know when she was killed."

"Have you ever fired a gun, Phillip?"

"Actually yes, when I was training. Ken thought I was a natural. I never missed the target."

CHAPTER THIRTY SEVEN

D.I. Chris Shaw spent the rest of his morning and afternoon interviewing the house staff at Stonebridge, going over their written statements, and trying to get more information about what exactly transpired that fateful Sunday.

In some aspects, he was very successful, but in others less so as nobody else confessed to the murder. He did discover that Cathy did indeed have sex with John Steele on Saturday night. She didn't know it had been taped at the time but she lied about knowing of its existence.

All the staff except the chef, said they were helping everyone leave at around 3p.m, that it was all chaotic, and anyone and everyone could have slipped down to the patio. No one saw anything suspicious and no one heard a gunshot. The chef said he was in the kitchen at that time, cleaning up still after lunch, but no one could confirm that.

When he pressed them all for the events leading up to the demise of Lady Baldwin, the consensus was that Phillip, the butler from Crompton Hall, had packed away much of Lord Baldwin's belongings for removal. As soon as the helicopter arrived, he began to load it all. The helicopter left at the same time as the guests did but Lady Baldwin wasn't seen by anyone. As far as anyone knew, she wanted to be alone so everyone left her to it. Even her children and husband concurred with this. They hadn't sought her out to say goodbye or anything, they just left, apparently as quick as they could.

After a long staggered breakfast that morning, no one was really sure what anyone had done for the whole period up to the murder. A couple guests had gone riding early that morning with Sophie. Lady Baldwin had been out walking. In fact, nearly all the guests had been seen by someone, going out for some air, but not all together. No one really took much notice, work needed doing and everyone was around at lunch time, either outside, or like in Mrs. Roberts's case, having a sandwich indoors. She had been alone in the library. After a late lunch, Lord Baldwin had snapped, telling his wife to quite literally stop fondling Tristan, he was sick and tired of her behaving like a common whore with the likes of Simon. He announced that enough was enough, he was leaving her. There ensued a huge row with all sorts of accusations being hurled and truths told. Lady B confessed she loved Tristan but needed sex on a more regular basis, and she sure as hell never got it from her useless husband.

He accused her of manipulating everyone, even her own trusted staff, for her own amusement. She told him she'd take him for every penny he had, including taking his bloody factory, his stupid cars, and especially his estate in the north, which she always hated and would take great delight in selling. He told her he'd be happy for her to try, at least he would always know that their children hated her as much as he did.

The helicopter was approaching by this time so Lord Baldwin stormed away, very closely followed by the stunned and embarrassed guests. Cathy and Kay also tried to sneak

away but were ordered back by the livid Lady Baldwin, who

also told Tom to go and get Phillip's ass down there, but not

before telling Tom that he'd better get his wife back working

as they'd been hired as a couple, so if one quit then the other

did as well.

As Tom went to get Phillip, she turned on Cathy and Kay,

berating them both for not forewarning her about Lord

Baldwin, that they were both going to be going on a very

long trip with her, to arrange for all the locks to be changed

pronto at all the properties, and to fire all the staff at

Crompton Hall. She ranted on and on about finding the slut who

had obviously moved in on his Lordship, sending Mrs. Roberts

down so she could call the lawyers and the banks, and that

thanks to their ineptitude, her life was now in ruins and it

was all their fault. Before they could come up with sort of

reply, Tom was back with Phillip. Lady B then directed her

venom at him, accusing him of being behind all of this, that

he was fired never to find another position and he wouldn't be marrying his stupid bloody American girlfriend, not after she told her a few truths.

Phillip told her to fuck off and a couple of other things which made the other staff smile before turning his back on her and walking away. That seemed to fluster her. She told all of them to get out of her sight and to send down Mrs. Roberts who had been in the library that directly overlooked the patio.

There were a couple of other developments that afternoon for D.I. Shaw. A bullet was found lodged into a tree, and a constable found one of the locks that a key fitted. It was to an unoccupied but furnished staff house on the estate so Steve had the remaining forensic technician look it over just as soon as he retrieved the bullet.

CHAPTER THIRTY EIGHT

"Kay," spoke Lord Baldwin softly, "if you feel you're up to it, we'd like you to organize Lady Baldwin's funeral arrangements."

By 'we', he was meaning Charles and Sophie also who were also present in the library.

"Yes, I'll be able to handle it. Would you like her to be buried on the estate at Crompton Hall?"

Lord Baldwin's first wife and his parents were laid to rest in a plot there, along with a couple of pets he'd had over the years, and it was a place he often visited.

"No, we'd like the service to be held here in the village chapel. Her remains can be buried in the graveyard there. This was her place so we think it only fitting that she remain here."

"I'll see if it can be arranged, milord. Will you want a large service?"

"Only invite a few of her friends. We can offer some tea after the service, we don't want any overnight guests or any of the fuss and extravagance that Lady Baldwin would have done. If any of the staff wish to attend, that will be fine. We'll expect you to ask all the other staff if they wish to come, and if so, to arrange transport if they need it."

"Okay, do you know when they'll release her body?"

"It should be by the end of the week so if you can get in touch with the local undertakers, we'll leave you to pick out a casket for her and see what day they can do the service ."

"And flowers?"

"Of course, order us a wreath but if her friends want to get flowers, tell them we'd prefer it if they donated the cost to their favorite charities instead."

"I'll get busy then. Is there anything else I can do?"

"You can give Sotheby's a call. We've decided we no longer wish to keep this estate."

"Oh!"Kay had only thought about this just this morning. She didn't think Lord Baldwin would want to keep this place but it still came as a shock. She was losing her home too.

"We want to look after you, Kay. You were a great nanny for Charles and Sophie but they're grown up now and can look after themselves. We love you, Kay, we can't just toss you out and we want to see you as much as possible. You can keep the car you've been using, and we could also get you your own apartment if you like somewhere. You're welcome to stay here until it's sold, with pay which will no doubt be months from now. Have you any thoughts on this, Kay?"

"I don't know, I suppose I could have gone a long while ago when Sophie and Charles moved out but I never had the courage. I don't want to stop seeing you all but I don't know where I want to live or work, so this needs some thought. I will be able to keep seeing you?"

"Oh yes, Nans," cried Sophie, calling her by the name she used to use and rushing over to hug her, "it was you and daddy who raised us."

After they all hugged, kissed and cried a little, Kay asked what would happen to the other staff.

"We're going to have to let them go", explained Lord Baldwin, "but at their own convenience, providing of course it's before we turn over this estate to its new owners. The only exception is Cathy who, and I've already informed my estate manager, is being given a month's notice. I don't wish for her to see out her notice. She is welcome though to attend the funeral."

"Can I ask why she's being dismissed? She was really only following orders. She really wanted to go back working at Crompton Hall."

"I know what Lady Baldwin had you doing, Kay, but Cathy just went too far sometimes. She even tried telling the staff up there that they were all fired this morning, even after what happened to C, so there's no way they'd tolerate her working there again."

"Lady Baldwin told her to do that."

"I realize that, Kay, but she had no authority to do that, even if her ladyship was still here. I and my staff there can't trust her."

"Has she been told yet?"

"I believe so. You may want to go and say goodbye if
you
wish."

"I'll do that, I'll let you know about the arrangements."

They all hugged again and Kay went to say goodbye to her
friend.

CHAPTER THIRTY NINE

Chris had taken his work home with him and after he and Megan had eaten dinner, he began to re-read all the interviews he'd conducted, comparing them with the background checks and previous statements.

"Found your killer yet?" asked Megan, stretching herself out on the sofa and glancing at the picture on the TV.

"I think I could charge about a dozen of them and make a case for it," he replied amidst the reams of paper.

"So Lady Baldwin wasn't well liked?"

"From what I can gather so far, she was adored and detested all at the same time."

"How do you mean?" asked Megan, sitting herself up but leaving her legs outstretched.

"Her maid, for instance. She's been with her for many years, yet because of Lady Baldwin's interference, her marriage is in ruins, she had an abortion, she was taped having sex with a guest, and lives apart from her children. Yet she was the most upset at the loss.

Then we have the nanny, or personal assistant more like these days. She too had her personal life interfered with, was made to do all the nasty things like fire and admonish staff, tell tales on them like the maid had to do as well, has no life of her own it seems, yet she was with her for years as well.

Two butlers. One was going to be fired because his wife had just quit so he faced having to go live with his hated in-laws. The other butler, who I haven't spoken to yet, was fired by Lady Baldwin and told that his forthcoming marriage would be destroyed.

A chef, who apparently was gazzumped out of a restaurant he'd actually moved into by Lady Baldwin purely to make him go back to working for her.

A husband, who stood to lose everything he'd built because of her, a very considerable amount. Then there are rumors saying there's another woman in the picture as well.

A movie star, who was humiliated by Lady Baldwin when she announced that not only had she been having sex with her boyfriend for many years but also that she loved him.

The two children, neither of whom showed much grief at their mother's death and are strong allies of their father.

The secretary, who's already confessed and by all accounts was the last person to see Lady Baldwin alive, has a strong motive, and would be quite willing to be sentenced."

"Hmmm, she obviously upset a lot of people. Is that it for suspects?"

"It is for now but god knows how many others there could be. The only blessing is that I have the names of everyone who was there. If she'd been shot in the street, I don't think I'd have had a restricted list of suspects."

"You seem to have found out quite a bit from the statements."

"Not really from the statements," Chris explained, "Lord Baldwin told me quite a bit of stuff, probably to deflect from him."

Megan got up from the couch and approached Chris at his desk, "Can I see what she looked like?"

"Sure, this is how we found her," he handed her a couple of the photos that didn't show the gaping hole in her head. "She was better looking than the photos on the news, I can see why she was popular with men."

"She seemed to like dangerous situations, with men she shouldn't have been looking at, like the boyfriend of her friend."

"It was probably the fear of being caught that turned her on. I bet she flirted right under her husband's nose."

"Seems that she did that before he left her."

"She had a good surgeon."

"What do you mean?"

"Well, she hardly has any lines on her face, her breasts are pert, no fat on her tummy, and her legs are way too good to still be all natural," Megan pointed out to Chris all the pertinent areas she was talking about.

"She was in great shape."

"Your instincts are good, Chris. Who do you really suspect?" Megan asked, as she continued looking at the photos.

"At the moment, the only instinct I have is that the secretary didn't do it."

"Well Sherlock," teased Megan, putting the photos back down, "I'm going to bed. Maybe you can come and check me out and tell me if I too need some nip and tucking."

"Be glad to," he smiled up at his wife, "I'll be there as soon as I check some more of these statements"

CHAPTER FORTY

The following morning when D.I. Shaw arrived at work alongside his Sergeant who had picked him up as normal, there was a message waiting for him in that Dr. McBride wished to see him, so they both headed down to her laboratory.

She was seated at her desk at one end of the sterile white room, head down as she studied some kind of report.

"You wanted to see me, Doc?" inquired Chris as he and the Sergeant sat themselves down on the opposite side of her neat desk.

"Oh, I didn't see you come in," she replied looking up from her report, "yes, we have a little news for you." Without pausing for pleasantries, she picked up a clear, sealed evidence bag and continued, " this bullet we retrieved from the tree is the bullet that killed Lady Baldwin. It is a 38 as I

thought, and if you're able to find a weapon, hopefully we'll

be able to find a match." She put the bag back down and

picked up the report she'd been reading when they arrived,

"and in the cottage, we've found traces of semen and vaginal

fluid, several fingerprints, footprints outside the cottage

windows which I'm having cast as we speak, but they look as

if they were made by both a man and a woman."

"You think these footprints are important?" Chris asked.

"Possibly. Someone was having sex inside there. We think,

from the fingerprints we've lifted from there and from the

house, that it was Lady Baldwin with John Steele, and the

boyfriend of the movie star," she replied, looking at her notes

again, "Tristan?" she asked.

"Tristan Squires" said Steve.

"We haven't matched their DNA yet, but we have got their

fingerprint results, and the maid, Cathy Jones, could also have

been involved as her fingerprints are in there as well and it

may be her vaginal fluid we found."

"Why do you think the footprints may be important?" asked Chris.

"Because they're fairly fresh, any rain would have washed them away, and although both sets are on different sides of the house," and she handed over the report so they could see the drawing that had been made, "they both could have seen the spot where we think someone was having sex, without knowing that someone else was also watching."

"It also seems feasible" Chris opinioned, looking at the drawing that had been made, "that they were having sex while watching the TV."

"Let me look at that again," said Dr McBride, taking the report back, "Hmm, you know what I think?"

"Let's hear it, Doc," answered Steve.

"I think," she continued, consulting another report, "that it probably was Lady Baldwin who was having sex, and she was watching the videotape and recreating the sex scene that was taped the previous night in the maid's room. It would certainly explain the finger marks we found on her thighs. It would also explain why she was in possession of the tape."

"I think you're right, Doc," agreed Chris, "will you be able to find out whose footprints they are?"

"It's not an exact science like fingerprints and DNA but we can match the shoes and give you the weight of the person in them, even how they walk if we're lucky."

"That'll be great. We need whatever you can get but you look like you need a break," replied Chris, who'd noticed from the second he came in that the doctor wasn't looking as good as she normally did.

"Are you telling me I look a mess?" smiled Susan.

"You could never look a mess but you do look tired."

"I am but the Chief wants me to get results to you as soon as possible so the lab is working overtime on this."

"We appreciate it, just don't wear yourself out, okay?" Chris got up to leave, quickly followed by Steve, "give me a call on my cell if you get any updates. We're going to the other house to see this other butler."

"We are?" asked Steve.

"Yes, we are, right after you get someone to go through all the trash cans at Stonebridge and see if they can find a gun or some gloves."

"I know they looked through them all for a gun, but why gloves?"

"Because the doc here tested everyone for gunshot residue and they were all clean so maybe they wore gloves. They can collect all the gloves inside the house as well, like the rubber ones the housekeepers use and the ones the butlers use for handling plates and silver."

"I already have those, Detective Inspector, we just haven't been able to process them yet," interrupted Doctor McBride.

"I thought you would have but I still want all the trash cans looked through, like in the stables for example just in case we inadvertently missed something. We've got the bullet now, it would be real nice to find the weapon it was fired from."

"I'll meet you at the car, Sir," replied the Sergeant with an evil grin, "as soon as I get the right copper to rummage in the refuse."

CHAPTER FORTY ONE

"Hey, you old fart, how's the world treating you?"

Phillip was calling his friend Ken.

"About time too, I was beginning to think you'd been arrested and that I'd be forced, out of our friendship, to marry my darling Natalie."

"It's a wonder you didn't shop me to the cops."

"I'm not a snitch but I did think about making an anonymous call."

"You think Natalie would marry you?"

"If she had sense she would, I know she fell in love with me when I gave her the grand tour of our wondrous capital city which she thought was marvelous after being stuck in the dark north with you."

"She may have given you that impression but she was just being kind. She has a soft spot for senile raconteurs."

"It was more than that, my friend. I saw the twinkle in her eyes whenever she gazed in my direction which was most of the time."

"That was her contact lenses, dummy, it's the way they catch the light."

"We'll send you a piece of our wedding cake when they send you to prison, you'll believe me then."

"Just make sure you put a file in the cake."

"Count on it," turning serious, he went on, "So my friend, I've been worried about you, I haven't heard from you since the news broke, have they found who did it yet?"

"Not that I've heard, and there's a couple of detectives on their way up here to interview me, so I've just been informed."

"Who told you that?"

"The police called, told me to stay around until these guys visited."

"They might take you back with them."

"If they do, I'll tell Natalie to go and marry you, spend all your money on my defense, and when I get cleared she can divorce you and we'll throw you out of your home."

"She'll forget all about you once we get married, she'll realize just what a mistake she made in not picking me first. So my friend, who was it who killed the wicked witch?"

"No one knows yet."

"Well, who do you think did it?"

"I have my suspicions but she could really have been killed by anyone. Virtually everyone had a grudge against her."

"Was it your guvnor?"

"No, he couldn't have done it. He's never so much as raised an arm against her, never mind shoot her."

"Well, somebody did it. Do you think you'll be a suspect?"

"I suppose I have to be, I was there and it was so chaotic at the time with everyone going in different directions, it wasn't like a bunch of us were in a room and we heard a gunshot. I didn't even know she was dead until we got back."

"At least you and Natalie are okay. It could have turned into one of those massacres where everybody gets shot."

"I suppose, Natalie is amazed that no one seems to be mourning Lady B."

"Are you going to the funeral?"

"I don't think so. I don't see the point, and His Lordship is trying to keep it as small as possible. I think he's had his fill of over elaboration."

"How is my darling Natalie doing?"

"She's doing okay. It's a shock to her of course but she seems okay."

"I'll get Fran to give her a call. They got on famously you know when they met."

"So I heard, but then Fran has good taste. Give her our love when you see her."

"Will do, buddy, she's been worried about you. Keep me informed about what happens , will you? That's one thing that never happened to me."

"What's that?"

"No one I ever worked for ever got killed. "

"I will call back later when the detectives leave."

"Okay, until later then. Give Natalie my love. Be careful."

"I will. Bye for now."

"Bye, buddy."

CHAPTER FORTY TWO

Kay had been on the phone all morning. She'd managed to get a vicar to do a funeral service in the village chapel, gotten the undertakers arranged, picked out an outfit for Lady Baldwin to be buried in and selected her coffin. The seldom used chapel was being cleaned , a plot had been picked, she'd ordered the marble headstone, narrated the very simple inscription, and chosen the wreaths for the family and the staff. She had also called all of Lady B's friends to invite them to attend the service. Most had declined, especially the ones she'd had relations with. They didn't, it seemed, want to be involved in a murder investigation. Nor did much staff want to attend either, the only one from Crompton Hall was, surprisingly, Maud, who no doubt just wanted to nosey around and be a part of it all.

Cathy, of course, wanted to attend but she was a wreck now having lost both her employer and her job. Finding out that no one wanted her back at Crompton Hall really upset her, she couldn't fathom why none of the staff there could understand why she'd had to tell them so many lies over the years.

An obituary had been done in the local paper, several in the national papers and another in the local paper back at Crompton Hall. Most had dwelt on Lady B's philanthropic side, her love of horses, and her lavish entertaining. The paper at Crompton Hall had also mentioned the shooting parties she organized, with a little reminder to everyone about how a dog had been killed during one of them. It was a small community there, so the dog had been big news. In all the years she'd worked here, Kay never thought for one second she'd ever have to organize a burial, especially for her employer. But that is what she was doing, and also trying at the same time to come to terms with her whole life now being turned upside down.

She was also thinking of the interview she'd had to endure yesterday with the police, who seemed to know all about her. Since she'd been the one to report the dead body, she was a main suspect. Not that she'd been told that of course, it was just implied. Nevertheless, it was a scary thought.

Paul though was being very supportive, telling her not to worry about anything. She was welcome to move in with him, that he was going to ask her to do so anyway even before Lady B was shot.

That was very exciting for her. She thought her personal life had long since gone. It was just scary to start afresh. But first, she had to deal with all this stuff, and Cathy, and not strictly in that order.

She still hadn't gotten her head around the family practically abandoning Lady Baldwin. She knew she'd done bad things but for them to have her buried down here, and sell the property, was like saying they were never going to visit her grave which seemed harsh.

They hadn't though short changed her as far as costs were going. Lord Baldwin wasn't asking how much it was going to cost him. Rather, when Kay said she ordered an expensive casket, he asked if she wanted to get a better one.

She had to go through Lady Baldwin's things though. Lord Baldwin said that all her jewelry would go to Sophie so she was carefully boxing everything up. Most of it had come from him or heirlooms from her own mother, but some little things hadn't so she was keeping them off to the side. She'd kept things her whole life, small silver photo frames with faces even Kay didn't know, small trinkets and bracelets, but Kay was especially on the lookout for engravings.

Lord Baldwin had told her that if she wanted any of her clothes she was welcome, otherwise she could dispose of them as she wished, but preferably to somewhere with a charitable contribution. Paul said he knew of a place in London that would be happy to take her stuff, they specialized in just this kind of thing and had the clientele that would pay for the used designer clothing. He said he would arrange for it to be picked up.

Kay didn't know how she'd have managed without Paul during all this. He'd been offering to come back and help her with all the arrangements, help with the belongings, or give her a shoulder to cry on . He was coming for the funeral, as was Larry. They were both sorry to lose a good customer like Lady B.

He also realized the police would want to talk to him at some stage, as he and Larry also had been hurriedly departing that day. She'd be glad to see him again.

"Oh god," she thought silently, when she found Lady B's sex toys, "Sophie will not want these," especially this vibrator that says 'think of me' on it along with a couple of Polaroid's. Kay was able to keep a few things, not much, as barely anything was her size, and she took those away along with the damaging material.

CHAPTER FORTY THREE

It was Phillip who answered the door to the detectives. He was in casual clothes as his employer was not in residence.

"Mr. Phillip Scott?" asked Chris.

"Yes, that's me. You must be the detectives I've been expecting. Can I see your badges please?"

"I'm Detective Inspector Shaw and this is Detective Sergeant Greene," Chris replied, both proffering their ID's, "may we come inside?"

"Of course," smiled Phillip, "come in. I hope you'll excuse me for asking for your identification but there have been a couple of reporters sniffing around here so I need to be careful. It's part of my job to know who's entering my employer's home."

Phillip was leading them into the main kitchen which was just off to the right as you entered the house. It was a big kitchen with a large island to work on to the right, a big range on the left and a table with chairs at the far, south facing side by some windows.

"Can we talk privately?" asked Chris, hearing some chatter from the left which was the laundry room.

"Yes, of course. I'll close the door and no one will disturb us," Phillip replied, leading them over to the table and asking them if they'd like some coffee or anything.

"No, I think we're fine," said Chris, seating himself down, "this shouldn't take long. Why don't you sit across from us?" Phillip sat down opposite the two detectives.

"First of all," said Chris, "can you give us a statement of what transpired the day that Lady Baldwin was murdered? The sergeant here can write it down as you tell us, then you can sign it after you read it. Is that okay?"

"Sure, no problem."

"Just give us a brief outline to begin with and I'll ask questions to fill in the gaps."

"Okay, well to begin with, I got up pretty early around six I think because I had a lot to do. I believe you know now that his lordship was leaving her ladyship so not only did I have to get his things together, I also had to do my own. I spent much of my time packing. I'd already gotten a lot of his stuff done, but that early in the morning it's quiet so I was able to get a few more of his things."

"Did you see or hear anyone else around while you did that?"

"No, it was very quiet."

"Continue."

"At about seven I went downstairs. Tom was already there and he'd made some tea. He told me what was going on for the rest of the day, that they would have lunch downstairs by the patio, then the guests would probably leave. He and the chef would be able to handle most of the lunch but if I could help with the setting and clearing up that would be great. During lunch itself I could check on whether anyone needed anything packed. After lunch I could help with bringing their luggage down and bringing around their cars."

"Tom, meaning the butler at Stonebridge?" asked Chris.

"Yes."

"Did he know you were leaving that afternoon?"

"Not as far as I know, no."

"Did anyone else?"

"His lordship knew, Ian the pilot , and my girlfriend Natalie .
Also my friend Ken, but the only other person I think that
knew was Kay."

"Did you tell her so?"

"No, I think his lordship's daughter, Miss Sophie did."

"Why did your friend, girlfriend and pilot know?

"The pilot needed to know because of flying and the weight,
and he was also picking up my girlfriend from London early.
As my friend had been taking care of her, he had to know
also."

"Did your friend and girlfriend come here on the helicopter?"

"No, he lives in London and she was taken to Crompton Hall
before Ian came here."

"Okay, so tell us how the day went?"

"Well, it was fairly non eventful until later on. Breakfast took
forever as it always does here, they don't have a set time for
it so everyone ambles in and out all morning. In the
meantime, we're trekking up and downstairs with all the lunch

stuff. In between, I'm trying to get all our luggage ready to throw onto the helicopter."

"I see," replied Chris, "so what happened during the time they had lunch up to your departure?"

"As always happens down there," said Phillip referring to Stonebridge Manor, "lunch was late. It should have been 1pm and it was closer to 2pm. Her ladyship wasn't ready so we all had to wait."

"Why wasn't she ready?"

"I have no idea but she and a couple of guests weren't around so we had to wait."

"Do you know which guests?

"No, everyone was here there and everywhere all morning long, but without her ladyship, lunch wouldn't begin."

"Couldn't Lord Baldwin have started lunch?"

"Sure, but he's too much of a gentleman to have started lunch without everyone being present."

"Even though he was leaving?"

"Yes, even though."

"Do you think he could have killed his wife?"

"No."

"That was a quick answer. What makes you so sure?"

"Shooting her was too quick. If she'd been strangled or pushed off a cliff then maybe so, but not being shot like that. There is no way he did it though, he's just too nice. "

"Who do you think did it?"

"I have an idea, but that's all. Not enough of one to point the finger at someone and say they did it."

"Did you kill her?"

"No."

"You had motive."

"Yes, I did. The woman was a bitch and I haven't shed any tears at her demise. I also won't be going to her funeral."

"Did you not tell her to fuck off and go screw herself?"

"I did, yes."

"And she fired you?"

"Yes."

"Told you she'd ruin your life?"

"Yes."

"Yet you didn't kill her or feel the urge to?"

"No. I was able to tell her what to do to herself and that made
me very happy"

"If I was spoken to like that and felt myself and my family
threatened, I'd have killed her. Why wouldn't you?"

"Because his lordship was leaving her. He's my employer, not
her. I knew he wasn't going to fire me. That's why I said
what I did, I was free to. I'd rather have seen her go through
a divorce and lose her precious title, if she married someone
without one."

"So lunch was late?"

"Yes, then his lordship told her a few truths and it went
crazy."

"Did that surprise you, him doing that?"

"Yes, but it's been coming for a long while."

"Were you witness to that?"

"No."

"Would Lord Baldwin have been prepared to lose his business
if there'd been a divorce?"

"I suppose so. I think he'd just got to the point where it was worth losing his business if it meant saving his relationship with his children, and his own self esteem."

"Do you think one of his children could have killed her?"

"No, they didn't like her but they still loved her."

"After you had words with Lady Baldwin and she fired you, did you see her again?"

"No."

"Where was she when you last saw her?"

"Downstairs on the patio."

"Could you have sneaked back down there without anyone seeing you?"

"I don't know, I had no reason to go see her again."

"We found a couple of keys in her possession, do you know where they could be for?"

"She had no reason to carry keys, she doesn't have one for here although his lordship does. One of them may be for her place in London but I have no idea about the other one."

"Do you mean the house they own near Harrods."

"No, she doesn't need a key there, the housekeeper is always there. I mean her apartment in Soho."

"I thought the Baldwin's only owned one property in London," said Chris, rifling through some of his notes in his notebook and looking at his sergeant who looked equally puzzled.

"They do. The apartment is owned exclusively by her ladyship, paid for with her own money, maintained by her, and his lordship is totally oblivious to it."

"She has her own money?"

"Oh yes. She's always kept her own bank account secret from his lordship, that way she can do what she likes without him hearing about it."

"And she had this apartment for what reason?"

"Come on, detective, you can guess. It was for meeting her men friends privately and without having to check into a hotel."

"How long has she had this place?"

"Years, I believe."

"Did anyone else know about it?"

"Apart from the men? Maybe Kay and Cathy did. She used to tell them about her exploits I believe. But I don't know if they knew about the apartment, because they never let it slip when they gossiped."

"They'd gossip?"

"Sometimes, when they were in a good mood and only with me as they knew it wouldn't go any further. I don't think they knew of the apartment."

"Have you got the address for this apartment?"

"No, sorry. I know it exists is all."

"Do you think Lord Baldwin felt threatened by Lady Baldwin?"

"Maybe I suppose, but he wouldn't have shot her."

"Does he own any guns?"

"Sure, a bunch. But they're all shotguns."

"No handguns?"

"No."

"How can you be so sure?"

"Because I'm the butler here and also his valet. If he had a gun, I'd know about it."

"Do any of the children own a handgun?"

"If they do, I don't know about it. They certainly have never had one while I've been around."

"Did you see anyone while you were departing Stonebridge Manor who looked like they were possibly heading toward the patio?"

"Not that I noticed, no."

"Did you see Mrs. Roberts when she was there?"

"Yes, the poor soul was left waiting in the library."

"Would she have seen, or heard, what was going on down at the patio?"

"Yes, if she was in there. The library is directly above the patio and the windows were open."

"How do you know the windows were open?"

"Because I opened them myself when she arrived, she thought it was a little stuffy in there."

"Can anyone vouch for your movements at, or around, 3pm on Sunday?"

"Not really, no. It was just crazy."

"Do you own a gun?"

"No."

"So you wouldn't mind us looking around?"

"No, not at all."

"Did you kill Lady Baldwin?"

"Nope."

"Do you know who did?" A little frustration was showing now.

"Not for sure, but it sure as hell wasn't Mrs. Roberts."

There wasn't much more the detectives got out of Phillip. The sergeant finished the statement which Phillip read then signed and it wasn't long before they returned south, stopping quite quickly to have a bite to eat and for a coffee.

"So what are you thinking, sergeant?" he asked after they'd sat down with their coffees and sandwiches.

"I think that he may have a better idea than we do, as to who killed one of his employers."

"Do you think he did it?"

"No, I don't."

"Neither do I, but I still have no idea who did it. Have someone try and find this apartment and get a search warrant and forensics down there. Tomorrow we'll go and interview the weekend guests who live in London, so tell them we're coming and to expect us. I don't want us knocking at empty houses. Also, have someone take a swab from Mr. Scott and take his fingerprints."

CHAPTER FORTY FOUR

The two detectives had a long and frustrating day in London, nobody was cooperative with them and they learned little, if anything.

They met Jane Robins in a theatre's dressing room where she'd agreed to play a small part for a lot of money. She didn't particularly want to do the play, but after what had happened she thought she needed the distraction. She made a statement which only confirmed what they already knew except that she'd declined to return home with Tristan, getting a ride instead from Simon Ward-Davis. She hadn't seen Tristan leave and hadn't seen him since. She also stated that although she felt very humiliated and betrayed, she hadn't killed Lady Baldwin.

Simon Ward-Davis confirmed he'd given a ride to Jane

Robins, and he didn't see Tristan leave either. Tristan himself,

was very open with the detectives. He readily admitted having

a long affair with Lady Baldwin, but never envisaged it

becoming permanent. He was quite happy with Jane Robins

and was genuinely sorry it was over. He wouldn't be going

to the funeral out of respect for Lord Baldwin but would visit

her resting place as soon as he deemed it fit to do so.

Liz Price didn't leave with who she arrived with either.

Instead she left with Charles and Sophie Baldwin. Her

statement didn't come up with anything new really, apart from

John Steele having to also drive home alone, and no, she

didn't see him leave.

Suzy Walker, having met the detectives away from her

home, flirted with them virtually nonstop. She seemed the only

one to truly miss Lady Baldwin, and was ever so grateful to

her for introducing her to Simon who truly was a friend. She

would attend the funeral. It was the least she could do to pay

her respects.

Robert and Mandy Mills didn't shed any light either. Chris thought Robert may have had a close relationship with Lady Baldwin at some stage, purely because of his mannerisms during some of the questions. Perhaps his wife Mandy suspected that and took her revenge but that was a long shot. And when the weekend ended, they left the estate together.

Paul and Larry had no reason whatsoever to kill her. They'd just earned a sizeable amount of money for their endeavors and Lady Baldwin was a frequent customer. They seemed entertained with the whole weekend.

Chris really took a dislike to John Steele. He tried avoiding every question, didn't like admitting to making the tape with Cathy, didn't know why Lady Baldwin was in possession of it, didn't know of her apartment, and didn't know why Liz Price didn't leave with him.

"We're getting nowhere fast it seems, Sergeant," commented Chris on their way back.

"I agree . Apart from Mrs. Roberts, nobody wants to tell us anything and we don't think she's telling the truth either."

"I think I'll talk to the Chief when we get back, see about formally charging Mrs. Roberts and see if that makes someone relax and tell us something. I doubt it, but it's either that or we get lucky."

"It's the funeral tomorrow. Are we going?"

"Yes, and have all the family and staff available for some further interviews. Just tell them that we want to tie up all the loose ends, but we'll do the interviews before and after the funeral."

"Right, Sir."

CHAPTER FORTY FIVE

D.I. Shaw interviewed Lord Baldwin after speaking to his children. He now was in possession of all the background checks for all the suspects, but as far as the family went, there was nothing.

"Good Morning, Lord Baldwin. I'm sorry to have to ask you more questions, especially on the day of your wife's funeral, but I just need to tie up some loose ends."

"That's okay, but I think you've got the wrong person in custody."

"Why do you say that? She has confessed. Who do you think should be in custody?"

"If you knew Mrs. Roberts, you'd know she was incapable of taking someone's life even if she wished it to happen. I don't know who killed my wife but I still refuse to believe it was Mrs. Roberts."

"Were you prepared to go through a divorce?"

"Yes."

"Despite it probably taking away your business that's taken you a lifetime to build?"

"Yes, if that's what happened. I hoped to reach a settlement that would have saved it, but I was prepared to lose it."

"Is there another woman?"

"Yes, but who told you that?"

"You'll find out anyway but one of your children let it slip."

"That's okay. It's not a secret. I just want to protect her from all this."

"Did your wife know you were seeing someone else?"

"No, she didn't."

"How can you be so sure?"

"Trust me, detective," Lord Baldwin smiled, "if she'd known, I'd have heard about it."

"Did anyone else know?"

"I'd told my children and some of the staff at Crompton Hall"

"Where was she that weekend?"

"She was up in that neighborhood, not that far from the Hall."

"Can I call her to confirm that?"

397

"I suppose so, but really she has nothing to do with this."

"Like I said, Sir, I need to tie up loose ends is all."

Chris excused Lord Baldwin shortly after getting Victoria Harrop's name and contact information. He passed it along to his sergeant to check up on.

After reading through some of the background checks on the staff, they both took in some fresh air by walking down to the funeral service that was shortly due to start.

Although there was a sizeable contingent of press, there weren't a lot of mourners present. The family were well represented. A few locals, mainly Lord Baldwin's friends, who knew her from dinner parties were present, along with the staff who worked at Stonebridge, but from the overnight guests who attended the weekend only Suzy Walker and Liz Price came. It was clear the latter only because she wanted to support Charles. The bulk of the tears came from Cathy who seemed inconsolable, then from Suzy Walker, and surprisingly from Maud, the housekeeper from Crompton Hall.

Chris wasn't too surprised that more people didn't show up, but he watched and observed just in case someone broke down and confessed. It could happen, he thought.

CHAPTER FORTY SIX

"I thought you might have gone down to the funeral," said Natalie, who'd gone over to Crompton Hall to see Phillip. "No, his lordship didn't expect me to and he knows what happened when she spoke to me. It would have been hypocritical to go."

"Even just to show respect?"

"I could have done that. I even thought about it but it's best I stayed away."

The gardeners were working outside and the painters hadn't shown up today. Maud, of course, had gone to the funeral so they were alone for now. They were in the main kitchen where Phillip was making them both a sandwich for lunch.

"Do you still think you know who did it?" asked Natalie, smiling as she watched him put together the sandwiches 'American' style by using mayonnaise instead of butter.

"The more I think about it, the more I think I know. I just couldn't swear to it or even point the finger at someone."

"So who do you think did it?" implored Natalie, obviously getting a mite frustrated.

"I know you want me to say but I'm probably wrong. Let me write the name down in a sealed envelope, and if they ever charge someone other than Mrs. Roberts, you can open it. You could do the same thing."

"I have no idea who did it."

"I've told you everything I know, make a guess. You were a paralegal so you know this stuff. We could make a wager."

"What's the bet?"

"Come with me a minute," he said, taking her hand and leaving their sandwiches behind, leading her out to the outside of the house which overlooked the valley, which today was bathed in sunlight.

"Why have we come out here?" enquired Natalie, although she loved the view.

"Something I need to tell you and ask you. His lordship has offered us a bigger house, the new one that is just up the lane, and also given me a raise."

"Oh-kay" replied Natalie, drawing out the single word to sound like two separate words. She wondered where this was leading.

"Well, and I realize this may not be the most suitable time," Phillip continued, a little sheepishly now, "but with the bigger home and the salary, and with us already declaring our love for one another", he dropped to one knee, "would you agree to marrying me? I adore you and would really like for us to spend the rest of our lives together"

Natalie looked stunned, dumbstruck.

She took in the surroundings and Phillip's face was full of hope and more importantly, love.

"Yes I will Phillip, I just love you so much!"

He got off his knees and they hugged and kissed, deliriously happy.

"So what's the bet?" she finally asked curiously.

"We each put a name in an envelope and if one of them is the killer, then whoever picked it chooses the wedding menu. If we're both right or wrong, then we both choose the menu."

"We have a bet. Let's kiss on it."

CHAPTER FORTY SEVEN

Chris sat down again with Rene once the funeral was over and everyone had left.

"So, you still have no alibi for when Lady Baldwin was killed?"

"No sir, but hasn't Mrs. Roberts confessed?"

"Yes she has. But we just have some things to tidy up. You bought a restaurant and then lost it?"

"Yes, I was , as they say, gazzumped."

"Do you know who by?"

Rene contemplated this, you could almost hear him thinking.

"Yes, I know who did it. It was Lady Baldwin ."

"And you did your national service in France?" asked Chris, rifling through the background check papers. For the moment he was ignoring Rene's reply.

"Yes, two years."

"So you know how to use a firearm?"

"Yes."

"Rifles and pistols?"

"Yes"

"So why, when you knew it was Lady Baldwin who'd taken away your restaurant, did you come back? For revenge?"

"I didn't know then it was her. It was only recently I found out."

"And you wanted revenge?" asked Chris, calmly.

"Yes, but I didn't shoot her," replied Rene, his voice going up an octave in a slight panic.

"Do you own a gun?" Chris was throwing the questions at him, looking for a slip up.

"No sir."

"You didn't keep one from your national service?"

"No sir."

"Did any of your friends?"

"Maybe."

"So you have access to a 38mm handgun?"

"I don't know."

"What do you mean you don't know? Your friends have guns."

"They do but I don't know what kind"

"What kind did you use in the service?"

"All kinds."

"So then one of your friends must have a 38mm?"

"I suppose so."

"And when did you borrow it, or steal it from them?

"I didn't," replied Rene, sweating now.

"Can you prove that?"

"Prove what? I don't have anybody's gun."

"And you still maintain you were alone when Lady Baldwin was shot?"

"Yes."

"And you were full of revenge?"

"I suppose so."

"So did you kill Lady Baldwin?"

"No sir."

"Are you thinking of leaving the country soon?"

"No sir."

"Very well," Chris's tone relaxed, "thank you for seeing me again today. I may have further questions for you at a later date. You can go now."

The visibly shaking Rene hurriedly left the room while the detectives busied themselves shuffling papers.

"So what do you think, Detective Inspector?" asked D.S. Greene after the chef had closed the door behind him.

"I think we either need to get lucky or find some evidence. Bring Cathy Jones in."

The detectives were once again using the estate manager's office at Stonebridge to do these interviews. It wasn't far removed from the interview rooms back at the station, the biggest difference was this had a window instead of a mirror. Chris took a sip of water from a plastic cup as he waited, tapping his fingers on the table to an unknown beat.

The red-eyed Cathy finally entered the room, along with D.S. Greene who asked her to sit down after offering her some water. She declined the water but pulled a tissue out of the Kleenex box to dab her eyes.

"I'm sorry for your loss, Ms. Jones, and I'm sorry that I need to ask you further questions, especially today. I just need to clear up some minor details," said Chris, directly across the table from her and again looking through his background notes.

Cathy didn't respond so Chris continued.

"Would you have had reason to cause Lady Baldwin any harm?"

"No," replied Cathy rather defiantly, her eyes beginning to water again, "why would you think that?"

"So whatever her ladyship did to you over the years, nothing comes to mind that made you angry?"

"No," she answered, but a little hesitantly.

"Was she always nice to you?"

"Most of the time."

"You never had cause to complain?"

"No", still with a hesitant edge.

"She never made you cry?"

"Sometimes, but not much."

"Always gave you ample time off to be with your family?"

"Yes" Cathy avoided eye contact, a little perspiration beginning to appear on her forehead.

"Did she ever set you up with any men?"

"No, what do you mean by that?" asked Cathy, a little annoyed now.

"Like a date, or to have sex with?"

"No," yelled Cathy, "that's a lie."

"It's you who are lying, Ms. Jones," Chris replied forcefully, "is it not fact that after Lady Baldwin had set you up with a worker here, that she later paid for the abortion of your baby? Isn't it also true that she made you come back to work when you should have been spending time with your family? Isn't it also true that she made you tell lies to other members of staff and to tell her personal things about those same staff? Isn't it also true that she had John Steele spend a night with you and tape it? Is it not also true that you stood outside your own house on this very estate, and watched as Lady Baldwin and John Steele recreated the sex scenes you and he performed, while they watched that tape? Isn't that the truth, Ms. Jones?

By now Cathy was crying in great sobs. She mumbled something between sobs.

"What was that?" asked Chris.

"Yes. I said yes, it's all true."

"And that's why you killed her?

"No, I didn't do it."

"You expect me to believe that?"

"You have to," she pleaded, "I didn't do it"

"Doesn't your husband have a firearm's license?"

"Yes."

"Does he have any pistols?"

"Yes."

"So you took one of his pistols and shot her, for all she'd done to you. Now what did you do with that pistol?"

"Nothing, I never had a pistol. I didn't do it," she pleaded again, trying to stem the flood of tears.

"Okay, Ms. Jones. Then do we have permission to go and search your husband's firearms?

"Yes, please do. I implore you. I didn't do it."

"If we find one missing, Ms. Jones, the only time you'll ever see your children again will be on visiting day. Unless you confess to me now, in which case I'll have the court go easier on you."

"But I didn't do it, I swear. Please, you've got to believe me."

"Can anyone vouch for your movements around the time of Lady Baldwin's death?

"I don't think so, no," she sobbed.

"You can go now, Ms. Jones. Thank you for your time, we'll be in touch."

She was practically out of the door before he'd even finished the sentence.

Tom though, couldn't be rattled. He just stayed calm and collected, rather like Phillip had been at Crompton Hall. He admitted that he didn't want to live with his in-laws but he saw no reason why he'd kill to avoid that. He didn't have an alibi either but he did say he could shoot. Most butlers who've been trained can shoot as it's a part of the training.

Kay reiterated what she'd said previously. She'd found the body, she was alone, she hadn't seen anyone else, and yes, she supposed she had motive as well. But no, she hadn't done it.

CHAPTER FORTY EIGHT

First thing the next morning, Chris called Phillip at Crompton Hall and asked him if he could shoot a pistol.

"Sure, what do you want me to shoot at?"

Ignoring the not so funny remark, Chris also asked if he would have access to a 38mm handgun.

"Yes I do. My friend has one."

"He has a license for it?"

"He sure does, keeps the thing in a box bolted to the floor."

Chris learned from Phillip that the gun belonged to his friend Ken and got his address so he could check it out.

"You'd better send one of your deaf coppers to check it," continued Phillip, "he'll either have Beethoven blasting out of his stereo or he'll want to regale the policeman with all his life's stories. If you send a policewoman, you may as well say goodbye to her. It won't matter to him how old she is or how she looks. If there is one thing he likes, it's a woman in uniform."

Chris actually laughed.

"Care to enlighten us yet on your theory?" he asked Phillip.

"No, but I do have a hunch that you'll find your gun because if I'm right then it was only borrowed."

"Have you borrowed a gun lately, like Ken's for instance?"

"Nice try detective, but no, I haven't needed one lately."

"We'll see about that, Mr. Scott. You'll be hearing from me," Chris ended the call.

D.S. Greene was entering his office as he was finishing his call, carrying a report.

"What's that, detective?" Chris asked his sergeant as he sat down.

"Looks like we found the London apartment."

"Good, did you get a search warrant and dispatch forensics?"

"They're on their way as we speak."

"Good job, have them pick a gun up from this address while they're down there and have someone interview the owner of it," he wrote down Ken's name and address on a post-it and passed it across. "Also, while they're there, get them extra help if necessary and have them collect fingerprints and DNA samples from all the guests. I know we have all the samples from their rooms but just to be sure, let's match them all up 100%. What else do we have, Sergeant?"

"Confirmation about the footprints outside Cathy Jones's house. The female one fits her size and weight which she admitted to," the D.S. read from the report. "The other footprint was male, probably around six foot, about 160 to 170 pounds. Slight emphasis on the outside heels, size ten and a half. If we get a suspect and the shoes, we can match them up. There's a photo of the shoe sole we can look for. Also, although we now know some of this from what we learned from Cathy Jones, Lady Baldwin, John Steele, Tristan and Cathy were in that house. It's almost certain that it was Tristan's, and more recently, John Steele's, semen that was found in the house, as well as inside Lady Baldwin. Also, it's almost certain that Simon Ward-Davis spent the night in Suzy Walker's room, Liz Price spent a night in Sophie Baldwin's room, and John Steele spent at least part of one night in Cathy Jones's room. Forensics also found evidence of a sexual encounter in the family room, they're almost certain it's from John Steele again but definitely with Lady Baldwin."

"Okay, good, keep me up to date with any developments," Chris told him, "I need to get these reports done," his eyes signaling the stack that waited his attention.

CHAPTER FORTY NINE

Cathy left Stonebridge without much fanfare. The staff, of course, said their goodbyes without many tears, apart from Kay who was her closest friend. For Kay, it was now exciting to be leaving. She could barely sleep now thinking of it, but for Cathy it was trepidation.

She had no job to go to, her children were indifferent to her these days, she didn't have much of a relationship with her husband, and her mother now, in effect, thought of herself as the children's mother.

At least his lordship was going to let her keep her car now. He'd shown how kind he was after the funeral by telling her to keep the car which was less than a year old, and also giving her a check for six months pay. She would still have liked to have gone back to work at Crompton Hall but knew now that wasn't going to happen. Maybe she could call in from time to time.

Kay had told Lord Baldwin she was going to move in with Paul. He and the children were amazed, yet delighted. They reiterated that she was always welcome to visit at any time. Kay didn't have to do any packing but she wanted to do a little. Paul had come to help. Going through all her stuff brought a tear or two as she recalled all the years, especially with the children. But she wasn't too old to have her own children, not yet, though the clock was ticking. She couldn't put it to the back of her mind like she had done previously. She was in very good spirits when she and Paul left after saying their goodbyes, giving everyone hugs and kisses and lots of smiles.

The Chief Inspector asked Chris the following morning if he was any closer to finding another suspect. Chris explained to him how he had a bunch of them but was still trying to find the hard evidence they'd need to convict.

"Keep looking,. It'll be out there somewhere, just try to find it before we have to go to court with Mrs. Roberts."

"Understood, Sir."

Chris found his sergeant at the coffee machine and they both took their coffee down to forensics, finding Dr. McBride in her office. She looked up as the sergeant knocked on the door before they both entered.

"I'm sorry if I'm rushing you, Doc. I just wondered if you'd got anything for me?" asked the apologetic Chris.

"Well, thanks to a couple of my technicians who put in a lot of overtime last night, which I expect you'll approve?" looking for and getting the nod from Chris, "I can tell you this much.

The 38mm we retrieved from a London apartment was not the murder weapon."

"And by all accounts," interjected the sergeant, "the detective I sent there was there most of the day."

"Was the detective female?" asked Chris, a slight smile on his lips.

"Yes, she was. Why is that funny?"

"It isn't, sergeant," replied Chris stifling a giggle, "why don't you carry on, Doc?"

"Before she does, I should also inform you that the search at Cathy Jones's home came up with nothing either, apart from a lot of high end price clothing."

"Lady Baldwin was always giving the stuff she didn't want to her nanny and maid. It was part of their perks. Carry on, Doc."

"The key we were given fit the lock at the apartment we went to that was owned by Lady Baldwin. We found twelve sets of fingerprints, one set belonged to a maid, who very conveniently had left her name and number on the fridge, and three of the other sets belonged to Lady Baldwin, Tristan

Squires, and Simon Ward-Price. Although the bed had been freshly made, the maid thankfully hadn't yet washed some soiled sheets. She said there had been a leak in the washing machine and it hadn't been fixed yet so we are certain it contains Lady Baldwin's fluids and we're testing the semen. Those tests take much longer, as you know.

The apartment was well stocked with frozen foods and lots of champagne, great linens and towels, and other expensive toiletries. The maid said that it was very rare that anyone ate there. In fact, she never saw anyone there. She was just called to clean either before or after anyone stayed there.

We got the fingerprints and the DNA samples from everyone with no problem. Except that is, John Steele who refused to give us anything but we have his anyway from his room, the maid's room and the maid's house.
That's about it really. We just need to find the gun that killed her."

"Great work, thank those technicians for me and as soon as you can tidy up all the paperwork, that'll be great. I have some more questions about the other cases we're working

but I'll call you later about them.

C'mon Sergeant, let's go."

As they left Dr. McBride's office and began to walk down the empty corridor, Chris stopped and wrote some notes before tearing the piece of paper out of his notebook and handing it to his sergeant.

"Find out who this person is and call when you have a number. Ask these questions and get a faxed reply. Okay?"

"The sergeant read the note, nodded, and Chris added,

"And don't call London to get the name and number" before he carried on walking.

Sergeant Greene hurried to fall back in step.

"You can also get someone, or do it yourself if you like, to get a search warrant to go and rummage through John Steele's home. See if you can find a gun there but even if you can't, drag his ass back here for an interview. The guy pisses me off and if the media happen to see us dragging him away, I have no problem with that. If he doesn't come on his own terms, arrest him for withholding evidence."

"I can do that, sir, with the utmost pleasure," replied the smiling Sergeant.

"But see to the note first."

CHAPTER FIFTY ONE

"Well, at least you didn't finger me for murder and have me arrested" were Phillip's first words when Ken answered the phone.

"Hang on a sec, me old bean, let me turn this down," Ken went to adjust the stereo, "despite my misgivings, I had to cover for you this one time."

"You're such a kind old fart. It makes me wonder how I used to get by without all of your help."

"With a great deal of difficulty is how."

"So how did your brush with the law go?"

"It was actually quite a day, thank you," Ken continued, getting into his stride, "they sent over the most striking young lady to interview me and she was smitten with me I'm sure. She spent hours chatting with me, was totally fascinated and enchanted, and even gave me a hug and kiss when she left."

"Get out of here, I bet you had her chained to the chair."

"No, my dear man, I tell you the truth. She was quite a bit of all right. If you didn't have that sweetie in America, I'd have set you up after I'd finished with her. I can still do so if you're lonely."

"I'm fine, Ken, but thanks for the offer."

"She was all over me. She liked my piano playing, laughed and laughed at my anecdotes, and she was very impressed with all the folk I know."

"You should marry her."

"I did ask her out, I even asked her to stay the night."

"You didn't?"

"I most certainly did. If you ever get to my age, you have to take your chances where you can."

"She didn't stay, did she?"

"No, but she has my number."

"I'll bet she does, has she called?"

"Not yet but she will, mark my words."

"So, did she take your gun or totally forget it after being enchanted with your divine presence?"

"You may scoff but you'll see. Some young feller came in with her wearing hospital gloves, and took it away in a bag. He was only here a minute. The lovely detective asked if I had any more weapons so I told her she was more than welcome to rummage through my drawers."

"The only thing she'd have found down there would have been a pea shooter."

"Now less of your cheek, my drawers contain a still working member of my aging body. You should be so lucky," he replied, in good humor.

"I haven't seen anyone else arrested yet. Do they still think that secretary did it?" Ken continued.

"I don't know. I heard they put a couple of the staff through the grinder but they didn't arrest anyone."

"Is it all settling down again up there?"

"Yes, it is, and I'm moving into a bigger house on the estate."

"Why do you need a bigger house? Is Natalie coming back for a visit?

"She said she would. But this house is great, it's not as draughty as the other one and there's a lot more room."

"You don't need much."

"I do if I get visitors from London."

"Is that an invitation?

"Whenever you want. At least I wouldn't have to take you back to the railway station after a couple of hours."

"I'll make plans, I could do with a few days in the country. So when is the darling Natalie coming back? Will I get to see her?"

"I hope so, it's one of the reasons I called."

"I'm at your disposal."

"Well Ken, I'm going to need a best man. Will you do me the honor?"

For only the second time ever, Phillip had totally stumped Ken for words. Phillip thought he heard him sniff a little.

"Oh, my dear man," he finally muttered, " I just can't express how happy I am for you both. Wait until I tell Fran."

"So are you going to be my best man or do I have to ask somebody else?"

"Not on your nelly are you going to ask anyone else. Of course, I'll do it. I'll be absolutely delighted to do so."

"Glad to have you onboard."

"I wouldn't miss this for the world. Now when did you ask her and where? Didn't she say she'd rather marry me? Where are you going to get married? What can I do to help?"

Phillip smiled as he listened to Ken's excitement. He was so happy.

"Who are you protecting Mrs. Roberts?"

She was dressed now in a more normal attire for her, in a long skirt, flat shoes, blouse and cardigan, virtually everything was in a shade of brown except her blouse which was more of a pale yellow.

"I'm not protecting anyone," she stated defiantly.

Despite Chris having gotten her legal help, she insisted on seeing Chris alone.

"You didn't kill Lady Baldwin. But I do think you saw who did from your vantage point in the library."

"I did kill her. I didn't see anyone."

That was her first mistake, she had no reason to say she didn't see anyone if, of course, she fired the bullet.

"Okay then, Mrs. Roberts, let's just go through this again. You waited all through lunch time to see Lady Baldwin, in the library, with the window open. You heard the commotion and the arguing, probably saw it all as well, with Lord

Baldwin leaving. Then a while afterward, you went down to see Lady Baldwin."

Mrs. Roberts wasn't saying anything so Chris continued.

"What was Lady Baldwin's mood like?"

"Foul." was her simple reply.

"Can you explain that a little further?"

"She was in a terrible mood. I'd heard her shouting at all the nice staff, like Kay and Phillip and Tom. I've seen her in a bad mood before but this was far worse."

"Wasn't she also shouting at Cathy?"

"Yes, but she's not as nice as the others. She lies too much."

"I see, so did Lady Baldwin shout at you?"

"She was barking out orders but I wouldn't say she was shouting at me like she did the others."

"What orders was she barking out?"

"To get hold of her lawyer pronto so he could freeze Lord Baldwin's assets, to secure her own assets, to safeguard all her records and correspondence, and to find out who had moved in on her husband."

"Why were you asked to go there that Sunday?"

"Asked?" She humphed. "I was told to go there as I was told that there were invoices I had to deal with, correspondence, her diary, and various other paperwork."

"So that was basically your job, you managed her finances and her appointments and so on?"

"Yes. Although Kay was doing a lot of her appointments, I was still doing her finances."

"Weren't her finances tied in with Lord Baldwin's?"

"Most of them, yes, so I had to coordinate with his office."

"Lady Baldwin had her own finances, separate from Lord Baldwin?"

"Yes."

"Did he know about this?"

"I don't think so. He never asked me, nor did his office, and I doubt if Lady Baldwin told him."

"Why do you think that?"

"She once told me never to mention it to anyone."

"Did you?"

"No, only to my husband."

"Where did Lady Baldwin get her finances from?"

"Inheritance, before she married. Her parents were quite well off and as she was the only child. She got everything when they died."

"So how much was she worth, in her own right?"

"Oh, somewhere in the region of nine million pounds. It didn't start off there, it was about half a million to begin with. But she also got some financial advice and the money grew. It still is."

"Who gave her this advice?"

"I don't know, one of her friends I believe."

"Didn't you have to pay for this advice? There'll be invoices, won't there?"

"No."

"Was her friend male?"

"Yes."

"Okay, so did Lady Baldwin use her own money a lot?"

"No. She spent Lord Baldwin's money on just about everything."

"Even her charitable donations?"

"Yes."

"So what did she use her own money for?"

"Basically just for her apartment in London, the upkeep and supplies and so on."

"Anything else?"

"Sometimes for travel tickets or hotel rooms."

"You were aware that Lady Baldwin had, shall we say, extra marital affairs?"

"Oh yes, I knew that. I would even have to buy gifts sometimes, with her money, and mail her cards. I knew."

"Were you comfortable doing that?"

"No, but it was my job and with my husband being ill we needed my salary."

"You never thought about spilling the beans or letting it slip somehow?"

"I thought about it sometimes, especially as Lord Baldwin was so nice, but I never got around to doing it. But she can't do it anymore."

"Who did you see shoot her, Mrs. Roberts?"

"I didn't see anyone. I shot her. She deserved it."

"So after she gave you your instructions to contact her

lawyer, you did what?"

"I went back to the library."

"Why didn't you just stay down there?"

"Because she told me to go back to the library. She said she wanted to be alone for awhile, that she was all stressed out, still angry, and needed to calm down."

"So what happened then?"

"I went back upstairs and she went to lie down on a lounger."

"Your gun was in your purse?"

"Yes."

"So why didn't you shoot her then?"

"I don't know."

"You had your purse with you?"

"Yes."

Her second mistake.

"So you went back to the library, waited a little while, then returned and shot her?"

"Yes."

"Did anyone, in the period you went upstairs and waited, go and see her?"

"Not that I know of, no. She wanted to be alone."

"But it's feasible, when you were going upstairs, that someone could have seen her?"

"I suppose so, but no one passed me on the way up."

"Did you see anyone on your way to the library?"

"No, but I did hear a couple of cars leave the driveway as I passed the front door."

"Do you know who left?"

"No."

"Did you see anyone on your way back down to the patio?"

"No."

"And you still maintain, that you put a gun to Lady Baldwin's temple and pulled the trigger, throwing your gun and your gloves into the lake?"

"Yes."

Third mistake. She forgot to mention the cushion.

"Very well, Mrs. Roberts, thank you for being so cooperative" Chris said, rising from his chair to leave, "I'll talk to you again soon. Take her away, constable."

CHAPTER FIFTY THREE

As Chris was interviewing Mrs. Roberts, his sergeant was hammering on John Steele's door.

"You sure he's home?" Steve asked one of the constables, as he continued to knock and ring the doorbell for good measure.

"Security said he was. He was logged in very early this morning with a guest and he hasn't left the building."

The apartment John Steele lived in was very high end, very expensive, and supposedly very secure here at the wharf. The old dockyards of London had been cleaned up. New buildings had replaced the decrepit ones, and for a view of the water, the tenants had to pay for it.

"Who the fuck is banging on my door?" they heard finally from inside.

"Police, sir, please open the door." Steve replied.

"Go the fuck away, I'm still sleeping."

"Can't do that, sir. Please open the door."

"I don't want to talk to you assholes. If you have anything more to ask me, call my lawyer."

"Sir, you need to come to your door right now or I'm going to rip it off its hinges. Now open this door." Steve yelled, signaling the two policemen with the battering ram to make themselves ready.

"This had better be god damn serious or I'm going to fucking sue your asses" His voice grew clearer as he got nearer the door, "show me your god damn badge."

Steve held his badge up to the spy hole, hearing him unlock the door and finally opening it.

"Now what the fuck do you want now?"

"Mr. John Steele?" Steve politely asked.

"Yes. Who the fuck do you think I am, Charlie fuckin Chaplin?"

"That will be enough of the swearing, sir. I'm Detective Sergeant Greene and I have a warrant to search your property," Steve told him, brandishing the warrant, "now move aside please and let my men conduct their search." Steve moved inside closely followed by his crew.

"What the fuck is this all about? I haven't done anything. I'm calling my lawyer and he'll sort out you motherfuckers," yelled the bedraggled, unshaven, almost naked pop star.

"As you wish.   For now, you can sit down and stay quiet while we go about our business," Steve got right into his face, "okay?"

He sat down mumbling to himself.

The apartment would have been gorgeous if it had been kept tidy. As it was, clothes, food, drink, dirty china and crystal were scattered everywhere. It was a mess. Steve pitied the maid who probably had to come into this mess every day or so, although with the amount of stuff lying around, it was probably once a week.

"Sergeant, you'd better come and look at this," called one of the constables.

Steve made his way over to where the voice had come from, leaving someone to watch over Mr. Steele.

The constable signaled with his eyes toward the room he was standing at, it was the master bedroom, and upon it, totally oblivious to what was going on, was a still sleeping,

blonde young lady only partially covered by a black satin

sheet.

"Go and find PC Higgins, will you," Steve told the constable,

as he took over sentry duty at the door. As he waited, he

looked around the room. He noticed Mr. Steele had his camera

set up and god knew what that stuff was on the nightstands.'

"You wanted me, sergeant?"

"Yes, good, you've got your gloves on. Go into this room,

close the door behind you, and wake that young girl up. Find

out who she is, how old she is, and what she took that is

keeping her asleep. As soon as you have her decent, let me

know as I want forensics in here to check out all that shit on

the nightstand."

"Right sir."

PC Higgins was one of the two policewomen that had come

with the Detective. She was very good with people and

wouldn't scare the young lady. She was also young and

attractive, not much older than the sleeper. 'God' he thought,

'it's a good job Chris didn't come. That girl looks younger

than his daughter and this guy has to be in his fifties now, surely. He makes me sick' and he looked over disgustedly at the still sitting John Steele.

The door opened after about five minutes or so and PC Higgins peered out, seeing just the sergeant she spoke quietly with him as the girl sat on the bed, head down and obviously upset.

"I think we need her checked out sir, at the hospital."

"You think she was drugged?"

"She's taken something, sir. She has no needle marks but she could have swallowed something. She's very groggy still."

"Was she raped?"

"I don't know, she doesn't want to go there. She was certainly taken advantage of but she knows where she is and remembers coming here, even having a couple of drinks when she arrived, but it's a blur after that. She faintly recalls having sex but can't remember if she said no or not and she feels very embarrassed."

"How old is she?"

"She says nineteen and that she's a struggling model. She thought it would do her career good to be seen on his arm."

"Don't they all? Have you got her name and address?"

"Yes."

"Then call in an ambulance and go with her to check her out. See if she's telling the truth with her age and name. If at any time, she wants to press charges against this scumbag, call me right away. Understood?"

"Yes sir."

"Then get right on it and leave as soon as the ambulance gets here. Tell them to treat her like a rape victim just in case she changes her mind."

"Yes sir."

"Now stay with her while forensics does their stuff," Steve signaled them to get into the master bedroom before he walked over to one of the big windows overlooking the dock and watched as some folk cruised around in their motor boats. It was roughly forty five minutes before forensics reported to Steve, a guy named Richard who Steve knew fairly well. He was quite the nerdy looking guy with his large glasses, but nonetheless, he was always thorough.

"We found an old 38mm amongst other things, sir."

"You're kidding," replied the delighted Steve, "do you think it's the one we're looking for?"

"I don't know, sir. We'll have to test it of course but it doesn't appear to have been fired for a long time," said Richard, a little dejectedly.

"That's disappointing, but you said there were other things?"

"Yes. We found twenty two ecstasy tablets, seven ounces of marijuana, two grams of cocaine, and a bunch of amateurish porn movies with what look like very young girls."

"Really, how surprising," replied Steve, rather sarcastically. "How young would you say?"

"Definitely teenagers. They look eastern, possibly Thai."

"I suppose I'd best look. Constable," he called out to the nearest policeman, "go and arrest Mr. John Steele. He's sitting by the front door. Tell him he's being charged with unlawful possession of illegal narcotics. Also ask him if he has a gun permit. If he hasn't, charge him with unlawful possession. Let him put some clothes on, then take him back to the station and book him in. They can also take a DNA swab."

"Yes sir."

"Okay Richard, let's take a look at these movies," he added with a sigh.

There was quite a collection of movies. It seemed like Mr. Steele tried keeping a record of all of his conquests. Although most of them were with much younger women, there were a few older women, but extremely attractive older women. Then there were the really young looking girls. They did look Thai and Steve knew that it might be a hell of job discovering how old they all were but it looked like child porn to him.

"Pack them up, Richard. Let's see if we can determine anything with them and make sure there's nothing else lying around."

CHAPTER FIFTY FOUR

Three or four miles away from the wharf in a different apartment, Suzy Walker was lying face down, naked, on Simon Ward – Davis's equally naked chest. Both were heavily perspiring and breathing hard as she folded her arms and placed her head on her hands. She stared at his upturned chin as he stared straight up at the high ceiling, his chest still heaving at their previous exertions.

They'd been having these liaisons ever since they'd gotten together at Lady Baldwin's and always at the request of Suzy. Simon didn't call her as he didn't want her husband to pick up the phone. Neither did Suzy. But she'd called him a lot since getting back to London, and as his employer was away, he had the time and an empty apartment.

"Simon?" she asked softly, wondering if he'd fallen asleep.

"Hmmm?"

"You know about my husband, don't you?"

"Yes, you've never made any secret about it," he replied, keeping his voice low as well and his eyes still closed.

"Bob, my husband, has a form of MS. There is a medical term for it but it's just a variation of MS. It's gradually taken hold of him. He just used to have attacks, but now he's severely disabled. Thank goodness for the nurses who come in and look after him. I don't know what I'd do without them. I could never leave him but he is getting weaker now and gradually losing his will to live. It's just very difficult," She took a deep breath before continuing, "He knows I need some intimacy and he knows he can't do so anymore. He's often told me he wouldn't mind if I did which is all well and good but I can't tell him about you. I know it would kill him."

Simon wasn't stirring, all he did was put his arms around her waist and clasp his hands to let her know he was still awake and listening.

"I think what I'm trying to say, Simon," she continued, "is that in the very short time I've known you, I've become very fond of you. I can't tell you how grateful I am to C for introducing us. I just wish I could tell her."

"I know what you mean," Simon answered, opening his eyes and bending his head forward so he could kiss her on her forehead.

"Do you miss her?"

"Sometimes."

"Where you sleeping with her for a long time?"

"I wouldn't say we ever slept," he said good naturedly, "but we got together sometimes, just not often enough."

"I was surprised she introduced me to you. I thought she'd have kept you to herself."

"She wasn't in the least bit possessive like that, not to me anyway."

"Did you know about Tristan?"

"I did know about Tristan from when I used to work for her."

"Did you know about her loving him?"

"No, I didn't."

"Do you think Tristan killed her?"

"No, I think Lord Baldwin did it. He was angry enough."

"Mmm, maybe. He sure was angry. Are you seeing anyone else, Simon? Do you have a girlfriend or anything?"

"No, I'm only seeing you."

"You know I'm a huge flirt but I do have to confess something."

"What's that?"

"Well, although I do flirt with practically everybody, I don't actually sleep around. There is only you that I'm sleeping with at the moment."

Simon peered down to see her smiling, and smiled back.

"At the moment?"

She removed a hand to dig him in the ribs before bringing it back to under her chin.

"You know what I mean."

"I know and I appreciate it."

"Do you like living in the city, Simon?"

"It's okay. I'm used to it now and it is handy having everything within walking distance practically. But I do miss the country. That's where I'd prefer to live if I had the choice."

"I would too. I promised myself that once Bob passed away, that was what I'd do. I wouldn't need any more money and I don't feel safe in the city anymore. You hear too many stories. Even though C was killed in the country, I still feel safer there."

"Just watch out for jilted husbands," Simon replied, his hands moving down from her waist to stroke both cheeks of her still small and firm bottom.

"That's nice," she whispered seductively, moving up on him to graze around his neck, "it feels like something is stirring. Maybe we could shower together later if we have any energy left?"

"It's a good job I work out," he panted, raising her mouth toward his lips, "because you're just wonderful."

CHAPTER FIFTY FIVE

By the time John Steele had gotten to the police station, a small smattering of press were waiting, probably tipped off by his own apartment's security and his lawyer.

Mr. Rees - Jones, the dapper Savile Row suited lawyer, was not at all impressed. He didn't like the fact his client was being incarcerated and thought the charges were trumped up, not to mention the search warrant. Like his pin suited attire, his grey hair was also perfect, the side parting so straight it could have been put there by a laser. His half spectacles, perched on the end of his nose only made him look even more lawyerly which was probably why he wore them.

Chris had made Mr. Steele wait in his cell before seeing him. He was in no rush to do so after seeing a couple of the tapes and was hoping against hope that the gun would be the murder weapon. Unfortunately, Dr. McBride's department had just informed him that the gun hadn't been fired in years and would probably have backfired if it had as it hadn't been cleaned in a very long time.

John Steele still looked like he'd just got up. His hair uncombed, chin unshaven, wearing just a t – shirt and torn jeans, he didn't look happy either.

They were in the same interview room that Chris had used previously with Mrs. Roberts and the fourth chair was occupied by Steve.

Mr. Rees – Jones didn't wait for a pause before complaining he'd waited long enough. "On what basis did you obtain the bogus search warrant of my client's apartment?" he protested.

"On the basis that your client, Mr. John Steele, is a suspect in the murder of Lady Baldwin. He was having an affair with her, nobody saw him leave, he's been uncooperative with our enquiries, and he was there when she was killed."

"Absolutely preposterous. My client had no motive to kill her and is totally innocent."

"Well maybe he did. Is it not true, Mr. Steele, that Lady Baldwin had in her possession a tape that you made, a tape that put you in a very compromising position with one of her staff? A tape that could be very embarrassing to you?"

"There's no need for you to answer that, Mr. Steele," his lawyer advised, "this is just nonsense. My client will readily admit to having an affair with Lady Baldwin, just as he will to making a tape with a member of her staff, who by the way was fully compliant. The tape was made purely for Lady Baldwin. It was her idea and it was hers to keep. My client wasn't interested in keeping it. So now that I've answered your questions, my client can leave here?"

"Not so fast. Unfortunately for your client, we found some things in his apartment that will force him to stay the night at least until he sees the magistrate in the morning. You'll probably be able to get him bail at that point."

"Oh come on detective, it was just some recreational paraphernalia that people in Mr. Steele's circles are expected to have. You know this so just let my client go. He'll make a glowing statement to the press about our wonderful police, apologize publicly for wasting your time, and we can all forget about this."

"You know, Mr. Rees – Jones, I would normally tend to agree with you. But I do have a problem with the cocaine we found, and more especially with the young girl that had been taken advantage of, not to mention the child porn he possessed."

"That's fucking bullshit, you motherfucker! That is not child porn and you know it! Those are personal tapes and that piece of skirt last night was born stupid. She knew exactly what she was doing and was privileged to do so." yelled the irate John Steele.

"Sir, you need to stay quiet and let me deal with this. This is why I'm here and you'll be best served by letting me do your talking," responded Mr. Rees – Jones very calmly.

"Okay, but this is a fucking set up ."

"I've had experts look at those tapes, Mr. Steele, and they are all of the opinion that none of those girls are above the age of fourteen at the most."

"All those little bitches told me they were eighteen. They're small in that crappy city and I didn't pay good fucking money for children." Mr. Steele yelled again, nodding his head at his lawyer as a kind of apology for speaking again.

"I always thought that Bangkok was a great city," stated Chris.

"It's a fucking slum," replied Mr. Steele.

"Mr. Steele, you really need to stay quiet," admonished his lawyer.

"What did you give that young lady last night?" asked Chris.

"He's not going to answer that detective. The young lady in question has not pressed any charges against my client and is not going to so the question is null and void."

Chris was well aware of this. He thought she'd been quietly paid off after speaking to someone earlier. Oh well, that was her mistake, at least now he knew the tapes were made in Bangkok and that these kids had been prostituted. That might get them somewhere.

"Very well, we're going ahead with the charges of unlawful possession of narcotics and unlawful possession of a firearm so Mr. Steele will be spending the night here. This concludes our interview."

As soon as Chris and Steve left the interview room, Chris was telling his sergeant to get on to the foreign office to contact the Bangkok authorities, send them copies of the tapes, and see if they knew of these kids, and how old they were.

Later the same evening, Chris was home with his wife chatting while commercials were running on the television. Chris was still tense

"We brought the pop singer into the station today."

"The one from the Baldwin Murder, the one I used to like before he went solo?"

"That's the one. I was going to give him a rough time but he came with his fancy lawyer."

"Did he do it?"

"No, but I wish he had."

"What's he like?"

"A prick. Most of the murderers I've ever met are way nicer than he is. His lawyer was telling us he doesn't mean to be but that he thinks he's supposed to act the way he does."

"In what way?"

"Oh, just being uncooperative, abusive, talking down to folks, taking advantage of the young women who think he's a big star, the way he is with women."

"So he plays the big star with attitude?"

"That and way more. In his home, we found all these home movies he made and stuff like ecstasy he gave to drug these young girls. Even worse was some child porn starring himself. If the Sunday Papers got hold of any of them, they'd have a field day."

"Child porn movies?"

"That's right. He also taped himself with the girls he took home. They were probably so out of it, they probably never realized. The child movies were done in Thailand, all these tiny young girls, I wish I could have arrested him for that but there's no way I can determine their ages. Not yet anyway, but I'm trying."

"That makes me sick. I hope you got him for something?"

"Not much, he's going to spend the night in a cell but his lawyer will have him out in the morning. All we could do really was charge him with possession of the gun and the drugs. Hopefully he'll fight us for possession of his tapes."

The phone rang and Chris took it in the kitchen, getting refills for their wine as he listened. All Megan heard was what Chris said, "Hi Sergeant. No it's not too late. Did you speak to him? Did he have one? Do we have permission to retrieve it? Did he tell us where it is? Did you get a fax?

Excellent work, Sergeant. Get yourself home. Pick me up first thing in the morning. Goodnight and thanks again. I needed some good news."

Chris returned with the wine and a smile that Megan hadn't seen for a while. All his tenseness seemed to have vanished in an instant.

"Is everything okay?" she asked him, taking her wine.

"Yes, fine," he casually commented, making himself comfortable, "what did I miss?"

CHAPTER FIFTY SIX

At five a.m. the following morning, Phillip was on the phone with Natalie. He was in his own house, the new one was still being made ready for he and Natalie to move into. Now that Lady Baldwin wasn't around, he didn't have to spend nights in Crompton Hall. The dogs had returned here and they slept in the butler's pantry all together.

Phillip had been hastily putting together a wedding plan for he and Natalie. they were going to get married in a local registry office once all the paperwork was completed. The registrar needed Natalie's divorce papers and birth certificate and so on. Then after they got wed, they'd go and have a little reception in the pub. Lord Baldwin had offered to pay for that, He would be away at the time but he also offered to pay for the honeymoon.

Phillip's family who lived near Manchester were surprised that he was finally getting married. They all thought he was a confirmed bachelor who would remain that way forever.

They were all going to attend, and Phillip's sister was going to act as witness for Natalie, as her parents wouldn't be able to come over.

"Hi, how was work today?" Phillip asked, still thinking it was very odd to be saying that when it was early morning for him, almost daylight.

"Oh, you know, tiring more than anything."

Although she'd dropped one of her jobs, she was still doing two, an executive assistant during the day and a cashier in the evening. She was quitting both soon.

"At least you haven't much longer to do."

"No, but there's a lot to do here before I come over. We are all so excited."

" So how are the girls?

Natalie had two boys and two girls, and she'd had them in that order. The two boys had their own lives, one was in the navy and the other was doing landscaping, both living away. The girls however were still at school, the oldest, Tamara, had another year to do at high school and her younger sister

458

had two years to do. Both were very excited about going to England, neither had ever done so but they were very nervous about not only Phillip but also about having to finish their schooling there.

"The girls are good, very eager.. They're not sure what to expect."

Phillip had spoken to them sometimes. They seemed nice, but he knew how scary this may be for them with their mother marrying this guy they'd never met and having to move to another country.

"Tell them to expect cold weather and rain. You were lucky when you came over."

"I think their biggest worry is school. Foreigners in a strange land, and they have no idea if they'll be ahead or way behind in their studies."

"I know they'll be popular, the guys will be all over these two California girls with their cute accents. The local school, which by all accounts is very good, have told me there'll be no problem. They'll just give them a test to see where they stand and take it from there."

"Did you go and see the school?"

"Yes, it's very nice, and like I said, it has a great reputation."

"I won't tell them about the test."

"No, don't. It would only give them something else to worry about."

"Have you moved yet?"

"No, not yet, it still stinks of paint. There are a couple of carpets to go down still and some furniture to come in, but it's almost all done. Like I said, if it didn't smell like a paint factory still, I'd have moved in already."

"Will I like it?"

"You'd better. You chose everything."

"Yes, but that was all from brochures. Does it look good?"

"It looks great. You're going to love it."

"I can't wait. You're still sure you don't want to pull out?"

"Still sure. What do you want to do about a honeymoon?"

"I don't know. It would be nice to have one but do you think we could do it later? Until after the girls have settled in and the weather will be warmer?"

"Sure, that will be okay, much better probably."

"Maybe we could go to Scotland or Ireland or Greece."

Phillip had told her that he used to go to the Greek islands quite regularly when he got time off, it was hot, guaranteed sunshine virtually, and he'd just sunbathe, drink, and eat. Maybe read a book or two.

"I haven't been to Scotland since I was a kid so I don't remember much of it and I've never been to Ireland. Greece is very hot, last time I went it was about 110 degrees in the shade."

"I'd really like to go there one day and to Italy. Venice in particular."

"You'll have to get some travel brochures when you get here, try and pick a spot somewhere. If we go to Scotland or Ireland, we'll need to learn to golf. There are courses everywhere."

"You've never played?"

"No. I always watch it on the television but I never got to play."

"Me either, yet my whole family play. No one ever thought to teach me or take me with them. Wouldn't it be something if I

could go and play St. Andrews? That would really tick
them off."

"It's not a bad idea. I'll have to talk to my brother. He plays
golf and can tell us what it entails to play there."

"I'm very nervous about meeting your family."

"There's no need to be, they're friendly."

"Especially your mother, I'll be taking away her youngest
child."

"She's thrilled. She said it was about time I got married, I
was too miserable."

"She said that?"

"Yeah, and there I was thinking bachelors were always happy."

"You can still pull out."

"No, it's okay. I'm not pulling out."

"You'd better not. Have they arrested anyone else yet apart
from that secretary?"

"No. I saw on the news last night that John Steele was
arrested but only for drug possession I believe."

"You didn't like him, did you?"

"No, not at all. I wouldn't have thought he'd done it though."

"He wasn't your guess then?"

"No, I'm just hoping Mrs. Roberts doesn't have to go to prison for it. I can't believe she's still being held."

"Maybe she did do it and confessed. If they have evidence and she admits to it, they can't very well convict someone else as well. Maybe she did do it."

"I just can't buy it. Out of all the folk who were there, she'd have been my last choice. Poor old girl."

"Well don't you get arrested for it, I'm already working my notice."

"I'll try not to, but you sound sleepy."

"I am, I should go. I'm falling asleep."

"I do love you, Natalie."

"I love you too. Goodnight."

"Goodnight."

CHAPTER FIFTY SEVEN

On the stroke of seven this same morning, Chris clambered into the unmarked car driven by Sergeant Greene. They're followed by a patrol car containing two armed policemen and a technician from forensics. Chris wasn't expecting any trouble but if there were guns in the residence then it was quite feasible that someone may try to use them. The only surprise he wanted was the one he was hoping to pull himself. He took along the technician just to handle the weapon, hopefully. Thankfully avoiding much of the traffic, a patrol car works wonders in those circumstances, Chris and his sergeant were ringing the doorbell by 8am. The two armed policemen were on either side of the entrance, concealed from the view of the security camera, and the technician was out of harm's way should any occur.

"Good Morning, Sir," greeted Chris to the occupant as he opened the door, "you may remember, but I am Detective

Inspector Shaw and this is my partner, Detective Sergeant Greene," and they both proffered their badges.

"Yes, I remember you. Good morning to you both too. Is there something I may do for you?" enquired the fully dressed, alert, and always very polite Simon Ward-Davis.

"May we come inside, Sir?" asked Chris.

"Well actually, Detective, I was just about to go out. Will this take very long?"

Simon didn't seem at all flustered or nervous.

"It may only take a jiffy," confessed Chris if they didn't find anything.

"Very well then, come on in for a moment, " Simon replied, opening the door wide for them to enter, a tiny look of surprise showing in his demeanor as the two detectives were quickly followed by the two policeman who moved close to him.

"You won't mind if we just frisk you down, will you sir?" asked the sergeant, although the question was rather redundant considering it was already being done.

After the two policemen signaled he was clean, Chris asked Simon to sit down, which he did on the adjacent dining room chair with the two policemen keeping him within close proximity. The sergeant went back to the front door to signal the technician to enter. Already with his white overalls on along with his gloves, he entered carrying a small case. The door was then closed.

"Can you tell me where the gun safe is please, sir?" asked Chris. He already knew its whereabouts, but wanted to remain polite and see how cooperative his suspect would be.

"I don't have one, sir," replied Simon, still calm, "and may I ask if you happen to have a search warrant?"

"You may not have one, sir, but your employer certainly does. We were in contact with him yesterday and he told us we were more than welcome to check it out, as you'll see from this signed fax he sent us," Chris stated, brandishing the fax before Simon. "Now would you like to tell us where it is?"

"I'm sure then you already know where it is so go ahead," Chris nodded to his sergeant and the technician who headed off left toward the apartment's office. The sergeant had gotten the floor plan yesterday before talking to the owner so he knew exactly where he was going. He had also been told where to locate the key.

Chris waited and watched Simon who was still calm, wasn't drumming his fingers or anything, not sweating, no rapid movement of the eyes. Chris was not feeling very optimistic right now.

After a very long five minutes, Sergeant Greene reemerged, closely followed by the technician and his case.

"Did you find it?" asked Chris worriedly.

"Bagged and tagged," declared the sergeant triumphantly, "it's in the case."

"Then Steve, isn't it?" he continued talking to the technician, "why don't you take it back to the lab and ask Dr. McBride to test it as soon as she can, Police Constable Woodhead can take you, and the Police Sergeant can come back with us. Do you have anything to tell us, Sir?" asked Chris, now diverting his attention to Simon.

As he did so, one of the policemen left with the technician.

"Nothing whatsoever, sir, but I could offer you some tea or coffee."

"Tell me, just out of curiosity, why do you call yourself a personal attaché and not a butler?"

"I don't sir, that was a term that Lady Baldwin used but I do act as a personal assistant sometimes, just as most butlers do."

"Would you mind accompanying us back to Oxford to answer some questions?" Chris requested.

"Actually, sir, I would. As I said when you arrived, I was about to go out."

"Then unfortunately , I am going to have to arrest you on suspicion of murder and take you into custody. Sergeant, cuff him and read him his rights."

After he was cuffed, sat back down again and read his rights, Simon was asked if he understood.

"Yes, I do, and I would like a lawyer please."

"Sergeant, get one of the local policemen to come and secure this place until we can get a crew to do a search here, will you?"

"Right away , sir," responded his sergeant, walking away with his cell phone.

It was only minutes before two policemen arrived. They obtained a front door key from Simon and stationed themselves outside the closed front door until they were relieved, while the three policemen and Simon left for Oxford. Although Simon would reply to casual conversation, he wouldn't do so to anything pertaining to Lady Baldwin or her death. On the drive back, Chris at numerous intervals would try to get him to say something and although he thought he saw some reaction at times, Simon would just sit and stare out the car window. It was the same in the interview room at the station. He had his lawyer and he would be polite and answer questions if his lawyer told him to but nothing about Lady Baldwin.

It was late afternoon before the divine Dr. McBride arrived at Chris's office, as usual she had a lot of heads twisting as she hurried by.

"What do you have for us, Doc?" asked Chris anxiously.

She sat down opposite him, alongside Sergeant Greene who had also just arrived.

"The 38mm we retrieved this morning contained no fingerprints, it was as clean as a whistle. Our tests could not determine if it had been recently fired. So extensively cleaned it had been, that it seemed almost like new," she stated, reading her notes from the folder she had brought with her.

"But?" pleaded Chris.

"But", she continued, deadpan, "our tests indicate that this indeed is our murder weapon. Ballistics show a 99% match," she beamed a satisfied smile.

"Wonderful!" exclaimed the visibly relieved Chris.

"I'm flabbergasted that he kept it," commented Steve.

"He was actually quite clever. He knew that it wasn't registered in this country so when he borrowed it from his boss, he could put it back thinking his boss would never admit to owning it. Now if he'd replaced it with another 38mm while his boss was away, we'd have been screwed."

"So how did you convince his boss to admit to it?" asked Dr. McBride.

"Mainly by having our good sergeant appeal to his nicer side. That and telling him in writing, we wouldn't prosecute him for having an unlawful firearm."

"What if he'd said no?"

"Again, we'd have been screwed. We would never have got a search warrant. Which reminds me, has the search commenced sergeant?"

"Yes sir, about an hour ago."

"Good, we have the murder weapon but we need whatever else we can get. Mr. Ward – Price is saying nothing so we need to build our case."

"My staff will process whatever we can find just as soon as we can. But what made you suspect him, Chris?" asked Dr. McBride, reverting to his first name.

"I didn't. It was only when I found out that he was having an ongoing affair with her, yet he didn't appear to have had sex with her at her home. He wouldn't have gone there if their relationship had been over. Then knowing his boss was a very wealthy American who I understand is also a member of the National Rifle Association, I just played a hunch. I think

somewhere along the line someone suggested the gun was
borrowed, and it just fit."

"Do you want to interview him now, sir?" asked Steve.

"No, he's not going to say anything, and I don't have much
to get him to. Let's leave him be until Dr. McBride's staff
have done, maybe we'll have something then. Sergeant, release
Mrs. Roberts and have someone take her home. Then let's all
go home."

"I think I'll go and ask for volunteers first to do some
overtime." said the doctor.

"I'll approve it. Now go, the two of you, and let me just
say, great work."

As the sergeant and the doctor were leaving Chris's office, the
sergeant turns around and says, "I told you it was the butler."

CHAPTER FIFTY EIGHT

It was closer to lunchtime the next day before the two detectives and the doctor finally met up, all three had thoroughly enjoyed their previous evening. They all had thought the gun would never be found and without it, the whole case was lost.

They met again in Chris's office. Steve had already got some coffee for them, so they all made themselves comfortable. "Okay then, doc," Chris started after he'd said good morning to her, "you'd better tell us what we have to work with." "To begin with," she was looking at one of the files she would continue to consult, " Mr. Ward - Price did not leave a confessional note anywhere. We did find a pair of shoes that matched the prints we took from outside the maid's house at Stonebridge Manor. The tread of the shoe is exactly the same, the weight matches, the heel matches. It was Mr. Ward – Price who was standing outside that window." She passed over two of the evidence bags, one containing the cast, the other a shoe, and Chris and Steve both looked at the bags and nodded.

"You know about the gun," she continued, putting that file down along with the evidence bag, "and we also found some personalized jewelry, photographs, and notes, all we think from Lady Baldwin," and she laid out the evidence bags for Chris and Steve to look at. It was expensive stuff, one of the watches was a Rolex, Chris noticed, and peering through the bags he saw that after the sentiment, if they contained one, was a simple 'love C xxx'. The photos were mainly of Lady Baldwin alone in a variety of attire that ranged from dinner gowns to tiny bikinis, mostly unsigned, and the ones that were written on were just the symbol to signify kisses. There were some that contained the two of them but nothing suggestive, the locations were anonymous and looked innocent. The notes were a little more helpful, they were obviously little notes she'd written probably after intimate relations. The notes were like: 'Oh darling, this afternoon was wondrous, I wish I could stay for even more, love C xxx' or 'hope you like the

watch and chain, time is short and we have to make the most

of it, C xxx.'

"This is Lady Baldwin's writing?"

"Yes, a complete match," replied the doctor.

"We'll need to match the merchandise to the invoices that

Mrs. Roberts kept , Sergeant. Will you get on to that?"

"Yes sir," immediately picking up the phone.

As the sergeant made his call, Chris asked the doctor,

"Where was this all found? I never saw any photographs

while I was there."

"They were all in a box in his closet. Everything, and the

watches were all still ticking."

"I see. Anything else?"

The sergeant had now finished his call.

"Mr. Ward – Price has been continuing to see Ms. Suzy

Walker. Her fingerprints were all over the apartment, fairly

recent semen traces, female fluids and as the only other set of

fingerprints we found belonged to an unknown male, we're

fairly certain that the fluids are Ms. Walker's and that she and Mr. Ward – Price are still having intimate relations."

"Anything else?"

"No, sorry, that's all we have."

"It would have been nice to have had more direct evidence, rather than all this circumstantial stuff," Chris took a mouthful of coffee and relaxed back into his chair, "but let's see if we can piece all this together," he added, getting out his notebook, as did Steve.

"So, Mr. Ward - Price, Simon, let's just use their first names," Chris continued, "was having an affair with C."

"He used to be her butler so probably the affair started then," added Steve.

"And they met up frequently in a private apartment in London," contributed the doctor.

"Right. Now Simon knew about Tristan, that had been a long lasting relationship so he could cope with that. He knew Tristan would never leave Jane . He may well have thought that C was in love with him. After all, she gave him expensive gifts, wrote him notes, and met with him at the

London apartment. And who knows what she used to say to him?"

The other two nodded as they went through their notes.

" He gets invited to a weekend party at her house so he probably thinks he would have a chance to be intimate with her," Chris continued as he also read through his notes.

"And instead, she gets intimate with Tristan and John," stated the doctor.

"While he is paired up with Suzy," Chris added.

"Do you think that was willingly? Or do you think he was forced into it?" asked Steve.

"Very good question sergeant. I think he was forced into it. At that time, he didn't seem to have another interest in any other woman, there were no signs at his apartment. I think he's a one woman man. The only person he was interested in when he went to her house was her."

"But why would he take a gun to her house? It doesn't seem like he went there to shoot her?" asked Steve.

"No, I can't explain that one. There must have been some reason or maybe he did plan on shooting her," Chris gave a nonplussed reply.

"So do you think he was jealous?" asked the doctor, ignoring the gun question.

"This is what I think happened. He goes to her house thinking he would have sex with her. He believes they're in love and instead she hooks him up with her friend. Because he loves C, he does it and probably enjoys it. But then, maybe he sees C flirting, I didn't see in his inventory that he was in possession of the apartment key so maybe she asked for it back. Then he goes on a walk and catches her with John, and maybe Tristan as well. Then to cap it all off, she announces she's actually in love with somebody other than himself so he kills her."

"No, we didn't find a key for that apartment in his possession," confirmed the doctor, perusing her notes.

"Sounds good to me," commented Steve, putting away his notebook and finishing his coffee.

"It's just circumstantial for the most part, apart from the gun. I do think Mrs. Roberts either witnessed him doing it or saw him going there or walking away but she wants to take the blame so won't testify."

"The gun is going to convict him, Detective," said the doctor optimistically.

"Sergeant, arrange to have Mr. Ward – Price brought to the interview room at one p.m. and let his lawyer know. We should grab some lunch first."

Steve went through the interview preamble. Simon's lawyer was a Mr. Hughes, a balding middle aged guy with glasses and a paunch, and Simon was still dressed as he was yesterday. Yet he still looked smart and fresh.

With introductions over and Simon confirming who he was and why he was being interviewed, Chris launched straight into his questions.

"Did you kill Lady Baldwin?"

For what was going to be a pattern, and one that had obviously been arranged, at each question Simon would look at his lawyer, who would either nod or shake his head, to indicate if he should answer.

"No sir."

"Were you invited as a guest to Lady Baldwin's home on the weekend she was killed?"

"Yes sir"

"Were you in the vicinity when Lady Baldwin was killed?"

"My client will need to know the time she was killed before answering that question, detective."

"At, or around 3pm on the day you left."

"Yes sir."

"Did you witness her death?"

"No sir."

"What were you doing at the time of her death?"

"Leaving."

"Did anyone see you leave?"

"Yes sir, Ms. Jane Robins. I gave her a lift home."

Chris remembered that now but he also knew she hadn't suspected anything so she'd be a useless witness.

"Did you see Mrs. Roberts just before you were leaving?"

"No sir."

"She said she saw you."

"My client is not going to answer that question."

"Why don't you just admit to killing Lady Baldwin? We do have a witness, you know."

"My client is not going to respond to that statement, detective."

"Why were you in possession of your employer's handgun that weekend?"

"For my protection."

"Why did you need protection?"

"I'd been mugged a few weeks previous. I didn't want it to happen again."

"Did you make a police report?"

"No sir."

"Why not?"

"I'd read that muggings were rarely investigated by the police. It wasn't a priority so I didn't think it was worth spending a couple of hours in a police station making a report that would be just ignored."

"Were you badly hurt?"

"I was bruised up on my head and ribs but nothing was Broken."

"Is there a doctor's report or hospital record?"

"No sir."

"But surely you didn't think you'd be mugged at Lady Baldwin's estate?"

"No but when I was mugged, I was in my car. I was stopped and the next thing I knew I was being dragged out and beaten up."

"So you carried the gun. Can you now explain to me how this same gun was used to kill Lady Baldwin? And then found its way back to your boss's gun cabinet?"

"I can't explain that but I believe it was taken from my overnight bag and put back there before I left her house."

"How could someone have done that?"

"My bag was by the front door, I left it there while I went back to my room to ensure I hadn't forgotten anything."

"How long was it there for?"

"About ten minutes I suppose."

"Who knew you had a gun?"

"I don't know, but I didn't hide it in my room. The staff were in and out of there the whole time, so they probably saw it."

"So you get home with this 'replaced' gun, yet you don't notice that it's been fired or that a bullet is missing?"

"No sir. The gun wasn't clean anyway and I never kept it fully loaded. As my employer was going to come over to London soon, I thought I'd better clean it."

Chris had to admit to himself this was clever as he looked at his dejected looking sergeant as if to say, "so this is your defense."

"Did you love Lady Baldwin?"

"I was very fond of her, sir."

"Were you jealous of her?"

"My client is not going to answer that detective."

"Why were your footprints found outside the maid's house?"

"I'm not sure which house it was but I did look inside one that was empty."

"You didn't observe Lady Baldwin having sex with someone?"

"No sir, the house was empty. I was just being nosy."

"Why don't you just confess, Mr. Ward - Price? Going to trial is just going to add years to your sentence. If you confess, we'll make it easier for you. We understand why you killed Lady Baldwin, she pushed you to the brink and you snapped, it's very clear. We don't want to send you away for the rest of your life. You would be so much better off to just tell us the truth."

"My client is not going to respond to that, detective. He is innocent and we intend to prove it. Now are there anymore questions or are we all done?"

"Just a couple, Mr. Hughes. Mr. Ward - Price, were you seeing Ms. Suzy Walker before the weekend at Lady Baldwin's home?"

"He's not going to answer that detective."

"He is going to have to at his trial, Mr. Hughes."

"That's all well and good but he's not going to answer now."

"You slept with her and have continued to do so?"

"Detective, I said he's not going to answer."

"Have you fallen in love with Ms. Walker? Have you banished Lady Baldwin out of your mind now you have found someone else to love?"

"Detective, I'm warning you."

"What is her husband going to think when we force Ms. Walker to testify that she's been sleeping with you, regularly? And that you'd like to marry his wife, that you can do things with her that he can't possibly do?"

"Detective, this has gone too far," interrupted Mr. Hughes.

"And how is Ms. Walker going to feel," continued Chris, ignoring the lawyer, "knowing her testament is probably going to kill her husband?"

"Detective."

"Can he force her on to the stand?" asked Simon to his lawyer.

"Let us just have a moment, detectives," said the exasperated lawyer. They whispered together for a few minutes out of earshot of the detectives.

"If, and I stress if, detective," Mr. Hughes said, "if my client were to make a statement that he was in some way responsible for the demise of Lady Baldwin, he would want to be assured that not only would his sentence not be severe but also that Ms. Walker would not have to go through the indignity of being forced to testify which would put her in a very embarrassing, and possibly, damaging position."

"As I said before, Mr. Hughes, I don't believe this to be a pre-meditated murder, more of a spur of the moment one, a crime of passion as the French like to label it. If Mr. Ward – Price makes a full written confession, I will testify that he was very cooperative and that he only merits a short sentence. Once the judge hears the full story, I am sure he or she will agree."

Again they whispered together, Chris thought he heard the lawyer say he could clear him in court, but finally Mr. Hughes broke off with his client.

"My client will make a full confession."

That plain and that simple.

The sergeant passed over some paper and a pen and Simon made out his statement silently. Once he'd finished and it was witnessed, Chris said to him, "Do you mind me asking you something?"

Simon didn't say anything so Chris went ahead.

"Did you love her?"

"Yes, very much."

"You saw her having sex with John Steele?"

"Yes, he's horrible and he taped himself with Cathy which he and C were watching as they recreated the scene. It was gross. I would have gotten over it eventually. I knew what she was like but then she asked me for the apartment key, probably to give to him. And then she says she loved Tristan. She was getting rid of me, made me go with Suzy, and the next thing I know I'm holding a cushion to her head."

"Why the cushion?"

"I've fired that gun before at the range. I didn't have my ear protectors on and it nearly deafened me. I guess that was an instinct. I remember holding the cushion and firing the gun. I didn't look at her, I just walked away, and that was it."

"Okay, Simon. Thank you."

With that, the two detectives left the room, leaving Simon with his lawyer and a policeman who would take him back to his cell.

"Congratulations, sir."

"Thank you, sergeant. I was worried there for a while. I sure as hell didn't want to go to trial."

"No, even to me it sounded plausible. Are you going to celebrate?"

"I don't think so. Maybe just a quiet night at home."

"Actually sir the wives have arranged a dinner out for us all tonight."

"They have? Then I guess we can celebrate after all."

CHAPTER FIFTY NINE

"Good Evening, Scallywag,"

Phillip laughed at Ken's opening line as he picked up the phone.

"Hey, you old dog. Is that book ready yet?"

"Actually, my dear man, I'm glad you asked. It's being proofed read as we speak."

"So you finally got it done. About bloody time. What's it called?"

"Jack of all Trades, Master of None."

"Perfect title. You must have been a butler once."

"Well thank you, I did dally as a butler once."

"And you've dallied ever since. Congratulations on the book, I'll be expecting a free copy, mind."

"Yours will be the first copy. So has my darling Natalie jilted you yet?"

"No, she's getting ready to get on the plane with her two daughters. They fly out tomorrow afternoon."

"She didn't get cold feet then or say she prefers your bestman?"

"No, maybe she's waiting to do that during the ceremony."

"I wouldn't be at all surprised. Are her daughters staying permanently?"

"Yes, I have them enrolled in the local high school. They are excited."

"How is our lovely bride to be?"

"Actually, she was pissed when I spoke to her earlier, thinks I'm a magician and played a trick on her."

"How so?"

"When I guessed about Lady B's killer, we put names in an envelope and she opened it today."

"Oh yes, that Simon fellow was convicted today, wasn't he?"

"Yes, he was."

"That's who you guessed?"

"Yes. Natalie thought the maid had done it"

"Good guess. Why did you think him?"

"Only because I thought he was the only one who really cared about her. I mean, he adored her. But I saw him after she'd admitted she loved Tristan and he looked devastated.

He was the only one who loved her enough to have killed

her. And I knew he worked for this gun crazy American."

"Jealousy is a terrible thing. People have always been jealous

of my looks and my personality, it's a curse."

"Oh, I know it," Phillip smiled, "Natalie is always saying that

she wishes I looked and acted like you."

"I knew that girl was made for me. So what else is going on

there?"

"Well, his lordship has gone to Palm Beach with Mrs. Harrop

for a holiday. He's having the house in Antigua redecorated so

went to Florida for a change. He is really happy. His two

children are happier now as well, they both have houses here

on the estate. She's riding again and he works the land. And

Liz Price, the model, is always visiting, as is the old nanny

Kay with her husband to be, the designer. She says she might

come to my wedding. Cathy, the maid, is back up here. She

seems to be doing okay, I heard she's working as a

housekeeper around here and she's living with her mother and

kids but we don't see her here. Let's see, what else is there?

Oh yes, Rene has his own restaurant now, and Tom, the butler at Stonebridge, got another job close by. Mrs. Roberts is doing okay, pops in sometimes.

John Steele got into trouble though. One of the tabloids got hold of one of his tapes from somewhere having sex with a very young girl so his career is going nowhere now. The Thai authorities want him extradited for child porn. Can't sell any tickets or any records, and the press are going for his jugular. Couldn't happen to a nicer guy. Then of course there's a big wedding this week."

"So I hear. Fran is so looking forward to it. You sure it's okay us staying with you?

"Course it is," replied Phillip, "you just have to promise me one thing."

"What's that, my dear pal?"

"Don't try to bed the bridesmaids'."

Made in the USA
Charleston, SC
22 May 2012